LYING
AND DYING

Josef Slonský Investigations
Book One

Graham Brack

SAPERE
BOOKS

LYING
AND DYING

Published by Sapere Books.

20 Windermere Drive, Leeds, England, LS17 7UZ,
United Kingdom

saperebooks.com

ISBN: 978-1-912546-69-5

Chapter 1

There are some beautiful parts of Prague, thought Bear, but Holešovice is not one of them.

He plodded on through the cold morning air, hands thrust deep into his jacket pockets and shoes crunching on the ice that was scattered in lumps on the pavement. Few tourists came to this part of town, though Bear conceded to himself that the Letná was a nice park, somewhere to take the children on a Sunday and unwind a bit. The looming bulk of the Arena reminded him that there was always the hockey to come here for, the regular winter entertainment that he enjoyed when he could afford it, which was not too often, and when he was off shift, which seemed to happen even less.

He glanced at his watch. 04:24. Whoever heard of a shift starting at a quarter to five? When the latest agreement had been reached with the railway management, the hours to be worked had turned out not to be easily divisible by the number of days to be worked, with the result that one of the team had to come in a quarter of an hour early each morning by rotation. Since they could do nothing useful until the others turned up fifteen minutes later, Bear failed to see any point in this arrangement, but rules are rules, so here he was, tramping in to work on a frosty February morning in Holešovice.

He carried on down Za Elektrárnou and rounded the corner into Partyzánská. Even the *bufet* was still shut. They had the good sense not to open until six, so he never managed to get any breakfast there. He could see the metro station ahead of him, and just below it the service road he followed to enter the mainline station where he worked. There was someone sleeping on the concreted area where a couple of cars could park. Poor so and so — it had been a cold night, hardly fit for sleeping rough, even if they were well bundled up.

As he drew closer, he wondered if he should wake the sleeper up and urge him to move before the police drove past and ran him in. It might be kinder to let him spend a couple of nights in a nice warm cell. Illogically, Bear decided that he would look at the sleeper's face. If he looked young and innocent, he would wake him. If, on the other hand, he was a wino, Bear would leave him alone.

Thus it was that Bear passed by around three metres from the sleeper's feet, only to see that the person was not sleeping. The staring eyes told him that. She also had a protruding tongue and what looked like a livid scratch on her neck. Bear had seen a few dead bodies during his military service, so he did not panic, but looked around for help. There was a man coming over the brow heading towards the tram stop, whom Bear hailed. It so happened that the newcomer had a cellphone, which they used to summon the police, but then he said he had seen nothing that the police could possibly want to know and he dared not be late for work, so he headed for the tram. As for Bear, he had no great love of work, and this offered a perfect reason to delay going there, so he sat patiently waiting for the police to arrive.

The uniformed police were first, but within moments they had summoned the detectives on duty and retreated to the warmth of their car. They allowed Bear to sit in the back, but kept the window wound down so that they could order people to keep well away from the body. After about twenty minutes a battered old police car pulled up behind them, and a battered old policeman climbed out, stretched himself, and turned his collar up against the sharp wind.

Josef Slonský had been a policeman in Prague for nearly forty years, working his way up from the lowest of the low to a position of almost no influence whatsoever. Although he was a lieutenant, he never expected to make captain, and did not care one bit. His remaining ambition in the police force was to make it to retirement age without any young yob bashing his skull in with a lump of wood, and needling his superiors just enough to satisfy his sense of insubordination without leaving him vulnerable to reprisals. In this he had done extremely well, and Captain Lukas regularly read the police handbook to see if there were grounds to let Slonský go early.

The old detective scratched his thigh thoughtfully and surveyed the crime scene.

'Navrátil?'

'Sir?'

'Had breakfast?'

'No, sir.'

'Me neither. Damn. Have a word with the troglodytes in the squad car while I go and see what's what.'

Navrátil was uncertain exactly what sort of word was needed, but after two days with Slonský he was beginning to understand his new boss. Slonský did not really want someone from the academy to care for, but he did want someone to be a gofer for him. In return for small domestic services like making coffee, he was prepared to dispense occasional pearls of wisdom that might benefit Navrátil's career. Lots of people told Navrátil that Slonský was a good cop. None of them actually wanted to work with him, but they were all agreed that he was a good cop.

Navrátil hovered by the window, hoping to be invited into the warm car, but there was no sign of such a courtesy from his uniformed colleagues. They explained that the guy in the back seat was the one who had called them, and they had then called the detectives' office. No, they had not called a pathologist, because that was a decision for the detective when he arrived on the scene.

Navrátil walked over to Slonský.

'Should I call a pathologist?'

'Bit late for a bloody dentist,' Slonský replied, and walked off to inspect the head from another angle.

Chapter 2

Dr Novák knew Slonský of old. Each had a healthy public contempt for the other's profession tempered by the knowledge that the other was a good exponent of it. The detectives let Novák do his work for a few minutes before curiosity got the better of them.

'Any idea who we're looking for?' asked Slonský.

'You're after a left-handed dwarf, red hair, slight stoop, smokes French cigarettes.'

Navrátil flipped open his notebook.

'Don't bother,' Slonský told him. 'Dr Novák always blames things on left-handed dwarves. If we ran them all in this would be a crime-free paradise.'

Novák smiled. Behind his thick glasses his luminous blue eyes glinted with pleasure.

'It's hard to get a good time of death because she wasn't killed here. There's no blood and the livid patch isn't the lowest point, so the body has been moved. I'll do the usual back at the mortuary, but for now I'm satisfied that she was strangled somewhere else and brought here. I know the temperature here, and I know her temperature now, but I don't know what it was when she was left here or where she was before that. My guess — but don't hold me to it — is that she was killed around midnight and brought here about two to three o'clock.'

Slonský nodded. 'There are people coming and going up until midnight, so the murderer would risk being seen. On the other hand, you don't want to be stopped driving around Prague with a stiff in the passenger seat.'

'How do you know she wasn't in the boot?' asked Navrátil.

Novák grinned. 'Tell him!'

Slonský put a fatherly arm around Navrátil's shoulder.

'You see, son, women are a lot heavier than you'd think when they're dead. Try lifting a dead one out of a car boot, even assuming you've been able to fold her into it, and you'll do yourself a mischief. Look at how she's lying. She was sitting in the passenger seat, probably with a seat-belt holding her upright. In the dark she would just look like she was having a nap to anyone who spotted her. Then when they arrived here the murderer reversed into the space, opened the door, and just gave her a nudge. Then he pulled the feet free of the car, checked no-one was looking, and took off.'

'How do you know he reversed?'

'Because you have to do any criminal the courtesy of assuming he isn't a complete idiot. First, he would want to tip the body out on the side away from the main road in case anyone passed by. Second, the front seat is marked by where she fell on the ground. If he drove in forwards, she would be almost on the grassy bank and nearer the end of the concrete. Unless, of course, she drove herself here after she was strangled, in which event we're looking at the wrong side of the car. But all in all, I think you'll find my hypothesis is more likely.'

Novák was directing the photographer's attention to the key points he wanted recording.

'He's a bright lad, is old Slonský. Listen to him, son, and one day you might make it to the dizzy heights of lieutenant.'

Slonský took it in good part. 'Haven't you got an anus to swab somewhere?'

'All in good time. Don't mind me. I'll carry on here while you go and talk to that nice man who found the body.'

Slonský could see no reason to put it off any longer and ambled across to the car. The policemen swiftly urged Bear to get out to speak to the lieutenant.

'Tell me what you saw.'

Bear told him.

'There wasn't anyone taking a length of rope off the neck of the woman when you got here?'

'Course not.'

'I know. Just hoping. One day, by the law of averages…'

Slonský turned back to look at Novák busily gesticulating to the photographer, the paramedics with their body bag, and a passer-by who was passing by too close.

'Thanks for calling us, Mr … Bear. Why do they call you Bear?'

Bear opened the top two buttons on his shirt to reveal a mat of black hair.

'Fair enough,' said Slonský. 'If we've got your address you can go.'

'Gave it to these boys,' Bear replied, and began to walk along the side road, keeping well away from the body on the other side.

Slonský called after him. 'Bear! One last question.'

Bear turned round and stopped.

'Where's the best place around here to get a sausage?'

Navrátil cradled the hot coffee.

'Not hungry?' asked Slonský.

'Had one.'

'I know. I saw you. But you're a growing lad.'

'I'm full.'

Slonský shrugged. Young men today! He took another slug of coffee, a bite of his *párek* and sighed with satisfaction.

'Not a bad sausage, this. For fifty crowns, that is.'

'Sir,' began Navrátil, 'shouldn't we be out … doing something?'

'We are doing something, Navrátil. We're preparing ourselves for a long day with a decent breakfast.'

'But the murderer —'

'Keep your voice down! He could be here, for all we know.'

Navrátil gulped. 'He could be getting away.'

'He could,' conceded Slonský. 'But since we don't know who he is and we can't arrest all one million, two hundred thousand inhabitants and hold them for questioning, it's not clear to me why we need to skip breakfast. Carry on like that, lad, and you'll fade away to nothing long before you make captain.'

This was not something likely to happen to Slonský, who was rather generously proportioned. There were three reasons for this. First, he had a genetic disposition to the fuller figure (he claimed), a propensity evidenced by his aunt whose backside he alleged had been the model for the plinth of the Stalin statue overlooking the river. Second, Slonský had a prodigious appetite and rarely missed a meal. He claimed that this did not affect him because the furious workings of his brain consumed any number of calories and kept him slim and trim. Third, he was without any doubt the laziest policeman in Prague, and probably in Central Europe. Slonský rarely saw the need to rush, and was frequently to be found conserving his energy with his feet on his desk. When Captain Lukas queried this, Slonský told him that complete physical immobility was a prerequisite if the mental processes were not to be interfered with by extraneous nervous signals from moving muscles. Since he solved the case he was working on within a couple of hours — a denouement made more likely by the fact (that he omitted to tell Lukas) that he already had a signed confession

— Slonský had been left to do his own thing thereafter. However, this was the first time that he had been trusted with an academy graduate of his own to corrupt.

Slonský finished his *párek* and grabbed his hat and gloves.

'Come on, Navrátil. We haven't got time to waste sitting here in the warm.'

Navrátil opened his eyes wide. He hoped he had not dropped off in the warm interior of the café, where the fire reminded him of his grandmother's house with its sweet smell of gas.

'Sorry, sir. Where are we going now?'

'Back to headquarters. We don't have any forensics to go on, we don't have a suspect and we don't have a motive, so I reckon our best bet is trying to find out who the victim is. She didn't have a handbag with her so we'd best see what missing persons reports have come in.'

They arrived at the car and Slonský opened the passenger side door.

'You can drive.'

'Forgive my asking, sir, but *do* you drive?'

'I've got a licence. Army gave it to me when I did my national service. They wanted me to drive a tank, Navrátil, so I took it for a spin round Hungary when we were on manoeuvres. Good place to learn to drive, Hungary is; big, flat, open plain and very few buildings.' He paused for effect. 'One less now. Those things turn on a fly's armpit, Navrátil. You should have seen the fraternal greetings I got from the Hungarian sitting on the outside privy.'

'You ran over a privy?'

'Of course not. No, I demolished his house while he was in the privy. If I'd run over the privy he'd have been salami and he wouldn't have been so upset. Still, he got some

13

compensation and a new house somewhere, I shouldn't wonder. Navrátil, that light was red. I know we're the police but it looks bad if you jump lights, son.'

'Sorry, sir. I must have been distracted.'

'Anyway, in answer to your question, I can drive, but I don't. What's the point of a car in Prague? The roads are choked, there's no parking anywhere and the metro is cheap and quick. Of course, I get a car, but then I can do my charitable bit by letting you drive, Navrátil, because you wouldn't qualify for a car, so I let you drive mine. Say "Thank you, Lieutenant".'

'Thank you, Lieutenant.'

'Think nothing of it, Navrátil. I certainly do. Hang on, I just want to get a couple of rolls at the bakery. Pull up on the crossing, I won't be long.'

The note of Novák's telephone message was succinct. "There is something here you will want to see", it said.

'We'll take him at his word,' said Slonský. 'Get the car started, lad, and I'll be down in a minute.'

Navrátil put his coat back on, grabbed his notebook and looked for a spare pen. When he reached the front door Slonský was already in the passenger seat.

'Sorry, sir. Thought you had something to do.'

'I did. And I did it. First rule of police work, Navrátil: never miss a chance to splash your boots. Who knows when it'll come round again?'

They drove to the pathology department where Dr Novák was in mid-autopsy, but they were ushered in.

'Is this one mine?' asked Slonský.

'She is. Mid to late twenties, a bit of cosmetic dentistry, probably locally done, no distinguishing marks.'

'No tattoos? I thought all young women got themselves tattooed now.'

'Not this one.'

'Inconsiderate bitch. Anything else?'

Novák paused for dramatic effect.

'Yes, there's something very interesting under her knickers.'

'You'll excite the boy. Navrátil, pay no attention to this sad old man. Every woman has something interesting under her knickers, so I'm told.'

'Not like this one, Slonský. This one is without parallel in my experience.'

Novák walked round the table to their side and prepared to re-enact the first part of the post mortem examination.

'We removed her clothing and laid her here —'

'Can't you get arrested for that?'

'You're the policeman, you tell me. It didn't take us long to notice that there was something very unusual in her vagina.'

Novák held out a tray, in which there was a small plastic bag containing a roll of coloured paper.

'You can handle it. I've finished with it now.'

Slonský donned some gloves.

'Have you counted it?'

'Counted and recorded,' Novák replied. 'Two hundred and forty-nine thousand, two hundred and fifty crowns.'

'My piggy bank had a slit in its back,' Slonský said, 'but I suppose this works just as well. That's a decent amount of money, but a hell of an awkward place to keep it if you need to pay off a taxi.'

'It would have been,' agreed Novák, 'but I don't think she put it there. It had urine on the outside.'

'Now you tell me,' Slonský complained, his face crumpled with distaste.

'I've washed it. And a bit of pee never hurt anyone. My point is that the likeliest reason for that is that her bladder emptied when she died and the urine got on the bag as someone inserted it.'

Slonský slowly walked around the table to inspect the body from all sides.

'I wonder why they didn't make it a round two hundred and fifty thousand? It would have been a smaller bundle of notes for a start.'

'Maybe that number means something, sir. Like the price of something, or a loan repaid.'

'Nice idea, Navrátil. Of course, it may just have been her life savings, but she isn't much older than you. Have you got two hundred thousand in the bank?'

'No, sir! Nowhere near. I'd have to work for over a year to earn that, and by the time I'd paid my rent —'

'Yes, I've got the point. I've worked a lot longer than you and that would be a very welcome sum for my savings. Novák, on the other hand, probably makes that each month.'

'I wish,' the pathologist muttered.

'So, we've got a young lady who has somehow managed to put together a nice little nest egg which she keeps safe by shoving it up her whatsit.'

'No, someone else shoved it up her whatsit. She was already dead. And you haven't given me a handbag, so I'm assuming there wasn't one there.'

'You assume correctly. While you're deducing you wouldn't like to tell me who she is and who did it?'

'No, that's your job. But I may have a little extra help for you. When we extracted the money I was able to do the usual little extras, and one of those tells me that there had been recent sexual activity.'

'How recent?'

'Very. Last night, I'd say. And my trusty little swab has collected a nice sample of semen, so I can do a DNA test. If you ever catch a suspect, I should be able to tell you if you've got a match.'

'She didn't use a condom, then.'

'No. But she seems free of germs, so I don't think she was a prostitute. You can't be certain, but there's no sign of a lot of use down there.'

Slonský's flippancy evaporated as he knelt at the victim's head.

'Navrátil, would you do me a favour? Nip out into the corridor and find me a good-looking woman in her twenties or thirties.'

'Sir?'

'I take it you've got one or two in this God-forsaken place, Novák?'

'Depends what you want them for. But yes, there are a few.'

Navrátil realised that he was not going to receive an explanation, and did as he was asked. In the reception area he found the receptionist and her supervisor, and asked the supervisor to mind the desk while he borrowed the receptionist. He had to offer his police identity card for close inspection before they agreed and he was able to conduct her to the mortuary.

Navrátil held the door open and followed her in, which put him in the perfect place to impede her running away when she saw the body on the slab.

'Don't mind her, she won't bite,' said Slonský. 'You've seen a naked woman before, I'm sure.'

'Is she … dead?'

Slonský considered his answer carefully.

'She's certainly a bit under the weather. But I'm no doctor, you'll have to ask Novák.'

Novák tutted.

'What I'd like you to do, miss, is come round here next to me and look carefully at this woman's hair. Now, I know very little about hair, but I reckon that's a pretty expensive hairdo. She's got those little red stripey bits hidden in the middle —'

'Highlights,' offered the receptionist.

'Exactly. And I've seen a few of those, and there's not many people tone them in as well as this lot. Am I right?'

The receptionist looked closely. As she bent over she inhaled sharply.

'French perfume,' she said. 'I'm not exactly sure which one but it's not cheap.'

'Excellent! Keep going!'

'Well, her nails are well kept, except for that broken one.'

Novák held up the hand.

'Broken in a struggle. She had tiny chips of leather under the nails, as if she had clawed the back of a pair of gloves.'

'Not unreasonable if you're being strangled. Carry on.'

'I don't think she does much in the way of housework. No wedding ring, see?'

Novák held up another bag.

'This gold cross and chain were in her clothes. I think they were probably wrenched off as she was attacked.'

The woman looked closely at the jewellery.

'Again, that's not cheap. It's real gold, not plated. Nice stuff! I've never had anything like this. In fact, I don't think I've seen one like it in the shops in Prague.'

'We can tout it round a few jewellers, Navrátil,' Slonský said. 'See if anyone knows where she could have got it.'

'The same goes for her earrings,' declared the receptionist. 'Not garnet or opal like most of us. Hoops with two real diamonds. She must have had a well-paid job.'

'You don't think she's a whore?' asked Slonský conversationally.

The young woman recoiled from the body.

'Is she? No, she can't be. I mean, I know she's got a few nice things, but she doesn't look … easy.'

'Dead people rarely do. And even a tart is somebody's daughter.'

'But if she was … like that, wouldn't her boss have taken the good jewellery off her?'

'They're called pimps and you're absolutely right. That stuff wouldn't have lasted five minutes in the lap-dancing places. I suppose she could be a hotel escort, in which event we're stuffed because no hotel is going to admit that she ever set foot in the place.'

'We could ask for the security videos,' Navrátil suggested, pleased that a sensible idea had come to him.

'We could,' agreed Slonský, 'and you can spend many a happy afternoon watching hours of people going in and out of doors. The thing is, Navrátil, that it takes the best part of twenty-four hours to watch twenty-four hours of live action video. We can do that if we can find a hotel that looks a likely prospect.'

The receptionist was inspecting the victim's toes.

'Nasty corn there. Badly fitting shoes, I suppose.'

Novák reached behind himself to retrieve a plastic crate.

'The very shoes.'

The receptionist cooed.

'They're nice! I wouldn't mind some like that. Italian leather slingbacks.'

Slonský beamed.

'Pay attention, Navrátil. You're going to have to put all this technical stuff in your report. That's a good expert you've found us.'

The receptionist smiled at Navrátil, who blushed slightly.

'They're not new,' she said. 'The heel is worn down. I couldn't walk in these without a bit of practice. They're quite high.'

'Can you tell the size?' asked Slonský.

'Thirty-eight,' said Novák. 'Did it with callipers. You can't read it on the inside.'

'What about the brand?'

'It's not easy to read, but it looks like something or other Gozzi.'

'Alberto Gozzi?' asked the receptionist. 'You wouldn't get them for under five thousand. There aren't many places in Prague you can get those.' She pondered for a moment. 'I've seen them in a place in the New Town, somewhere along Na Příkopě.'

'Write that down, Navrátil! It'll save you a lot of walking later.'

Within a few minutes Navrátil's notebook was filled with addresses of hairdressers, jewellers and shoeshops that might possibly have equipped the young lady, and the receptionist, suitably flattered by Slonský's encomiums on her intelligence and powers of observation, returned to her post to discuss her half-hour with anyone who would listen.

'Get on to headquarters, Navrátil. They've got a tame artist they use. Ask him to draw the girl with her eyes open. We can't put her picture in the paper looking like this. No rush, so long as he gets it done by tonight.'

Slonský swept out of the room without any acknowledgement of Novák.

'Is he always like this?' asked Navrátil.

'No,' conceded Novák. 'Sometimes he can be quite brusque.'

Navrátil expected to go straight out on his tour of the shops, but Slonský restrained him.

'Waste of effort until you get a photo, lad. Unless, of course, they've only ever sold one pair of shoes or done one hairdo. This is going to be a long day, so we'd best fortify ourselves with a bit of lunch. I'm off out for a sausage and a beer. Coming?'

'I'm not hungry yet, sir.'

'Suit yourself, but don't come running to me if you die of starvation. If anything urgent comes up, I'm at the café on the corner.'

He remained at the café on the corner for nearly two hours, and had not returned when Captain Lukas wandered into the office.

'On your own, Navrátil? Where's Slonský?'

'Gone to lunch, sir, but he suggested one of us ought to stay by a phone in case the artist had finished his picture.'

'Really? Well, I hope Slonský remembers you need a lunch break too. I don't want my trainees fainting in the street. Tell the lieutenant I'd like a verbal report when he returns.'

Slonský appeared behind Lukas in the doorway.

'No need, sir. I can do it now.'

'Ah, good! Well, how is it going?'

'The dead person is a woman, sir, with a quarter of a million crowns in a plastic bag up her private parts.'

Lukas' mouth opened and closed several times.

'That is extraordinary!'

'I'm not sure, sir. For all we know there may be women all over Prague with their life savings between their legs.'

Lukas frowned.

'Your flippancy is misplaced, as always, Slonský. This is a very serious affair.'

'Murder always is, sir. She was strangled somewhere else, taken to Holešovice by car and dumped near the mainline station. We don't have an identification yet but young Navrátil here showed great initiative by asking a receptionist at the hospital where the victim could have bought her clothes, and as soon as he has a likeness to work with, he'll be trawling indefatigably round town.'

Lukas beamed at the young policeman, who was blushing at the unexpected and unwarranted praise.

'Well done, Navrátil. I can see I was right to pair you with this old warhorse. Keep me posted, Slonský!'

He swept out of the door with the grace of a poorly hitched caravan.

'Why did you tell him it was my idea, sir?'

'Because I don't need the praise and you do. Captain Lukas is an honest man and a fair cop, but he's a shallow as a dried-up puddle. Never embarrass him, never let him down and try as hard as you can never to tell him anything you don't want the world to know. Now, any word from Novák?'

'Not yet, sir.'

'Damn! We don't need a work of art, just a good likeness. Hand me the phone, lad.'

Slonský dialled Novák's number and chatted briefly with the pathologist.

'He says the artist is there but it'll be another hour or two yet, Navrátil. Come on, we're off to the metro station at Holešovice.'

'Can I ask why, sir?'

'We're going to speak to the rough sleepers there.'

'There weren't any, sir, or we'd have talked to them this morning.'

Slonský stopped in his tracks, turned and sighed deeply.

'Now, Navrátil, I've built you up as a bright lad and you do this to me. Of course there weren't any rough sleepers there this morning. Who turned up first?'

'The squad car, sir.'

'Exactly. So when a car turns up with "Police" written on its side, what are rough sleepers going to do? Scarper! Only a dimwit would hang around to be arrested.'

'But if they'd seen anything, wouldn't they have reported it?'

'They might. But they're not supposed to be there, they may not have the money for a phone call, and they might be worried that the killer would turn on them. Having said all that, it was a cold night and I guess they squeezed under the canopy at the bus station side to keep out of the wind, so they wouldn't be able to see the parking area fifty metres down the hill. But if we're lucky one of them might have seen a car, and it's the only lead we've got, so get your skates on.'

The homeless men seemed to know Slonský and were relaxed when he approached, though a little suspicious of Navrátil.

'Good afternoon, gentlemen,' Slonský announced. 'I'm not interested in giving you any trouble. I need some help.' He waved his badge at nobody in particular. 'A young woman was found strangled down the hill there early this morning, and don't tell me you didn't know that.'

'We didn't,' one protested, 'but we knew it was something important when the uniformed guys didn't chase us off. Even so, best not be around. Police and homeless don't mix.'

'I couldn't give a toss about that. More important things than moving you on.' He counted heads, turned to Navrátil and shoved a banknote in his hand. 'Navrátil, get some coffee for us all, will you? There's a place in the station.'

The men nodded their appreciation.

'What I need to know is when the body was dumped and if anyone saw a car that might have done it.'

The small group stamped their feet to keep warm and shrugged their shoulders. Nobody had seen the body dumped, and cars had run past all night, so that was no help at all. Slonský was not surprised, but he had hoped that there might be some chance of a step forward in the investigation.

Navrátil handed out the coffees, and the men grabbed them in their frozen hands, wrapping long, blue fingers around them. The braver ones took a sip of the scalding, tarry liquid.

'I don't know…' began a young one with a tattoo of a snake wrapped round his neck.

'Yes?' asked Slonský.

'Well, it might have nothing to do with it, but there was a big German car that came by around two or half past two.'

'German?'

'BMW or Merc. Didn't really look too closely. I think it was beige or some similar colour. Anyway, I saw it come over the bridge and towards us here, then as it went past us it seemed to be slowing down. I didn't watch where it went, but I thought from the engine noise that it must have parked somewhere nearby.'

'What did you think they stopped for?'

'I guessed they were … courting.'

'You mean shagging?'

'Maybe. Anyway, there was no point in spying on them, because after a minute or so the car drove off again. But I didn't hear any other car slow down near us.'

The others furrowed their brows as if weighing his story against their own experience. One lifted his cap and scratched his head as if thinking was an unnatural act.

'There was a truck around one o'clock.'

'Closed truck or pick-up?' asked Slonský.

'Pick-up. Something written on the side but I couldn't read it from here. But I think the driver was on his own. He stopped at the bend down the hill but he didn't turn his engine off.'

Slonský smiled broadly.

'Thanks, fellas. I knew I could count on you.'

He waved goodbye and led Navrátil back to the metro.

'Shouldn't we take statements, sir?'

'They won't give them, Navrátil, and if we'd asked we'd have got nowhere. What would we use them for? If we find our killer, identifying his car isn't going to be the key to nailing him. But at least we've got a plausible time and a possible car.'

'Shall I ask the motor licensing authorities to give us lists of owners of beige BMWs and Mercedes?'

'Navrátil, do you like watching paint dry? There'll be thousands, and we can't say for sure it was beige. Let's find our man, then corroborate our suspicions with these snippets.'

The officer at the main desk had an envelope for Slonský when they returned to the station.

'What do you think, lad? Good likeness?'

'I'd recognise her in the street.'

'Doubt you'll see her there now, but it'll do us nicely. Be a little angel and run it over to the publicity department so they can get it in the papers for the morning. They'll want some flannel so tell them where she was found but leave it at that. What we want is big headlines saying "Did you know this woman?". Then go home — we've done enough for today and we're going to need all the rest we can get. See you here at seven tomorrow.'

Navrátil nodded and disappeared through the double doors, leaving Slonský leaning against the front desk.

'How's he doing?' asked Sergeant Mucha.

'Navrátil? He's all right. Got to learn to pace himself though. You get nowhere rushing.'

Slonský dumped his battered hat on his head, shrugged the coat back onto his shoulders, and turned towards the door.

'Fortunately he has the great advantage of having me to show him the ropes.'

The portrait duly appeared in the Prague newspapers, though it achieved less prominence in some than Slonský would have liked, prompting him to remark that a photograph of the naked corpse would certainly have made the front page in that kind of rag.

Navrátil occupied himself in a tour of the shops, clutching a single shoe in a plastic evidence bag and the jewellery in another. He found a jeweller who recognised the cross and chain, but admitted that he had sold a few recently and could not remember to whom. However, he had only had them in stock within the last year. Another thought it possible that he might have sold the earrings but was unable to say when or to whom, and it was with a sense of disappointment and failure that Navrátil reported back to Slonský in the evening.

'Can't say, or won't say?' Slonský demanded.

'He said he couldn't,' replied Navrátil.

'That's what his mouth said,' Slonský muttered. 'What did his eyes say?'

'Sir?'

'You'll have to learn to watch the eyes, Navrátil. You see, lad, villains lie. I've complained about it to Captain Lukas, but that's just the way it is. It's not like detective novels when you accuse a man and he stretches his arms out all ready for the cuffs and tells you it's a fair cop.'

'I understand that, sir, but I'm not sure I can tell if someone's lying as easily as that.'

'Navrátil, would it surprise you to learn that I was Bohemian downhill skiing champion in 1973?'

Navrátil's jaw dropped open. 'Yes, it would, sir.'

'So it should, Navrátil, because it's a complete lie. See, you're getting the hang of it already. Let's go and see the chap with the earrings and I'll give you a master class.'

As they left the shop, Navrátil hung expectantly on Slonský's verdict.

'Well, sir, was he telling the truth?'

Slonský bustled impatiently away.

'You never told me he had a squint, Navrátil.'

'But he hasn't…' Navrátil began, before realising he was talking to thin air, for Slonský was already sitting in the passenger seat.

Chapter 3

Slonský was, it seemed, a poor sleeper, which accounted for his early arrival — and dishevelled appearance — at the station on the following day. He was standing at a table which he had covered with pieces of paper stuck together with sticky tape to form a single large sheet on which some sweeping black lines had been drawn with marker pen.

'Holešovice, Navrátil. A bit of artistic licence, but it'll do for our purposes. Station here, metro here, bus station here, body here. Now, the first tram past arrives at this stop at 04:50. The metro starts a few minutes later. If our killer knows the area he probably knows the tram times.'

'How do we know he knows the area?'

'We don't, but it's unlikely he'd drive around town with a stiff in the front seat looking for a good site. Even if he didn't know this exact spot, he knew that Holešovice was the sort of place he'd find somewhere to dump her.'

'It's very public, though.'

Slonský paused, tapping the marker pen against his teeth.

'Yes, it is. So we deduce …?'

'He knows nobody will be around when he drops the body off. Or he doesn't care.'

'Or he wants the body found quite quickly. He could have driven on for a few minutes and hidden her in a quiet area of the park. Maybe he wanted her found, because he'd have realised that she would be seen within a couple of hours of being left there.'

'Why would he want her to be found? Don't criminals normally hide their crimes?'

A grave shadow passed over Slonský's face.

'Psychopaths don't.'

'You think it could be a serial killer?'

'No.'

'Why not, sir?'

'Grammar, Navrátil. To be a serial killer you have to have killed at least twice, and so far as we know, he hasn't, so he can't be a serial killer.'

Slonský picked up his coat and headed for the door.

'Where are we going, sir?'

'A matter of the utmost importance, Navrátil. Breakfast.'

The portrait was on the front page of most of the papers, but the Prague public were hardly running apace to the nearest police station to identify her. This seemed not to worry Slonský, who merely observed that if she was an "evening worker", her friends or customers were probably still fast asleep, as he wished he was himself. To Navrátil's immense frustration, they busied themselves all morning with other tasks, one of which was to console an elderly lady in Karlín who was convinced that someone had stolen her porch light although there was no sign that one had been over her door for several years. Navrátil tried to explain that since the paint on the building covered the area under the site of the alleged lamp, it was likely that the lady was mistaken, but she abused him, his mother and the Prague police in general. Navrátil returned to the car rather crestfallen.

'It's no good, she won't believe me.'

Slonský folded his newspaper meticulously and pondered for a few moments before easing himself out of the car.

'That's better,' smirked the old dear. 'You look like a proper policeman.'

'See?' Slonský commented to Navrátil. 'Not stupid at all. Now then, grandma, explain to me why you put the light up.'

Navrátil opened his mouth to protest, but Slonský silenced him with a fierce look.

'When they took the old one away after the war. I tried to tell him —' she jerked her head towards Navrátil — 'but these youngsters know nothing. He probably doesn't remember the war, not like you and me.'

'So the old light went and you sorted your own one out? Very resourceful of you.'

The old lady preened herself.

'You have to take care of things yourself. Can't expect the district council to do everything.'

Slonský pointed to the upper window.

'Navrátil, in that bedroom you'll find an electric cable that's been chopped off. It used to have a bulb on the end and someone's run off with it. Hooligans, I expect. Have you got your landlord's phone number? I'll ring him and get him to put a proper light up.'

The woman found a scrap of card and Slonský copied it into his notebook. Navrátil appeared with a length of frayed flex in his hands.

'How did you know?'

'Because, Navrátil, you looked for a light and couldn't see one, whereas I looked for a power lead and saw the chopped end dangling over the windowsill up there, a metre higher.'

'But she said the light was missing, not a power lead.'

'Exactly, Navrátil. It was missing. No point in looking for it, then, was there?'

Slonský smiled angelically and lowered his bulky frame into the car.

'My brain's slowing down. It could do with a pastry or two. Come on, lad, put your foot down.'

'Is detective work always like this?' Navrátil asked.

'No,' Slonský replied, 'sometimes it's even more boring.'

They were sitting in an unmarked car watching a building. Since it was in a rundown area of the city, they had left their normal car behind and had been allocated a ramshackle old Škoda with around two hundred thousand kilometres on the clock, a top speed that would have disgraced many a cyclist, and a patch of corroded doorsill that whistled as they drove along.

'Try to look less official, lad,' Slonský counselled. 'Take your tie off if you want.'

'Are you going to take yours off?'

'No point. Everybody knows me. Disguise is a waste of time when you've got a face like this.'

'But if they know you're a policeman, won't they know I'm one too?'

'Ah, spot the logical flaw in that argument, Navrátil! I said they know me. I didn't say they knew what I am. I've cultivated anonymity for many a year. Everybody knows me but they don't know my business. They've met me in a bar or having a sausage somewhere, but so far as anyone knows I'm just someone who works in some office or other. You don't get to be as nondescript as I am by accident, Navrátil. You have to work at it. I wasn't born grey, you know. I'm a self-unmade man.'

Slonský smiled, happy with the epithet he had just bestowed upon himself, and stored it away to use spontaneously later.

'I know I'm going to regret asking this, sir —'

'Then don't. Not worth putting yourself through any more humiliation than life is planning to send your way anyway.'

'… but why are we watching a pole-dancing club at four in the afternoon? It's shut.'

'Exactly. So if anyone goes in, we're more likely to get a good view of him, since it's daylight and the place is deserted. At one in the morning with a crowd of punters hanging around it'd be a lot more difficult.'

'But why should anyone turn up?'

'Because if our information is correct — which I increasingly doubt — a delivery of stolen pilsner is likely to be made, and I don't expect they'll leave it outside the door. They'll want cash, and a bit of help unloading the truck I shouldn't wonder.'

Navrátil drummed the steering wheel.

'They could come any day.'

'They could,' conceded Slonský, 'but today is favourite. If it was stolen last night, the chances are they'll want rid of it pronto. Ever tried to hide a letter from your mother, Navrátil?'

'A school report, once.'

'Then you'll know how difficult it is. So just think how hard it is to hide a truckload of beer in Prague, where every other male inhabitant can sniff out a bottle of beer at fifty metres through two locked doors. No, they'll get it moved on as fast as they can.'

There was a rumble as a lorry pulled into the street.

'Ah!' Slonský beamed. 'A beer delivery.'

'Yes, but this one's legit. A company lorry.'

Slonský stared at him.

'You poor devil. We're going to have to work hard on that innocent veneer of trust, Navrátil. If you were going to deliver beer without drawing attention to yourself, what sort of vehicle would be best for the job?'

'A beer lorry, I suppose.'

'Oh, look, that's what we have here! An odd coincidence, wouldn't you say?'

Slonský read the licence plate over his radio. A few moments later the disembodied voice told them what they needed to know.

'Should be a red Škoda Fabia, Lieutenant.'

Slonský climbed out of the car, and waited for Navrátil to join him.

'Come on, son, let's go and arrest the driver of that red Škoda Fabia full of lager.'

To Slonský's surprise, the afternoon and evening brought no identification of the body.

'She's a striking girl, well groomed. Somebody must be missing her, Navrátil.'

'Perhaps she lived alone.'

'Maybe, but we know she wasn't on her own last night. Somebody had her, and somebody killed her.'

'But the murderer isn't going to contact us, sir.'

Slonský sighed deeply.

'I suppose not. But you'd think they'd do it once in a while just out of cockiness. Make yourself useful, lad — fetch your notebook and start making a list of people who might be missing her. For a start, she had a decent amount of money and some expensive tastes, but Novák doesn't think she's a prostitute.'

'A mistress, then?'

'Could be. Or a young wife of a middle-aged man who has made his pile. If she had a regular job her employer ought to have missed her by now.'

'If only we had her handbag, sir.'

'Never mind that. If only her mother had sewn her name in her knickers like my mum did.'

'I don't suppose it's worth checking —'

'No. Novák isn't so dim that he'd miss a surname in someone's pants. We have to assume it wasn't there.'

'Maybe she's just one of those people that don't have anyone to miss her.'

Slonský's face clouded over. When he spoke, his voice was quieter than usual, colder and firmer.

'I've known some real villains in my time, Navrátil. Human filth of the worst kind. And they all had someone to miss them. I remember a party secretary who had a local rival fed into a furnace a few centimetres at a time; his mother was heartbroken when he was shot. Until someone proves otherwise to me, I'll go on believing that every human being matters to someone.'

He picked up his hat and moved decisively for the door.

'There's only one thing to do, Navrátil. Let's get a beer.'

Two hours later, they were surrounded by wet beer mats and Navrátil was beginning to think that he would go home — the moment he remembered where home was. Being slightly built, he could hardly match Slonský, who appeared to be a practised drinker.

'Another one over here,' Slonský called to the waiter.

'I don't think I can manage another one,' Navrátil protested.

'Nonsense.'

'Why are we drinking anyway? We don't have anything to celebrate.'

'That's not the only reason for a drink, Navrátil. If you only drank to celebrate the Czech Republic wouldn't have much of a brewing industry.'

'To forget, then?'

'On the contrary, Navrátil, I drink for a religious reason. I'm a beer Buddhist.'

'I didn't think Buddhists drank beer.'

'Don't they? Poor devils. No, I drink to achieve enlightenment, which is a religious state much desired by Buddhists.'

'Enlightenment?'

'Exactly. There is a point, Navrátil, at which the brain ceases to maintain its tenuous hold on reality and allows itself to be carried along in the flood of ideas. It casts itself free of all earthly shackles and enters a meta-existence of cause and effect beyond reasoning.'

Navrátil frowned and composed the next sentence as carefully as his brain would allow after eight beers.

'You what?'

'In the normal run of things, Navrátil, the brain proceeds like a train, along predetermined tracks. It can't free itself of these ideas and preconceptions because a lifetime of training and constraint stops it doing so. But consider for a moment the average two-year-old. If you tell him you have an elephant in a matchbox, he doesn't doubt you. He wants to know how you got it in there. His mind is free, Navrátil, to roam as widely as it wishes, like a soaring swallow. Nothing is impossible to such a mind, and that's precisely the state I aim to achieve.'

'And you think beer will help?'

'It always has in the past. You order another while I go and add to the Vltava.'

Chapter 4

The following morning was bright, warm and sunny. Outside the surviving birdlife of Prague was singing fortissimo, or so it seemed to Navrátil. A prolonged shower did little to help the sensation of devils prodding the backs of his eyeballs with their tridents, and nothing in his pantry did anything to make him believe that there was the remotest chance that it would stay down if he could once swallow it.

He was therefore more than a little surprised to arrive at work to find Slonský with his feet on his desk while he attacked a *párek* and a takeaway coffee.

'How can you eat that? Or anything else, for that matter?'

'I have a constitution moulded by the Communist years. If you'd been picky about your food then you'd have starved.'

'Don't you feel even a bit queasy?'

'Should I?' Slonský asked innocently, as if the idea that a heavy drinking bout might affect your appetite the next day had never occurred to him.

'Never mind. I'd better find some water.'

Navrátil was halfway down the corridor when he heard Slonský call after him.

'If you can't find water, try some Hungarian beer. It's the next best thing.'

When Navrátil returned, Slonský was looking thoughtful.

'It was something you said last night that inspired me,' he explained.

'I said? What did I say?'

'You said it was a shame she didn't have her name sewn into her knickers.'

'You said that, sir!'

'Did I? Then I'm brighter than I thought. Anyway, how did the murderer know that she didn't have her name sewn into her knickers?'

'Maybe he didn't care.'

'He took the handbag.'

'Well, since he made love to her, he probably got to see her underwear.'

'Do you look, Navrátil?'

'Eh?'

'When you're with a woman, do you check her pants out?'

'Well, I … I haven't … but if I did …'

'Exactly. It's an unnatural act. But whether he did or didn't, he might have handled her clothes. That's what I asked Novák.'

'And?'

'Nothing. Now, she may have taken off her own clothes and put them back on herself. And perhaps he wore gloves to dispose of the body. But I can't picture anyone going to bed with a girl and wearing gloves while he did it.'

'Which rules out a crime of passion?'

'Well, he was farsighted enough to have gloves there. It was a cold night so he may have just had them with him, but this begins to look premeditated. Which is good, Navrátil. Where there's a plan, we can discover it. It's the sudden, irrational killing that is hardest to detect.'

'So we have a man who takes a woman out, buys her dinner, takes her back to his flat or hers, makes love to her, kills her then dumps her body where it will be found quickly.'

'Where did you get the bit about dinner?'

'The stomach contents. Novák's report doesn't sound like the kind of meal someone would cook for themselves. Asparagus, for example.'

'We could waste a lot of time tracking down shops that have asparagus in February, but let's run with your idea for a minute. If that's the case, they must have eaten in a restaurant somewhere that has asparagus on the menu.'

Navrátil's face sank.

'I can see you're one step ahead of me, lad. But it'll take a lifetime to visit all Prague's restaurants. We'll do it if we have to, but for the moment let's try the wholesale greengrocers. See how easy it is to get asparagus and if anyone can tell us who has been buying it. Might narrow things down a bit.'

When Navrátil returned, Slonský had his feet on his desk, a coffee in his hand, and a broad smile on his face.

'Almost all the big hotels, sir. Not too many restaurants have bought asparagus lately, but it still gives us a lot to do.'

'Not necessarily, my boy,' Slonský replied. 'The great Czech public has come to our aid.'

He slid a brown paper envelope across the desk. Navrátil opened it cautiously to find a single photograph within.

'No note?'

'No note. Recognise the girl?'

'It's her! It's the victim.'

'And who is she having dinner with?'

Navrátil scrutinised the picture closely before his jaw dropped.

'Isn't that —'

'It is. Now isn't that a turn-up for the book?'

Slonský was promenading around the office, or as much of it as was accessible to him given his physique and the small gaps between desks.

'Now, the first question is when this picture was taken. I have an idea about that and with a bit of luck we'll have that confirmed fairly soon. I'm assuming that the Minister didn't send me the photograph himself. I like to think that if our public figures are knocking off women other than their wives they'll be decent enough to exercise a bit of discretion.'

'But he's having dinner with her in a public place.'

'Indeed he is, but men can have dinner with women for innocent reasons.'

'He's holding her hand across the table.'

'Ah, that's the way it looks. I'll grant that there's a degree of intimacy here.'

'There's also a near-empty bottle of white wine. But he's drinking mineral water. She must have drunk that bottle by herself.'

'And Novák found evidence of wine in the victim's stomach.'

Navrátil's mouth unaccountably ran dry.

'You think this was taken on the night she died?'

'Not necessarily. Perhaps our informant just wanted us to know how we'd identify her. But then he could have put the name on a bit of paper himself, so I jump to the conclusion that it's the link with our much beloved boss, the Minister of the Interior, that our informant wanted to emphasise. If, of course, this proves to have been taken on that evening then we can ask the Minister some pointed questions.'

'The clock in the corner of the picture shows twenty to nine.'

'And the clock in the corridor outside shows ten to six, but that doesn't mean everything in this station happens then. You see, Navrátil, your generation labours under the disadvantage of not having grown up under Communism. For people of my age, rampant cynicism comes naturally. We always disregard the obvious and assume that things are not what they seem.'

'That's fair enough,' conceded Navrátil, 'but I can't interpret that picture any other way than that the Minister was having dinner with our murder victim in compromising circumstances.'

'It certainly looks that way,' agreed Slonský. 'I suppose she could be his sister or niece.'

'Well, there are nieces and "nieces", but I wouldn't hold my sister's hand like that.'

'No, neither would I. You've got younger eyes than me, lad. Can you see what's on her plate?'

Slonský handed Navrátil a large, brass-handled magnifying glass.

'I didn't think detectives really used these!'

'Essential piece of equipment, Navrátil. Though I use it mainly for getting splinters out of my thumb. Still, it's not only Novák who relies on technology.'

'I can't see much — the angle across the plate isn't right.'

'Neither could I.'

'We might be able to recognise the restaurant, though.'

'Don't spend too long on it. Right, that's long enough. If you haven't got it by now, we'll fall back on the old-timer's technique of asking the suspect.'

'You think the Minister is a suspect?'

'No, Navrátil, not *a* suspect. *The* suspect. We haven't got another one.'

'But he's a Minister.'

'If you'd known some of the Ministers we've had in the past, strangling a woman and ramming a bag of money up her doodah would seem small beer, believe me. Status and position are no guide to honesty. You'd think a priest would be as law-abiding as they come, but we had one in Žižkov who was one of the great cat-murderers of our time. Used to take them out with a handgun from his back door. Good shot, too — there aren't many people who could get a running tabby right up the fundament from thirty metres.'

'There's a world of difference between killing a woman and shooting a cat.'

'Of course there is, but you might think differently if you were a cat. And who do cats have to protect them against lawlessness if not the Prague police department? Granted, cats aren't voters, or we might have a better government than we've got, but they're still entitled to our protection. And who's to say that the man shooting a cat today isn't practising to wipe out his wife tomorrow?'

'Well, the priest wouldn't be. He wouldn't have a wife.'

'And a good thing too, if he's going to go round shooting them up the backside. I rest my case. Hand me the internal phone directory, would you?'

Slonský thumbed through it and dialled a number.

'Technician First Class Spehar.'

'Lieutenant Underclass Slonský. I've got a photo sent in anonymously that needs your expert attention.'

'In an envelope?'

'Of course. My assistant and I have pawed it mercilessly but you may still get something off it.'

'Are your fingerprints on file?'

'Mine are. Don't know about Navrátil's.'

Navrátil shook his head vigorously.

'He tells me he hasn't given his dabs in. If I send him across with the evidence you can do the necessary at the same time.'

'How long have I got?' asked Spehar, suspecting that he knew the answer.

'Don't ask me, I'm not your doctor. But if you don't drink industrial spirits, it'll be longer.'

Slonský replaced the handset and thrust the photograph and envelope into Navrátil's hand.

'Copy the photo first, then run this over to the lab. Spehar will be waiting for it. Tell him that you have to swear him to secrecy about the contents and that he is the only person other than us to have seen it. That way he'll get the thing off his desk and back to us as fast as his little legs will carry him. In the meantime, I will go to the café and invest in some coffee and breakfast for us both.'

'Coffee sounds good,' Navrátil allowed, 'but you can hold the breakfast for me.'

'I'll get you one anyway,' beamed Slonský. 'If you don't want it I'm sure I'll find room for it.'

Technician First Class Spehar proved to be a slightly built man with a balding head, half-moon glasses and a neat grey beard. His name badge described him as "Technician First Class Spehar", leading Navrátil to wonder if that was what his parents had named him. It was quite possible that nobody knew his first name. I wonder what his wife calls him, pondered Navrátil, as he waited patiently for Spehar to complete the evidence receipt and attach a docket to the plastic sleeve.

Deftly, the technician flipped the envelope open and extracted the photograph with his gloved hand.

'Now, what have we … My God! Isn't that …?'

'Yes. That's why we'd like it back quickly, please.'

'And is that the girl in the newspaper?'

'I can't discuss that. Operational reasons.'

'No, of course. Silly of me. Right, I'll get straight onto it. We'll give it the works.'

Navrátil had no idea what 'the works' might be, but it sounded like a superior quality of forensic service so he thanked Spehar and left him to get on with 'the works' with all speed.

When he returned to the office Slonský was sitting with his feet on the desk and a broad smile on his face.

'Your coffee is on the radiator. I hope you haven't changed your mind about breakfast, because it's a bit late. I've almost finished yours.'

'What's that, then?' asked Navrátil, pointing at a cardboard parcel.

'That's mine. I thought I'd better eat yours first, while it was hot. Now, exciting things have been happening while you've been swanning around the forensics lab. The boys in the press office have come up trumps.'

'Why do these things always happen when I'm out?'

Slonský shrugged. 'Why do footballers always score when I'm in the toilet? One of the great mysteries of life, lad, and one that has taxed greater minds than ours. Now, where did you put that copy?'

Navrátil produced the copy of the photograph. Slonský placed it on the left side of his desk before opening a second envelope and spreading its contents across the right side.

'Photographs of the Minister provided by the government press office, showing him going about his various duties on the day before the body was found. Fortunately he likes having photographers around, so we've got a pretty good record of his day. Notice anything, Navrátil?'

'Same shirt, same tie.'

'Precisely. Now, we can assume, I think, that a ministerial salary will run to more than one shirt and tie. That being so, we have to compute the odds that these photographs were all taken on the same day.'

'Maybe he always wears that tie with that shirt.'

'A plausible assumption, but the suit is the same too. And notice that the gap from the underside of the tie knot to the top of the first stripe looks very similar, so his habits extend to always tying his tie in the same way. Possible, but surely the likeliest conclusion is that these were all taken on one day. And since we know when the press photos were taken, that enables us to date the dinner date.'

'The cautious side of me still thinks we shouldn't jump to conclusions.'

'And you should certainly listen to it, Navrátil. But as a working hypothesis we're entitled to think the two go together, and no doubt if we're wrong about that the Minister will tell us so when we go to see him.'

'We're going to see the Minister?'

'We can't ignore the evidence, Navrátil. Someone is dead, and the Minister was with her shortly before she died. We have to ask him about it. At the very least he can explain why he hasn't contacted us to identify her. After all, you would expect the man in charge of policing in this country to help the police do their job, wouldn't you?'

'He may be too busy to see us.'

'Standard rules apply, Navrátil. He can co-operate at his office, or we can bring him down here for questioning if he prefers.'

'Sir, aren't you a bit … wary of accusing a minister?'

'No, and if you think that way you'd better pack your things now. A criminal is a criminal, whatever else he may be, and he gets nailed whoever he is. And while there may be some question about what constitutes a crime as regimes change, strangling a woman is on everyone's list of bad things you shouldn't do. But we'll do things by the book. Let's go and see Lukas.'

Slonský may not have been wary of accusing a minister, but Lukas certainly was. Several careful examinations of the photographs persuaded him at last that there was a need to ask some questions of the Minister, but he insisted that he should make the appointment and accompany Slonský to the Minister's office.

'I want to hear what goes on for myself,' he said, omitting to add 'and intervene if necessary', though they both knew that was what he meant.

'Of course, sir,' replied Slonský. 'I shall be the epitome of respect and discretion.'

'No, you won't,' answered Lukas. 'You don't know how. You'll be a bull in a china shop as usual. But I can't deny that the Minister has some explaining to do.'

The Minister's secretary had booked them an appointment shortly before noon, so Slonský and Lukas were conducted into the Minister's presence precisely on time, while Navrátil waited in the anteroom.

The Minister was a small man, but he had a huge desk. Slonský computed its dimensions and concluded that if the Minister laid his head on the desk he would not be able to reach to the two ends. He also thought that the Minister might be sitting on a cushion to raise him up a little.

The desk's surface was highly polished and free from clutter. A blotter occupied the centre, with a telephone and a computer monitor to the Minister's left. He was wiggling a mouse around as they entered, and completed whatever he was doing on his computer before inviting them to sit in a pair of chairs a couple of metres from the far side of his desk.

'I understand you need my help with a delicate matter,' the Minister oozed. He stopped short of making a steeple with his hands but the motion was clearly in his mind before being dismissed as a cliché.

'Just so, Minister,' Lukas began. 'We are investigating the murder of a young woman and we have come across some material that requires some … interpretation.'

He rose and slid the dinner photograph across the desk. The Minister picked it up and examined it closely without any comment or change in his facial expression.

'I see. Is this the murder victim?'

'We believe so.'

'Then of course you must ask for an explanation. But I'm afraid my help will be limited. I barely know the woman.'

'You seem to be on quite close terms in the photo,' Slonský interjected before Lukas could frame a response.

'A dinner companion,' announced the Minister. 'Not someone I knew well.'

'But you didn't respond to our public appeals to identify the victim,' Slonský continued. 'Why was that?'

The Minister threw his head back to unleash a rolling chuckle.

'I don't read the news, Lieutenant. I make it. I don't need to look at newspapers because I already know the interesting stuff.'

'I'd have thought the murder of someone you had dinner with was of passing interest, sir. But no matter. We still need her identified.'

'Irina. One moment.' He reached into an inside pocket and extracted a slim pocket diary. 'Gruberová. Irina Gruberová.'

'And can you date this dinner, Minister?'

The Minister picked up the photograph again and frowned.

'I don't think so.'

'There were a number of such dinners, then?'

'A small number.'

'A small number like three, or a slightly larger number — ten, say?'

'Three or four.'

'Does the restaurant give it away?'

'Not really. It's a favourite place of mine.'

'If you'd give us the address the reservations book might help us.'

The Minister scribbled an address on a leaf from his jotter pad and passed it to Lukas.

'I don't usually make a reservation. I find I don't need to.'

'We understand,' Lukas assured him.

'Does your appointment diary give us a date, Minister?' asked Slonský, a little more deliberately than was strictly necessary.

'It's not the kind of appointment I would put in my diary, Lieutenant.'

'I understand. Perhaps I could help with a suggestion. It seems to us that it may have been taken on Tuesday evening, because the government press office has supplied us with these pictures taken on Tuesday afternoon. You'll see you appear to be wearing the same clothes.'

'It could have been Tuesday,' the Minister admitted. 'Irina and I had a working dinner then.'

Slonský opened his mouth to speak but Lukas had anticipated the next question.

'May we ask why you use the word "working", Minister?'

'Miss Gruberová was helping me to organise my wife's birthday party.'

'And her particular expertise was in …?' asked Slonský with the air of a man who did not believe there could be a satisfactory answer to his question.

'She wasn't formally trained,' explained the Minister cautiously. 'It was more in the nature of a natural gift.'

'And I suppose that, since this would be a surprise party, your wife would not be in a position to support your alibi because you wouldn't have told her about the meeting.'

'Why should I need an alibi?' asked the Minister.

'Because you seem to have been the last person to see Miss Gruberová alive, Minister. And it's normal practice to begin with the assumption that the last known contact is the likeliest murderer.'

If this perturbed the Minister, he hid it well.

'Of course. That is how things are done. I understand that. But I need hardly explain that I did not, in fact, kill her.'

'And I need hardly explain that almost every murderer I have ever known has said the same thing.'

The Minister frowned and ostentatiously pulled back his sleeve to check his watch.

'Do you remember what you both ate, Minister?'

'I'm sorry?'

'On Tuesday, at your working dinner. Did you keep the receipt for your expenses claim?'

'I don't think the powers that be would let me claim for a dinner on a family matter, Lieutenant,' the Minister chortled. Lukas joined in the laughter, as if to emphasise that he would not allow Slonský to put such a dinner on his expenses either.

'I don't have a family to discuss at dinner,' replied Slonský. 'The menu?'

'I'm not sure. I usually have soup and then something traditional. I think I had a pork steak.'

'And your companion?'

'She had melon, I think, and a schnitzel.'

'With asparagus?'

'Yes, I believe it was. We just ordered some assorted vegetables and shared them. I don't particularly like asparagus, so I didn't bother with it.'

An attendant entered with a tray of coffee, poured for the Minister, and then for Lukas and Slonský, in that order, despite having to walk past Slonský to serve Lukas.

'And after dinner, Minister?'

'I drove Miss Gruberová to her flat and then went home.'

'Perhaps you had some outstanding business to complete in Miss Gruberová's flat.'

'No, I walked her upstairs to her door and left her there.'

'I see. What time was this?'

'About ten, I think.'

'And was there anyone in Miss Gruberová's flat when you got there?'

'I don't think so. The lights weren't on inside, and so far as I know she lived alone.'

'Could you let us have her address?'

'I don't think I know it precisely. She gave me directions.'

'Her phone number then.'

'I'm not sure I have it.'

'You must have had it at some time, Minister, in order to arrange the dinner.'

'I suppose I must. Let me see.' After some leafing through his diary he recited a number.

'Thank you. We may be able to track her address from this.'

'I hope so. It wasn't far from the restaurant, somewhere near the Slavia stadium in Strahov.'

Slonský drained his cup.

'I'm sorry, I'm stopping you finishing your coffee, Minister. We may have to ask your wife to verify the time you arrived home.'

'Of course. I'm not sure she'll be able to help you — she was already in bed when I got in.'

'Yes, that's what she told me,' Slonský said, causing Lukas' eyebrows to jerk violently upwards. 'You see, Minister, we've been keeping something from you. Before she died, Miss Gruberová made love to a gentleman friend. Naturally, if there had been someone in the flat, we would have assumed that he was responsible. But since you say there wasn't, that poses a difficulty.'

'I said I didn't see any lights, Lieutenant. That doesn't mean there wasn't an intruder in the dark.'

'Understood. And of course we'll check out that line of enquiry once we know where the flat is.'

'Excellent. I'm sure we all want you to redouble your efforts to catch the man responsible for this outrage. Captain, I expect you to put all the resources you can into the investigation. If I can help in any way, please let me know.'

'That's very good of you, Minister,' Lukas answered, inclining his head in acknowledgement.

The Minister drained the last of his coffee from his cup. Slonský jumped to his feet, produced a plastic envelope from his pocket, and dropped the cup into it.

'I'm sorry, Minister. I was taking your consent for granted,' he announced guilelessly.

There was a long silence.

'Of course. Now, if there's nothing else …'

'That's very good of you, Minister!' Slonský mimicked Lukas' comment as they walked through the polished corridors back to their car.

'It would do you no harm to learn some manners, Slonský. Fancy snatching the Minister's cup like that.'

'It's evidence. His DNA will be on it.'

'You could have asked him to give a swab.'

'Men like him don't give swabs. He'd probably get an underling to do it for him.'

'Do you seriously expect to get a match with the swab from that young lady?'

'No. He's probably got an underling who does that for him too.'

'Slonský!'

'Well, his type makes me sick.'

'He is our superior, Slonský.'

'That's why he makes me sick. How can you look up to someone who cheats on his wife so flagrantly?'

'I remind you, Slonský, that he denied having intercourse with Miss Gruberová.'

'And that's another reason why he makes me sick. He's a liar.'

'Innocent until proven guilty.'

'Guilty as hell in my eyes. Does he take us for idiots? The girl is holding his hand in that picture. You only have to see the look in her eyes to know that she isn't going to be bonking someone else a couple of hours later. Even if he took her home at ten, which I accept, is it likely that he left her there and within a couple of hours someone had arrived, had persuaded her into bed, had her and strangled her? I don't think so.'

'I grant appearances are against him. What do we do now?'

'I drop this cup in to Novák. It might be good if you signed the evidence bag too. Then we wait for the DNA match. And if, as I expect, it matches the swab, we turn up at the Minister's office with a bunch of squad cars, throw a blanket over his head and march him outside while the press photographers click away merrily.'

'No, Slonský, you'll do no such thing. The arrest of a minister is a very serious business and must be handled properly. I must inform my superiors who will in turn report to the Prime Minister so that he can make arrangements for the continuity of government.'

'We mustn't give him the chance to destroy evidence, sir. He mustn't know we're coming. Please emphasise that to the Prime Minister.'

'I don't think I'll … do you think so? The Prime Minister?'

'Well, you're the senior officer. And your bosses are too spineless to want to tell the PM one of his ministers has murdered a young woman.'

'Yes, I see what you mean. But I can't ask the Director of the Police Service to act with discretion and tact. He won't listen to me. Perhaps the best bet is if the Director and I go to see the Prime Minister while you get your men into position at the Ministry ready for our signal.'

'My men? I don't have men. I have a man.'

'Yes, where is Navrátil? He was outside the Minister's office.'

'He's been doing a little job for me, sir.'

Lukas stopped dead, goggling at Slonský's back as the detective strode away.

'Slonský! Tell me there has been no impropriety here!'

Slonský carried on walking.

'All right, sir. There has been no impropriety here.'

'Slonský! Do I see your fingers crossed behind your back?'

Navrátil was in the back seat when they got in.

'Been waiting long?' asked Slonský.

'Long enough,' Navrátil replied.

'Well, we're here now. What did you find out?'

'His typist didn't know her. The doormen were sure she had never been inside the building, and she hadn't signed in.'

'False name?'

'You need formal identification to get in, sir. Unless she had something that persuaded the security men she was someone else, she hasn't been in.'

'She could have pestered him by phone.'

Lukas felt the need to interrupt. 'Look, what is this? Are you suggesting that she came to the ministry to make a scene?'

'Well, if she had we'd have a motive for killing her. A public figure can't have women turning up at his office alleging intimacy.'

'You've got her phone number. You can check the calls she made.'

'It's a landline. She must have had a mobile phone.'

'How can you know that?'

'She was the mistress of a busy man. There are bound to be last minute changes to plans and she can't sit by the phone waiting for instructions on the off chance. He must have been able to keep in touch with her. Besides, how many women of her age don't have mobile phones these days?'

'So we must see whether her address was used for billing a mobile phone.'

'And his. He may have given her a phone. She won't have called his office or home, so the chances are that she called a mobile phone he had. Which is probably now at the bottom of the Vltava. If you'll drop us off here, sir, Navrátil and I have some business in this area.'

The captain obliged, and Slonský watched him drive around the corner and disappear from sight.

'Nice uniform. Shiny buttons.'

'What urgent business do we have here, sir?'

'The Minister told us to redouble our efforts, Navrátil. So we're going for *two* beers and *two* sausages.'

The desk sergeant leaned over the counter in a conspiratorial fashion. 'Do I detect that substances are about to hit the fan?'

'You do, old friend. I am taking aim at this very moment. But how did you know?'

The lean figure reached under the counter. 'Technician First Class Spehar left this for you.'

'Good old Technician First Class Spehar! The title suits him.'

'He's always first class?'

'No, he's always a technician. Now, Navrátil, let's hide ourselves in some discreet place and see what Spehar has to tell us.'

Slonský opened the door to the main corridor and held it open while he bellowed. 'I hope this report explains why the Minister of the Interior denied shagging that woman who was found dead a couple of hours after he left her.' He winked at the desk sergeant. 'Uninformed gossip is a terrible thing, eh? Better to have facts to work on.'

'The right and proper order of things, Navrátil,' Slonský explained, 'is that I sit with my feet up scanning the report while you make coffee. Instant will do. Top drawer of the filing cabinet.'

'There are no files in this drawer, sir.'

'That's because it's marked "Unsolved Crimes", so I don't need a cabinet as big as that. Plenty of space for coffee and other essentials.'

Navrátil took the kettle to fill it, while Slonský read Spehar's report.

'Does it get us anywhere, sir?'

'A load of technical stuff about the paper used, but it's widely available. There are no fingerprints on the photograph except ours, but there are quite a lot on the envelope, presumably including the postman, someone at the sorting office, and so on. But it's not unknown for blackmailers to forget they've handled an envelope when they bought it, so we live in hope.'

'You think it's blackmail?'

'No, or our informant would have sent the picture to the Minister, since no doubt he would pay better than we do. I thought of blackmail because it involves stuffing pictures in envelopes. Anyway, if we get a suspect it may be that his prints will match.'

Slonský frowned. 'Sadly it's a self-seal envelope.'

'Sir?'

'He didn't need to lick it to seal it. Spehar has sent off a swab for DNA testing but he doesn't expect it to be very useful. Now, he says the address is more promising.'

'Address?'

'Navrátil, can you stop answering everything I say with a question? Yes, the address. My address. Somehow the sender knew that I was working on the case.'

'It was in the newspapers.'

'It was in one newspaper, Navrátil. The others that named me didn't come out until after this was posted. Incidentally, it was posted in the Ninth district. It shows no sign of being folded so it may have been posted at a post office rather than in a street postbox. Spehar says the address has been computer-generated using a laser printer.'

'Meaning?'

'There you go again, another question! Meaning that it's more likely to have been done at work than at home. Not conclusive, of course — there must be plenty of people with a laser printer at home — but most people with home computers will have inkjet printers. And Spehar, clever chap that he is, notes that if we find the computer his whizzkid colleagues may be able to prove that my address was in its memory.'

'It doesn't advance us too much, then.'

'Oh, I don't know. But then I've read the last paragraph. Of course, I already knew it, but it's good to know that Spehar comes to the same conclusion as me. Did you look at the envelope?'

'Of course. Plain brown, a bit bigger than A4.'

'The stamp?'

'Of course — he'll have licked the stamp!'

'No, he dipped it in a bit of water. No saliva on it at all, I reckon, but Spehar is checking that. Look at the address.'

Navrátil held the plastic evidence envelope at arm's length and tilted it to catch the maximum amount of light.

'He knows you're in the Criminal Detection department, and your rank.'

'It would be odd if it wasn't being investigated by the Criminal Detection department, wouldn't it? And my rank was in the newspaper. Look at the address, Navrátil!"

Navrátil shook his head. 'No, nothing. It's spelled wrongly, of course, but —'

'At last! It's spelled wrongly. He's missed the háček on the 'š' of Holešovice. Now, that suggests two things. First, he probably doesn't live in the district, or he'd have written it so many times it would be second nature. But the more important point is that it doesn't matter to him. He doesn't see any meaningful difference between an 's' and an 'š'. He's a foreigner, Navrátil.'

'Maybe his printer just doesn't print háčeks properly.'

'Ah, but Technician First Class Spehar has thought of that. "There is no sign that any attempt has been made to deposit laser toner in the háček field," he writes.'

'Okay, but maybe he deliberately spelled it wrongly to put us off the scent so we would think he wasn't a Czech.'

Slonský's face fell. 'You're not as green as you are cabbage-looking, Navrátil. He may indeed. But he knows who the Minister of the Interior is by sight, and not many Czechs would pass that one.'

'He's one of the more recognisable ministers, sir.'

'He's certainly one of the shortest, Navrátil. What do you think — one metre fifty-five? And did you notice his desk layout?'

'I was outside, sir.'

'So you were. Well, Navrátil, you'll have to rely on my powers of observation. The Minister used his mouse with his left hand.'

'So?'

'So maybe this time Novák has hit the nail on the head. Our Minister is a left-handed dwarf.'

Chapter 5

Sergeant Adamec was a lugubrious, slow-moving walrus of a policeman who had been detailed by the Strahov station hierarchy to help Slonský find Gruberová's apartment. The details given by the Minister were no use at all. He described a couple of landmarks and a very general description of the building that seemed to be applicable to most of the houses in the area. As for the telephone number, it proved to be an internet café and nobody there knew where she lived. Adamec had checked the station records but nothing had come to their attention, and the district council did not have a record of her either.

'Not surprising if she was renting, though,' Adamec muttered. 'It would be the landlord who appeared there.'

Slonský sighed. He had met some miserable swines in his time but it was depressing him just to be on the same planet as Adamec.

'It can't be every day that the Minister of the Interior comes to Strahov. Somebody must have recognised him.'

'Maybe it's because nobody recognised him that he came here,' said Adamec. 'Bit of peace and quiet. I could do with that myself.' He sat on a windowsill and mopped his brow. It was a cold day, but Adamec was struggling after this unaccustomed effort. 'It's all go, this serious crime lark. I don't know how you stick it.'

'Trying to find the killer of a fellow citizen helps to keep me going,' barked Slonský, who realised immediately how pompous it sounded. 'Let's apply a bit of lateral thinking. If you had a bit on the side and wanted to get a flat for her round here, where would you look?'

'I don't know.'

'But it's your area!' Slonský snarled.

'I know,' Adamec explained in his most reasonable tone, as if addressing a particularly dim five-year-old. 'But I don't have a mistress, so I don't know how a man who has one would think.'

'Humour me,' whined Slonský. 'Let's pretend.'

'I don't know if I can. It's so far out of my experience.'

Slonský removed his battered grey fedora to let the steam escape from his head, pinched the crown into shape, and replaced it carefully.

'Are you married?'

'Yes,' said Adamec, fishing in his pocket to produce an elderly black and white mugshot. 'Maria. Twenty-eight years together. She's a gem.'

'Yes,' said Slonský. 'She must be. Children?'

'Little Petr and Little Maria. That's them there. Of course, that was ten years ago. They're bigger now.'

'They would be,' agreed Slonský. 'Your name wouldn't be Petr, would it?'

'Yes!' Adamec cried. 'How did you know?'

'Lucky guess. Or detective's intuition. Well, suppose young Maria came to you and said "Dad, I want a flat of my own here, respectable area, somewhere I can keep nice", what would you say?'

'I'd say "You stay at home with your old dad until you're ready to get married, young miss".'

'And suppose she was ready to get married?'

'Then I'd keep out of it. She's her husband's responsibility then. Take my word for it, coming between a girl and her intended is a bad move, Lieutenant. You can't win. Anyway, why all these questions? Is your daughter moving out?'

Slonský was beginning to feel that murderers may not all be bad people. Some might just have spent an hour with someone like Sergeant Adamec.

'I don't have a daughter. I was trying to imagine how the murder victim would choose an apartment.'

'But didn't you say she was someone's mistress?'

'Yes. The Minister's.'

'Well, she wouldn't have chosen, would she? He would.'

'I thought that, but he says he doesn't know where it is.'

'So how could she afford this unless he was paying for it? Did she have another job somewhere?'

'If she did, they haven't missed her.'

'Maybe she did work that you don't have to clock in for. On the game, for instance.'

'Too clean.'

'Lap-dancing?'

'Possible. But then, how did the Minister meet her?'

'Maybe he goes lap-dancing.'

'That is too disgusting a picture for words, Adamec.'

'I meant as a customer, not a performer.'

'Thank goodness for small mercies. She must have had friends, though. Young women are sociable, aren't they? They all have friends. How come none of them has tried to contact us?'

'Perhaps they don't read newspapers. Watch a lot of television, though. Here, are you going to do one of those reconstructions on the television?'

'That depends.'

'On what?'

'On whether Tom Cruise is free to play you. Come on, Adamec, you and I are old-timers. We don't understand this modern world. If she doesn't have a tax number, and she doesn't seem to be on the game, how does she afford a flat?'

'Easy. Lover boy pays for it.'

'Then he must be paying in cash, because he knows we can get his bank records and then he'd be exposed as a liar if we find he's been paying her rent.'

Adamec chewed on a toothpick he had found in a pocket. 'Do you remember a case up here about five years back? Man who sawed his wife's head off so her body would fit in a trunk?'

Slonský pushed his hat higher on his forehead. What was the man rambling about? 'Yes. Little weedy fellow who got fed up with her talking while he was trying to read.'

'That's the one. We nailed him because he bought the saw at a hardware store and the shopkeeper remembered him. Then we proved the saw was used to lop her head off.'

'Yes, but we couldn't prove he'd killed her. He admitted it was his saw, but said he had nothing to do with the killing or the decapitation.'

'Where we went wrong,' mused Adamec, 'was that we tried to prove he had bought the saw in order to cut her head off. We were trying to prove he'd planned the whole thing. Whereas, as he subsequently admitted when he was locked in the loony-bin, there was no planning at all. He just flipped and grabbed the nearest thing to hand, which happened to be a distinctive saw.'

Slonský sighed deeply. 'If there was a point to this walk through history it has escaped me, Adamec.'

'Just that the lover might have hidden the payments if he planned the murder, but if it was an impulse he may not have realised that he left a smoking gun.'

Slonský showed an unexpected burst of energy in bounding to his feet.

'Adamec, if it wasn't one of the most disgusting ideas I've ever had, I'd kiss you! I'll get Navrátil onto it right now.' He took out his telephone and searched for Navrátil's number. 'Damn! I don't have his number. Never mind, I'll call the office and get someone to tell him. While I'm doing that, think harder! We have to find that girl's flat.'

Lukas listened carefully to Navrátil before shaking his head solemnly. 'It's out of the question. How could I possibly get permission to examine a Minister's bank account?'

'You could ask him, sir. After all, he voluntarily gave us his DNA sample.'

'Ah. Not quite. But I take the point. After all, if he is innocent, why would he object? And as our Minister he has to set an example, after all. But I'd better have a word with my superiors, Navrátil. Tell Slonský I'll speak to the Director of the Criminal Police about it.'

Navrátil coughed gently.

'Was there something else, Navrátil?'

'Lieutenant Slonský is concerned that if the Minister is alerted to our interest in him, he may destroy vital evidence.'

'Surely not! He is, after all, the Minister of the Interior, Navrátil. His job is to ensure the efficiency of the police, and destroying evidence would hardly achieve that.'

'No, sir. But he may be more worried about going to jail for the rest of his life.'

Lukas gaped as if the possibility of the Minister's guilt had just occurred to him.

'I can't imagine a minister in our government killing a young woman in such a vile manner. What is the world coming to?'

'Surely in the old days ministers did far worse, sir.'

'But that was under the old regime — ill-educated men who had no moral fibre, not elected politicians. The Minister is a university graduate, Navrátil. He holds a doctorate.'

'If there is the least chance that he may be guilty, sir, we can't be seen to be going easy on him just because he is our boss.'

'Of course not. Quite improper. Must be seen to be … without fear or favour.'

'So I can ask for a disclosure warrant, sir?'

'Can we do it discreetly?'

'Any judge will do, sir. I'll find one who'll keep it to himself. If you'll just sign the application here, sir.'

Lukas held the paper for some time with all the trepidation of a constitutional monarch asked to sign a death warrant.

'I'll take it with me, Navrátil, and get the Director to sign it.'

Navrátil knew Slonský had returned by the colourful language emanating from the office. 'They should pension off some of these old sergeants. Adamec must be eighty if he's a day.'

'He isn't retired yet, sir.'

'Mentally, I mean. Not a clue about his own patch. No idea where her flat could be. And the man is a walking photograph album. If I see another picture of his nauseatingly cherub-cheeked offspring —'

'Captain Lukas wants you, sir.'

'Me? Why?'

'He wants you to go with him to see the Director to get a warrant to examine the Minister's bank account.'

'Do we know who the Minister banks with?'

'No, sir.'

'Then getting a warrant may be a bit problematic, lad. We won't know what to do with it if we get one.'

'Isn't that always true?'

'Normally, Navrátil, we just ring round asking if the banks know Mr X of such and such an address. Sooner or later we strike lucky. It's a bit more difficult asking banks if a minister is a client.'

Slonský examined the floor in thought before marching out of the room.

'Come, Navrátil! We're going to see if we can find Klinger.'

Klinger was a slick-haired man in a dark suit and crisp white shirt who inhabited a nondescript office on the floor above.

'Why is it that visits from you always involve skulduggery, Slonský?'

'It's a gift. Can you do it or not?'

'I'm not sure. I'll have to make a couple of calls.'

'Fine. We'll wait.'

'The kind of calls I don't want people listening in on.'

'Fine. We'll wait outside.'

Slonský and Navrátil closed the door behind them. It soon opened again, as Klinger poked his head out. 'Outside and far away, where you can't listen in,' he insisted.

'You know your trouble, Klinger. A lack of trust.'

'Maybe that's why I'm a fraud officer,' Klinger replied, and watched as they made their way to the next doorway.

'Another couple of doors, please,' said Klinger.

'It's rubbing off on you, Klinger. You're developing an untrusting mentality. I could be very hurt.'

'Do you want the details or don't you?'

Slonský pushed Navrátil ahead of him. 'Don't dawdle, Navrátil. Do as the nice man says.'

Klinger emerged a few minutes later with a scrap of paper. 'I can't say it's his only bank account, but it's the one his salary gets paid into.'

'How did you get this?'

'Never mind.'

'No, I'm impressed! It can't be easy to get details off a government payroll department.'

'It is if you tell them you think he's been underpaid. Now hop off before someone sees you talking to me.'

'I owe you one, Klinger.'

'You owe me about eighteen, actually. But who's counting?'

'I was beginning to think you weren't coming, Slonský,' said Lukas.

'Tied up looking for the girl's flat, sir.'

'The Director is waiting for us.'

'Very good of him to work late for us, I'm sure.'

'Slonský, it's only four o'clock. He's hardly working late.'

'If you say so, sir.'

They were greeted by the Director's secretary and invited to sit down while she told him they were there.

'You could have smartened yourself up a bit, Slonský. It is the Director we're seeing.'

Slonský inspected himself carefully. 'I did. I never claimed to be a male model.'

'When did you last polish those shoes?'

Slonský furrowed his brow. 'When did the Berlin Wall come down?'

Lukas was deeply shocked. You could tell because his mouth fell open and he moved it like a landed catfish gasping for air.

'Joke, sir.'

'No laughing matter, Slonský.'

'No, sir. Anyway, I must have cleaned them at least twice since then.'

The secretary reappeared and held the door open. They entered, Lukas leading the way, and found the Director advancing towards them with his hand extended in greeting.

'Lukas. Slonský, isn't it? Sit, please.'

'Thank you, sir. You know why I asked to see you?'

'Yes, Lukas. Bad business. But if there are suspicions they must be investigated. Explain to me why you think a discovery warrant is needed.'

'The murder victim was last seen in the company of the Minister, sir.'

'And he admits they met?'

'Yes, sir. He left her at ten o'clock, he says, and forensic evidence suggests she died within two hours.'

'During which time someone had her,' interjected Slonský.

Lukas cringed with embarrassment.

'That's suggestive,' agreed the Director.

'That's what I thought,' said Slonský, 'but Captain Lukas is a stickler for doing things by the book and quite rightly said we needed more. The question is, who paid the rent on her flat in Strahov?'

'Nice area?'

'We haven't found it yet. But since nobody has missed her, we assume she didn't share.'

'Or he killed the flatmate too,' suggested the Director.

Lukas looked from one to the other as if watching a tennis rally.

'I hadn't thought of that,' admitted Slonský. 'That'll be why you're a Director and I'm just a humble footsoldier.'

'Anyway, sir,' Lukas continued, 'we want to know if he has been paying for the flat, since he says he doesn't know where she lived. If we find he has, then it casts doubt on his story.'

'DNA,' the Director muttered. 'If they made love, can we match the DNA?'

'We've got a sample from the girl, and the Minister gave us a sample of his.'

'Very public-spirited of him. Presumably he didn't know he was under suspicion. Did he waive his right to have a lawyer present?'

'Not exactly,' Lukas stammered.

'He didn't need one,' Slonský explained. 'He's a lawyer himself. He can be his own lawyer.'

'I'm not sure the court will go along with that when the time comes, Lieutenant.'

'He didn't object, sir. In fact, when I asked he said "Of course", didn't he, Captain?'

'Yes, I believe he did.'

'You were present?' the Director asked. 'That's all right, then.'

Lukas was unsure why his presence made it all right, and equally unsure whether he wanted to admit to having been there, but the Director's mind had raced ahead.

'The DNA will take a day or two. So we need to see the Minister's bank account to see if he has been paying for the flat?'

'That's it, sir,' agreed Slonský.

'Have you got the bank's details?'

Slonský offered Klinger's piece of paper.

'This looks a bit clandestine,' said the Director.

'Properly obtained, I'm sure,' Lukas interjected in a tone that indicated that he was actually very unsure of it.

'From the Minister's office, sir. His staff were sure he would want to assist us in every way.'

The Director smiled slightly.

'Very commendable. It makes things much easier for us, doesn't it? Nice when suspects co-operate.'

'Isn't it?' agreed Slonský, now certain that he had been rumbled.

The Director took the application and signed it with a flourish.

'I've amended it slightly. It now covers that bank account and any others the Minister may happen to have with the same bank, Captain.'

'Thank you, sir,' chorused Slonský and Lukas.

'You don't need a judge's countersignature. I've certified that for reasons of operational urgency we need to move quickly. I'll notify the appropriate people that it's been done.'

'What a nice man!' Slonský said. 'Very helpful. Easy to see how he got where he is.'

'Quite. Slonský, where did you really get that account number?'

'We already had it, sir.'

'Really?'

'Of course, it would be quite improper of me to divulge if any enquiry of a financial nature were under way elsewhere in the police, sir.'

'Of course. And I wouldn't need to know that.'

'Nor should you, sir. It might colour your thinking about him if you thought he might not have paid all his taxes.'

'Slonský! Don't tell me any more! I insist you keep the details to yourself and don't talk about it to me again.'

'As you wish, sir,' said Slonský, and allowed himself a roguish smirk.

Navrátil was feeling very proud of himself. He had a map of Prague on the desk and was busy putting pins into it.

'Amusing yourself, Navrátil?'

'I may be on to something, sir.'

'Say on, young prince. I am all ears.'

'Well, sir, they didn't recognise her at the internet café, but there must be a reason why she gave that number.'

'Except she didn't. I bet the Minister gave us that one to lead us into a dead end. He rang her mobile. If she'd gone to the café often enough to pick up casual messages, they'd have known her there.'

Navrátil was slightly upset that Slonský had already travelled along this line of thought, which he had believed was entirely original.

'Cheer up, lad. That's a map of Strahov and those pins aren't internet places, so give me the rest.'

'They're places where you can buy milk, sir.'

'Milk?'

'Everyone needs milk, sir. Almost everyone, to be more exact. But if you live on your own you just pick it up when you need it. So I thought Miss Gruberová must buy milk somewhere near her flat. And after a few tries, I struck lucky.'

'Well done, lad!'

'This one here, sir. The old woman recognised the photo.'

Slonský blanched.

'You didn't show her the picture with the Minister?'

'Not all of it, sir. I made a copy of half of it. She only saw the victim.'

'Thank heavens for that. And?'

'She said she didn't recognise the drawing in the newspapers because the eyes were wrong.'

'Wrong? You mean she had three or something?'

'No, sir. You can see what she meant from the photo. Miss Gruberová had hooded eyelids. The woman says she always looked half asleep.'

'If she was up all night getting bonked by the Minister she probably was. But pray continue.'

'She doesn't know exactly where the victim lived, but she says it can't be far away because she sometimes came to the shop without a coat.'

Slonský beamed with delight.

'You are destined for high things, son. When you are Director of Police, remember old Slonský gave you your first break and see if you can't bump the pensions up a bit. But why the other pins?'

'I wanted to see where she would have to live if that shop was the nearest to her flat. There are shops here and here, so the best bet looks like somewhere in these four streets.'

'Right. Ring Strahov and get Adamec to meet us. I don't care if he's finished his shift. Tell him we're going to do door-to-door along those streets and we could do with any spare men he can find. It's going to be a long evening, so I'm off to the canteen to get us some sausages and coffee. And because you've been good, you get a pastry too, young man.'

Chapter 6

Adamec had found three young policemen who stood in the cold night air blowing on their hands.

'Are they old enough to be out at this hour?' Slonský asked.

Adamec looked them over carefully. 'It's us,' he concluded. 'We're getting older. They say you know you're getting old when the policemen look young.'

'Fair enough. Gather round, lads! Now, Navrátil has a photo and a drawing for each of you. I want you to share these streets here and knock on everyone's door. We're trying to find the murder victim's flat.'

A hand was raised tentatively.

'Yes?'

'Sir, if she's the victim she won't answer.'

Slonský resisted the very real temptation to kick a police officer.

'Quite right, lad, she won't. So make a note in your little black book that there was no-one in. If someone answers, ask them if they know the woman in the pictures and where she lived. If you get an address, call your loving Sergeant, and he'll tell me.'

Navrátil and the three policemen trudged off through the snow, leaving Adamec and Slonský on the main road.

'What do we do now?' asked Adamec.

'No point standing out here,' replied Slonský. 'Let's find a nice warm bar and wait for a call.'

It was not too long in coming. A woman identified the victim as her upstairs neighbour, and correctly named her as Irina Something-or-other.

'Good enough for me, Navrátil,' announced Slonský. 'Anyone have a key?'

'She gave me the landlord's number, but there's no reply.'

'Adamec?'

'I'll get a locksmith. There's one we use.'

'There, that's what comes of keeping your brain warm. You lads go and warm up. Not you, Navrátil. I need you here with me. You should have thought of that before you made yourself indispensable.'

'Am I indispensable, then?'

'For the moment. But don't puff yourself up. I'm fickle like that. We're going to talk to the near neighbours. I want to know if any of them saw anything on Monday night, especially a car arriving around ten or leaving a bit later.'

'We didn't ask the Minister what kind of car he has, sir.'

'I asked his secretary. He has a beige Mercedes.'

When the locksmith arrived it took him only a few minutes to dismantle the lock and allow entry. The Scene of Crime team were quickly in action, dusting and measuring, while Slonský stood in each doorway in turn, silently inspecting the room and committing the layout to memory.

'Tidy place,' he pronounced. 'Some nice stuff.'

'No coffee cups waiting to be washed,' Navrátil noted.

'Interesting bedroom, wouldn't you say?'

'A bit girly for my taste, sir.'

'Undoubtedly. But I bet you have sheets on your bed.'

'I bet she did too, sir.'

'So our murderer took them with him, thereby removing a source of forensic evidence. I hope that doesn't catch on or our lives will get a lot harder.'

One of the Scenes of Crime team glanced over at them.

'No prints on the bedside furniture. But there are two nice thumbprints on the bed-head.'

'Really? How careless. You might want to check them against the cup I dropped in the other day.'

Navrátil appeared to be enacting some strange ritual.

'What are you doing, Navrátil?'

'I'm trying to think how the thumbs would be if he gripped the headboard while he was … occupied, sir.'

'I'm sure he gripped it nice and hard, son, so they'll be good prints. Well, I think we've done all we can here. Nobody saw anything, not even the murderer staggering downstairs with a dead woman wrapped in a sheet over his shoulder. Whatever happened to old women, Navrátil? When I was a lad all the women in our street knew everything I'd been up to and shopped me to my mother without a moment's thought. Now they don't even see a neighbour being murdered and carted off. Come on, let's get some sleep. It'll be a long day tomorrow.'

'It's been a long day today, sir.'

Slonský smiled faintly.

'I suppose it has, hasn't it? But it's what makes the blood rush in your veins, all this sort of thing. We're on the move, lad, and someone is going to be behind bars soon.'

Chapter 7

Slonský gazed out of the window as the rising sun reflected from the windows of the buildings across the street.

'I've got the report, sir. The Scenes of Crime team must have worked through the night.'

'That's because I told them to. What have we got?'

Navrátil scanned the cover sheet rapidly.

'The prints on the bed-head match those on the cup, sir.'

'Well, the Minister can hardly deny being in the bed, then. He lied to us, Navrátil. I can't wait to tell Captain Lukas. He'll be so shocked.'

Slonský picked a folder from his desk and handed it to Navrátil.

'Have a look at that, lad. The DNA on the cup matches the swab from the victim.'

'It's looking pretty bleak for the Minister, then, sir.'

'Look a little further, Navrátil. There are two sheets in that folder.'

'The Minister's bank statement?'

'Yes. And look at last Tuesday.'

Navrátil gulped.

'A cash withdrawal. Two hundred and forty-nine thousand, two hundred and fifty crowns.'

Lukas read and re-read the notes. 'I don't mind admitting I'm shocked, Slonský. Absolutely shocked. To think that a minister of the state could have a mistress, kill her and lie to us about it. Does he think we're fools? The very man who should know better than any other minister what we can do. It's … it's …'

'Shocking?'

'Exactly! I'm shocked. Well, our duty is clear. I must take this to the Director and arrange for the Minister's arrest. It's your case, Slonský. I'm sure the Director will agree to your being present to get the credit for the arrest.'

'That's not necessary, sir.'

'Nonsense. It's a job well done for the whole department. We have to be seen to have done our duty.'

'Will you be telling the Prime Minister we're about to bang one of his ministers up for murder, sir?'

Lukas performed his goldfish impersonation one more time.

'I think someone should, sir. It would be a shame if he read it in the papers first.'

'Well, it's hardly my place … surely the Director —'

'I'm sure the Prime Minister will want to be convinced of the strength of the evidence, sir, so he'll want to speak to the senior officer in charge.'

'It's your case, Slonský.'

'But you're my superior, sir. I must defer to you.'

'Slonský, why do I think that there is something you aren't telling me? Is this arrest unsafe?'

'You've seen the evidence, sir.'

'Indeed. It's clear we must arrest him. But it's going to cause a bit of a hoo-ha.'

'Well, it isn't every policeman that gets to arrest his own boss, I grant you.'

'So what will you be doing while I go up to see the Prime Minister, Slonský?'

Slonský grimaced. 'Navrátil is at her flat looking for an address for a next of kin, sir. Somebody ought to be told that she has died.'

Lukas dropped his head onto his chest. That was another job he would prefer not to have to do. All things considered, going to the PM's office with the Director would be more comfortable.

'Very well. You and Navrátil examine the flat and inform the next of kin while I tidy things up here. But come and see me as soon as you've finished. And don't speak to the press under any circumstances, Slonský.'

Slonský agreed readily. He hated speaking to the press at any time, a natural consequence of his belief that journalists were, in many cases, more morally repugnant than murderers. When he condescended to share a few words it was either to ask them to help him or to spread misinformation about a case. In any event, it was unlikely to be Slonský that journalists wanted to speak to, especially after he told them in strict confidence that Lukas had been the one who arrested the Minister.

The Director was a fast reader. Before Lukas had managed to arrange his uniform so he could sit without creasing the tail of his jacket, the Director was on his feet and reaching for his uniform hat.

'Clear enough, Lukas. It's not conclusive but the forensics prove he was there, the money is strongly circumstantial and his alibi stinks. I have a telephone call to make, then we'll take this dossier to the Prime Minister and ask him to help us arrest the Minister discreetly.'

'I'm sure he will appreciate that, sir. The Prime Minister, I mean.'

'I'm told there's no love lost between them, Lukas. Would you mind stepping outside and asking my secretary to order my driver round to the front? We'd best go by car.'

Slonský pushed the door open with his foot and slipped crabwise into the flat, each hand holding a cup of coffee with a pastry balanced on top.

'Keep your strength up, lad,' he explained to Navrátil, who was sitting at a small dining table on which he had arranged some small piles of papers.

'Nothing to connect her directly to the Minister, sir. No love letters, birthday cards, thank you notes.'

'There wouldn't be. He'd give her a few coins and tell her to buy her own. Family?'

Navrátil silently handed him a couple of sheets of cheap notepaper.

'Must be her mother. Not very educated spelling and a shaky hand equals an old lady who doesn't write much. Anything before this?'

'No, sir. It looks as if she had only been in Prague a year or so. Do you know the village, sir?'

'It's out towards Kladno, I think. Perhaps thirty kilometres away. We can radio in and check before we set out. God, it's depressing. Her own mother doesn't seem to know she's dead yet. Any signs of a father?'

'He's mentioned in the second letter, sir. "Dad sends his best." But no other family.'

Slonský scanned the room once more. He had already imprinted it in his memory the night before, but in daylight it looked a little shabbier. The furniture was neat, but not expensive.

'She had a bit of taste, bless her. Cheap sofa but some nice cushions on it. She's worked hard at polishing out the scratch on that table. Just missed a bit where it chipped the edge, look. How old was she?'

'I haven't found anything like that, sir. All her official stuff must have been in a handbag we haven't got. There are a few bags in the wardrobe but they're all empty.'

Slonský slurped his coffee and took a large bite from the pastry, chewing slowly and without enjoyment.

'Phone bills?'

'There's one for her mobile phone. We can get call records from that. I've started the ball rolling with the phone company.'

'Good lad. Well, best drink up, son. We can't put off going to see the mother.'

Lukas was sitting to attention. The Director seemed relaxed enough, but this was the Prime Minister they were talking to, and Lukas felt uneasy at proximity to the powerful. He had been offered a coffee and was paralysed with the fear that he might spill it on the carpet, as a result of which he was sitting bolt upright with the saucer wedged in his lap and had not tasted a drop.

'Never liked the shifty little devil. Doesn't surprise me if he topped his mistress. Let's get him over here and you can slap the cuffs on him.'

'I'd hoped to avoid that, sir,' the Director replied.

'Really? Shame. I'd have enjoyed that. Well, you know best. But if he falls down the stairs a few times during questioning, I won't take it amiss. I never wanted him but there was pressure from coalition colleagues to give him a top job. At least now I can put my own man in.'

The office door opened and a middle-aged man with an immaculate dark suit and white shirt slithered into the room noiselessly.

'Komárek, please telephone the Interior Ministry and ask the Minister to come here at once. No excuses. And don't tell him who is here.'

'Very good, Prime Minister.'

When he had gone, the three men sat in silence, the Director relaxed in his seat, Lukas rigid and watchful, and the Prime Minister doodling on a notepad.

'I don't suppose you'd reconsider the handcuff thing?' he asked hopefully.

Navrátil slowed as they approached the exit slip road, and was relieved to see the promised police car waiting there. He pulled in to the side of the road about thirty metres further on, and stepped out of the car to greet the local officers.

'Sergeant Tomáš,' announced a barrel-shaped officer who emerged from the driver's seat and flapped a hand like a seal's flipper in the general direction of his colleague. 'And that's Officer Peiperová.'

Slonský completed the introductions.

'Bad business,' said the sergeant.

'Do you know the family?' asked Slonský.

'I don't,' admitted the sergeant, 'or, at least, not particularly well. But Peiperová was at school with Gruberová.'

'She was a year or two ahead of me,' explained the young officer, who was a tall woman with thick, yellow-blonde hair which she had somehow managed to pile inside her uniform cap.

'Brothers or sisters?'

'There's a brother, but he's been away from home for a few years now,' Peiperová explained. 'I can't say I knew Irina well, but it's a shock to me so I can imagine what it will be like for her poor mother.'

'Father not around?'

'In body, if not entirely in spirit,' Tomáš interjected. 'He's well known to us. Likes a drink, then gets pulled in for some sort of hooliganism. Usually public nuisance, like urinating in someone's shop doorway. But he's quietened down a lot lately. Poor devil is a bit damaged now. Brain running on empty.'

'Let that be a warning to you, Navrátil,' Slonský snapped.

'Me? Why me?'

'I'm responsible for you, lad. We don't want that fine brain of yours turning to mush. Well, we'd best get it over and done with. Shall we follow you?'

They returned to their respective cars and smoothly pulled into the traffic. The squad car turned left and after two or three minutes took another left before following the road to the end of the metalled surface. A glutinous muddy track lay before them, but they continued barely fifty metres before the police car signalled right and they turned into a small yard. To the left of them was a fairly substantial old house, though in need of some redecoration and a bit of repair to the rendering at head level. In front there was a chicken shed and a fenced compound where the shed's inhabitants scratched and pecked their way through their days. On the right-hand side there was a barn of sorts, relatively derelict but still housing some old tools and a quantity of hay.

'Seen better days,' Slonský concluded.

'Haven't we all,' the sergeant replied.

The house's back door opened and a dumpy, grey-haired woman was framed in the doorway. She rubbed her hands on her apron and squinted into the low sun.

'Mrs Gruberová?' Slonský asked.

The woman nodded.

'I'm Lieutenant Slonský of the Criminal Police in Prague. This is Officer Navrátil, who works with me. And Sergeant Tomáš and Officer Peiperová are from the local police.'

'Is something wrong? Is it Irina?'

Chapter 8

If the Minister was surprised to see Lukas again, he hid it well. He stood in front of the Prime Minister's desk for a moment, then looked around for a vacant seat.

'No point in getting ourselves comfortable,' the Prime Minister barked. 'Unpleasant business, best done quickly.'

'Unpleasant business, Prime Minister? What unpleasant business?'

The Director stepped forward and formally cautioned the Minister before telling him he was being arrested for the murder of Irina Gruberová.

'But this is preposterous!' the Minister squealed. 'She was alive and well when I left her.'

'I would strongly advise you to say no more without your lawyer present,' said the Prime Minister. 'Needless to say, I shall have to relieve you of your office. I'll go to see the President later. Perhaps you'd leave any official keys on my desk before they cart you off to pokey.'

The Prime Minister turned his back and returned to work, leaving a bewildered Minister to walk to the car in the company of Lukas and the Director. As they reached the office door, the two policemen turned and saluted smartly.

'Shame about the handcuffs,' muttered the Prime Minister.

Mrs Gruberová cried silently as Peiperová sat beside her and patted the back of her hand.

'I know this is distressing,' Slonský began, 'but we need to ask you some questions to help us find the person who did this. I'm sure you'd want to help us if you can.'

The old woman nodded mutely.

'How long had your daughter been in Prague?'

'A bit less than two years.'

'Do you know what she did for a living?'

Mrs Gruberová looked away for a brief moment, sufficient to tell Slonský that she was unhappy with the answer she had to give.

'She got a job as a dancer in a club. A man saw her in Kladno and offered her a job. It was better paid than anything she could get around here.'

'But, if you'll forgive me, it sounds as if you weren't happy with the arrangement.'

'What mother could be happy with her daughter working in such a place? Irina always said nothing nasty happened to her, but if you go around showing yourself to men like that they're bound to get ideas about the sort of girl you are.'

'You don't happen to know the name of the club?'

She shook her head. 'No. But she stopped working there after a while. She told us last September that she had a boyfriend and he didn't like her working there, so he made her give it up and gave her money instead.'

'How did you feel about that?'

'I thought he would marry her, but I got to thinking that he must already be married and that keeping her like this wasn't proper. Irina never mentioned marriage and when I raised it with her she said I was silly and marriage was old-fashioned. Well, maybe I am old-fashioned, but who'll want to marry her after she's been living with a man?' There was a pause before Mrs Gruberová choked back a sob and corrected herself. 'Who would have wanted to marry her, I mean.'

Slonský let her cry for a while in the silence. When he finally spoke, his voice was unusually soft, and there was just a hint of pain in it. 'I'll find him, Mrs Gruberová. Someone will pay for what has happened to your daughter.'

The first interview with the ex-Minister was short and entirely unproductive. It was conducted by Lukas and the Director and was punctuated by demands for lawyers to be present.

'Of course,' said the Director. 'We just wanted to give you the opportunity to avoid the wasting of police time.'

'I'm innocent!' Dr Banda insisted. 'I have told you exactly what happened.'

'Unfortunately,' the Director responded, 'that is what you have not done. You have attempted to mislead us. You said you left Miss Gruberová at her door and drove home.'

'I think I said that, yes.'

'But you know that in fact you accompanied her into her flat and made love to her there.'

Banda lowered his head. 'I admit I did that.'

'So your first statement to the police was untrue?'

'Yes.'

'A deliberate lie?'

'Yes.'

'That presents us with some difficulty, Dr Banda. You were, after all, the Minister in charge of policing. It would be reasonable, I suggest, to expect a man in such a position to offer the police every assistance when investigating a crime.'

'I didn't want it known that I was consorting with a whore.'

Lukas' face reddened. Before he knew it, he had spoken. 'Nothing we have found supports that suggestion!'

Banda raised his head slowly and fixed Lukas with an intense gaze.

'Then look harder.'

Navrátil, Slonský and Tomáš were standing outside the door, getting some fresh air while Peiperová helped Irina's mother look for any useful documents and letters.

'Sir, why do you keep saying you'll find the man who did this when we already have?'

'Because, Navrátil, I don't yet have the evidence to convict him. It's all circumstantial and a good lawyer will get him off. I need more, and the best way of getting it is to let people think I'm still looking.'

Tomáš pricked his ears up.

'You've arrested someone? Is that the boyfriend?'

'Yes,' said Slonský, 'but don't talk about it yet. I'm not confident we'll be able to keep him in custody. He can afford a good lawyer and I wouldn't be surprised if the slimy creep was at the front desk now.'

'The boyfriend?'

'No, his lawyer. Although "slimy creep" fits both of them.'

Sergeant Mucha enjoyed this part of his work. The lugubrious desk sergeant had few pleasures in his working day, and aggravating an expensive Prague lawyer came high on his list.

'Come along, Sergeant! You can't mean to tell me you're expecting to keep my client locked up like a common criminal.'

'Well, from where I'm standing a common criminal is exactly what he is, sir.'

'Do you have any evidence for that assertion?'

'Not assertion, sir; personal opinion. As for evidence, that will be disclosed to the defence in the usual way at the usual time.'

The lawyer changed tack. If the sergeant could not be browbeaten, perhaps the unctuous approach would work.

'Perhaps if you gave us an idea of the evidence you have, we might be able to explain away any little … misunderstanding there might be and save you a lot of time.'

'Your client could have saved us a lot of time by telling the truth in the first place, sir. And you'll know that I am a mere desk sergeant, so I'm hardly likely to give out information on a case the Director has taken a personal interest in.'

'Perhaps I could see the Director and explain my client's position.'

'I don't keep the Director's diary, sir. You'd have to contact his office for an appointment.'

'Very well. I can see I'm getting nowhere here. You are being extremely obstructive, Sergeant.'

'Thank you very much, sir. One does one's best.'

Mrs Gruberová had little more to tell them. She had last seen her daughter at the New Year when Irina came home for a short visit.

'Did she seem happy?'

'Yes, very happy. She said she had been taking driving lessons and was going to order a new car, so she would be able to drive down to see us more often.'

'A new car? Did she mean brand new?'

'Yes. She said she would have to wait for the dealer to get the one she wanted.'

Slonský mimed to Navrátil to make a note of that.

'Do you know the make of car?'

'A little Škoda. I don't know all the types. Just a small one, she said.'

'Did she mention the colour?'

'She liked bright colours. She wanted a red one but she wasn't sure that they did them in red.'

'Well, perhaps we can find the dealer she went to. Did she tell you about any friends in Prague?'

'Just her boyfriend.'

'Did she give him a name?'

'Not that I remember. She said he was quite famous so she never talked about him because she didn't want the press sniffing round. I said it was coming to something when a girl wouldn't tell her own mother her boyfriend's name, but she wouldn't budge. She could be very stubborn sometimes. Do you think he really is famous?'

'If he is who we think he is, then you would know of him,' Slonský replied.

'Don't you know who I am?' shouted Banda.

'Yes,' said Sergeant Mucha, 'you're the noisy little sod in cell five. Now keep it down or we'll have to get the police doctor to give you a sedative.'

'I'm your direct superior! I'm responsible for the police in this country.'

'Then you've got a lot to answer for,' said Mucha. 'They're a complete shambles. Anyway, you're nobody's superior now. You're the prisoner in cell five in a borrowed jumpsuit. Still, you've made the evening paper.'

'What does it say?' asked Banda anxiously.

'I can't remember,' sniffed Mucha. 'I only read the sports pages.'

Chapter 9

The radio news announced the removal of Dr Banda as Minister of the Interior and introduced his replacement.

'Didn't take long to sort that out,' announced Slonský. 'I bet the Prime Minister had that up his sleeve all along.'

'But now everyone knows that we've arrested Banda,' protested Navrátil. 'Every step we take will be watched.'

'Probably. But we'll just keep saying we're not talking about it. After all, it's an active crime investigation. We can't go telling the press every little thing.'

'We usually do,' said Tomáš.

'I know,' replied Slonský, 'but that's when we want to. Now we'll keep our counsel and let him sweat a bit. If we put a bit of pressure on, he'll crack. Speaking of which, Navrátil, let's drop Sergeant Tomáš off at the police station and get back to Prague. We've got some questioning to do.'

'He's very stubborn,' said Captain Lukas, 'not to mention uncooperative.'

'Yes, sir.'

'The Director got nowhere with him.'

'I dare say the Director was constrained by the burden of his position, sir.'

'What?'

'He didn't feel he could give the suspect a slap, sir. Being the Director of the Criminal Police, sir.'

'None of us can "give the suspect a slap", Slonský. Is that clear?'

'I wasn't proposing to, sir. But it won't be long before that lawyer of his springs him from custody if we don't get some more evidence.'

'Yes, he's been ringing HQ all afternoon asking to see the Director. Fortunately the Director wasn't available.'

'No, sir, he wouldn't be. He's a clever man, sir; he wouldn't make himself available with this lot going on.'

'And the lawyer is complaining about the way Sergeant Mucha spoke to him. He says Mucha was uncommonly rude.'

'I doubt that, sir. Mucha is rude to everyone. I don't think he singled out Dr Banda's lawyer.'

'Well, the Director says it's our case, so I suppose there's no harm in your questioning the suspect. But nothing untoward, Slonský! I don't want this enquiry threatened by an excess of zeal on your part.'

'Thank you very much, sir. I've never been accused of an excess of zeal before.'

Navrátil had already conducted the same dialogue eight times when he struck lucky.

'I'm looking for a car dealership that may have ordered a car for a young woman, possibly in the name of Gruberová. The chances are that the car hasn't been collected.'

'Yes, that's us. A Fabia, I think, with a nippy little engine. Hang on — yes, she ordered one about three weeks ago. It came in on Tuesday but she hasn't collected it yet.'

'I'm afraid she won't. The lady has been murdered.'

There was a little torrent of street Czech down the line.

'Had she paid a deposit?' asked Navrátil.

'A small cash deposit, but not the usual.'

'How much was left to pay?'

'Forty-nine thousand, two hundred and fifty crowns.'

Armed with this information, Navrátil set off in search of Slonský, but there was no sign of him in his office. On the basis that if he had left the building he would have passed the front desk, Navrátil went down to the lobby and interrogated Sergeant Mucha.

'Has Lieutenant Slonský gone out?'

'No, he's behind me.'

Navrátil looked closely, but there was no sign of Slonský there. Anyone is entitled to a hallucination, he thought, but an imaginary Slonský was a real lulu of a vision. It was hard to imagine any street drug that could induce such a sight.

Mucha observed the puzzled look on the young policeman's face.

'Behind the wall. He's questioning a suspect in the cells.'

'On his own? Doesn't he have to have a witness?'

'Yes and no. Yes, if he were undertaking conventional questioning he would need a witness. But he's Slonský. He has his own methods.'

Mucha turned away with a grin and shook his head in admiration for the low cunning of the old detective.

Intrigued and not a little concerned, Navrátil pushed the swing door open and looked down the spartan corridor. It was bare, except for a power lead plugged into the wall by the third cell on the left, which then snaked into cell six.

Navrátil began to walk down the corridor, vaguely aware that he could hear music and that he recognised the piece. He could also hear the unmistakable sounds of a prisoner being assaulted. Dull thuds were followed by groans, expulsions of air, and an occasional slap on skin. Fearing the worst, he quickened his pace.

Cell five was across the corridor from cell six, and as he drew level with the doors he realised that his suspicions were unfounded. The ex-Minister was in cell five, and the top of his head could be seen at intervals as he jumped to look through the door grille. Cell six certainly offered a disturbing sight, but not the one that Navrátil had expected.

Slonský was sitting on the cot, clutching a pillow to his stomach. At intervals he punched it hard, followed by a cry of pain. When he spoke it was in a higher-pitched voice than he normally used.

'No more! I'll tell you everything if you just leave me alone!'

Navrátil opened his mouth to speak but was silenced by a signal from Slonský, who held a finger across his lips before continuing, in his own voice: 'You said that before. Why should I believe you this time?' He then hit the pillow again. 'Either you co-operate or you get another one!'

Navrátil now realised that the power lead was connected to a compact disc player that was belting out Frank and Nancy Sinatra singing *Something Stupid*. Slonský turned up the volume and then emitted a completely unprovoked howl of pain.

'Not the face, Navrátil! Never hit the face!'

'What's happening in there?' yelled Banda from cell five. 'Who are you beating?'

'Mind your own business!' Slonský responded. 'We'll talk to you later.'

The track ended, but now Navrátil discovered that Slonský had set it to repeat. He was about to protest when Slonský wrapped an arm round his shoulder and steered him down the corridor to the desk. Only once the door was closed behind them did Slonský speak.

'You nearly fouled that up, lad. Still, I think it went well.'

'He'll think I've beaten a prisoner!' howled Navrátil.

'I hope so,' said Slonský. 'That was the whole point.'

'I don't understand, sir.'

'I want him to be pliable when we interview him. I need something to break that arrogant shell of his, and the prospect that we might reach across the desk and give him a biff should do nicely.'

'But he's Minister of the Interior! He'll know it's illegal for police to hit suspects.'

'Oh, Navrátil, Navrátil! What do they teach you at the academy these days?'

'So young, and so innocent!' agreed Mucha.

'You two are winding me up,' Navrátil complained. 'All right, so I don't understand. Explain it to me.'

Mucha rested his elbows on the desk and leaned forward conspiratorially.

'It's because he was Minister for the Interior that this will work.'

'Exactly,' agreed Slonský. 'It's a dead cert winner with him.'

'As you rightly point out,' Mucha began, 'a police officer mustn't lay hands on a suspect. And, as you again are correct to remind us, the Minister would know that. But if police regularly slapped suspects, would they tell the Minister?'

'Of course not! He'd be the last …'

'Enlightenment dawns!' announced Slonský. 'Exactly, my lad. He'd be the last person to know. In fact, he wouldn't want to know, because he wants the police to be effective and clear up unsolved crimes, and if a sly poke in the ribs now and then helps them to do that, he's not going to cramp our style. So naturally our dear ex-Minister takes it for granted that prisoners get clobbered, but that he doesn't hear about it.'

'It stands to reason,' Mucha chimed in. 'Entirely logical.'

'So since he is expecting a bit of police brutality, it's helpful to fall in with his wishes. If he complains, Sergeant Mucha here will show the register that proves that there was no prisoner in cell six this afternoon, so one can't have been beaten up. The poor ex-Minister must be deluded. It happens to the finest of minds when they're in solitary confinement all day.'

'He's entitled to an exercise period though, isn't he?'

'Sadly, staff cuts mean that no-one can be spared to accompany him, so on grounds of security we are unable to let him out,' Mucha declared.

'Nice touch that,' said Slonský, 'on account of it was this Minister who said that if efficiency savings meant prisoners didn't get all their exercise breaks, who cares?'

'Well, *he* does — now,' said Mucha.

'It's been an educational experience for him, then,' agreed Slonský.

'But what about the Sinatra music?' enquired Navrátil.

'I like Sinatra,' Slonský replied.

'Me too,' said Mucha.

'And I don't have a CD player at home. If I didn't play it here I'd never get to hear it.'

Mucha began to sing.

'And then I go and spoil it all by saying something stupid, like —'

'— *I love you*,' chorused the two older men.

'You're barking mad, the pair of you!' Navrátil announced. 'You pretend to beat up a prisoner and you play music at the same time so you can sing along.'

'Ah, no,' Slonský interrupted, 'allow me to correct you there. I don't sing while I'm thumping suspects. As you've just discovered, my singing voice definitely constitutes cruel and unusual punishment.'

'You're not kidding there,' said Mucha.

'No,' continued Slonský, 'Sinatra has to manage without me. But he does a good job of masking the noises, which means

93

that our diminutive friend in cell five only catches snatches of what is going on, which makes him doubly suspicious. His imagination will come up with things we couldn't begin to stage.'

Mucha chuckled. 'Remember that hoodlum who convinced himself that his mate was being anally gang-banged by the Prague police?'

'Yes,' said Slonský. 'I never knew how he arrived at that conclusion. But he confessed double quick when we opened his cell door.'

'But when they discover they've been conned, won't they tell the court we've obtained a confession under duress?'

'No, Navrátil, because they know by then that there was no duress and that they'll look like grade A idiots if they claim that there was. Who wants to stand up in court and say that they only confessed because they thought that the sound of Sergeant Mucha pumping up his bicycle tyres was actually due to their colleague being gang-banged by a bunch of shirt-lifters?'

'Lucky he's so short,' opined Mucha. 'It enhances the effect.'

'Too right,' agreed Slonský. 'There must be a lot of things in life he doesn't quite see. Fortunately he's too short to see that there was nobody in cell six. Leave him to stew a few minutes, then go and retrieve the CD player.'

'Will do. I might give the floor a quick mop too.'

'That'd be good. There's a theatrical side to you I hadn't anticipated, Mucha.'

'That's me,' agreed Mucha. 'Give me an audience of one and watch me perform.'

Navrátil had collected the car dealer's statement, which Slonský was reading through.

'That's clear enough. So that explains the forty-nine thousand two hundred and fifty crowns. But what about the other two hundred thousand? If Banda withdrew the smaller sum to pay for the car, what was the two hundred thousand for?'

'Rent? Deposit on a flat?'

'Who knows? And why insert it in Irina's whatsit? Why not take it back again if it links him to her?'

'Forgot it?'

'No, he can't have done. Any way you look at it he inserted it after he strangled her. Why give away the money?'

'Maybe it was an impulse.'

'But he came equipped with a plastic bank bag. They won't have given it to him like that. He put it in there. Do we know for sure that it was the Minister that withdrew the money?'

Navrátil waved a videocassette.

'Bank security footage from the branch by the castle. You can see the Minister making the withdrawal, and the time and date stamp on the tape matches the date on the bank statement.'

Slonský laid the cassette next to the bank statement and the car dealer's statement and scrutinised each in turn.

'What's wrong, sir? It all fits.'

'Yes,' said Slonský, 'it all fits. Except for one thing. Banda isn't an idiot. And we still don't know why he killed Irina.'

'He doesn't seem to be heartbroken. Maybe he fell out of love with her and was worried she would spill the beans.'

'She knew the score. There would be nothing traceable. If it got out it would hardly damage him terminally. One day he would dump her and she'd just have to dust herself off and get on with her life. And why draw out the money if he was about to strangle her anyway?'

'To lull her into a false sense of security? Put her off her guard? If he gave her the cash for the car she'd think he still loved her. Perhaps he'd promised the money — after all, the car was due in that weekend. You can imagine her telling him she needed the money that night to get the car a day or two later.'

'But if he was having second thoughts, why didn't he tell her to take a running jump before he gave her the money?'

'A pay-off? Sort of "Leave me in peace and I'll buy you a car".'

'Possibly. But why take her out to dinner, then?'

'So he could tell her in public and she couldn't make a scene.'

'But then he drove her home and they made love. I haven't had much to do with women for many a long day, lad, but I can't see a girl you've just dumped inviting you into her bed.'

'I suppose not. Not that I would know,' Navrátil added hurriedly.

'Well, there's only one way to find out. Let's go and interview him.'

'When you say "Interview him"…'

'Cassette recorder, no violence, all above board, Navrátil. What do you take me for?'

Mucha and a junior officer were standing guard over Banda, who sat at the interview table, a hunched figure in a jumpsuit that was at least one size too big for him. The ends of the legs flopped over his shoes and he had turned the cuffs back to allow his hands some freedom.

'Official interview,' announced Slonský. 'The caution still stands.'

'I don't want him near me,' squealed Banda.

'Navrátil? Why not?'

'He hits people! I heard you tell him off for doing it.'

'I don't think so. Navrátil, have I ever told you off for hitting a suspect?'

'No, sir.'

'That would be a very serious disciplinary offence indeed. But since Dr Banda has concerns, why don't you sit by the door over there, out of arm's reach. I mean, out of harm's way.'

'What did you do to that unfortunate in the cell opposite?'

'What unfortunate? What cell? Mucha, do you know anything about this?'

'No, Lieutenant. That cell isn't occupied and hasn't been since Sunday night.'

'You were in there earlier,' Banda screamed. 'I saw you go in. And there were those horrible noises.'

'I don't think Mr Sinatra would be pleased to hear you describe his singing as horrible noises. You want to watch that — he had some bad friends, you know.'

'Good thing he's dead,' Mucha added, 'or he might have been upset by that.'

'I think you must be over-excited,' said Slonský in his most soothing voice. 'Shall we get on with the interview?'

He recorded the date and time, and listed those present. On hearing his name, Mucha pointed to the door and slipped out.

'Sergeant Mucha has just left the room,' Slonský said. 'Why he couldn't do that before I recorded his name, I have no idea.'

'I'm saying nothing without my lawyer present,' declared Banda.

'Very wise, sir. But of course your co-operation or lack of it may be a factor in court.'

'I used to tell my clients not to talk until I got there.'

'Well, you are here,' Slonský pointed out, 'so we can begin. The account you gave of your evening with Miss Gruberová contained, as you have admitted, some inaccuracies. Would you now like to tell us what really happened?'

Banda sat with his arms folded.

'The accused declines to answer. Then I'll tell you what I think happened. You rang up and arranged to meet. At the end of your working day, around eight o'clock, you met up for dinner at the restaurant you named. The waiting staff confirm that you were both there that evening. During the evening you presented Miss Gruberová with the money for a car that you had promised. She was very grateful. She invited you in when you drove her home, and the pair of you made love. At some time after you climaxed you strangled her, inserted the car money in her vagina, dressed her again and drove her to Holešovice, where you dumped her body by the main railway station.'

'Fiction. Pure fiction,' said Banda.

'It can't all be fiction,' Slonský retorted, 'because some of it is lifted directly from your statements. And when I dropped in on the restaurant last night they agreed that the two of you had dinner there.'

'It's accurate enough until we get to the climax. Then I dressed and left.'

'Did she dress?'

'I think she said she was going to take a shower. She wasn't dressed when I left.'

'Did you see anyone else on your way out?'

'No, but there must have been, I suppose, given that someone killed her soon after I went.'

'Or you did it yourself, of course. So where could this invisible man have been hiding, do you think?'

'I don't know. Since I didn't see him, how could I know where he was?'

'Let's return to the matter of the car money. Do you admit going to a bank near your office on the morning of the killing and withdrawing the money for the car?'

'Yes.'

'Why?'

'I'd promised it. I like to keep my promises.'

'There's a bit of a fine distinction between refusing the money, and giving it but then murdering the recipient, wouldn't you say?'

'This is preposterous!'

'So you wouldn't agree with me?'

'No!'

'So the accused sees no distinction at all between refusing to keep his promise and keeping it but snatching the money back.'

Banda's hand snaked out and switched off the cassette. Slonský stared him down for a few seconds, then he turned the recorder back on.

'The recorder was turned off by the accused and was off for less than twenty seconds,' Slonský recorded. 'Isn't that the case, Dr Banda?'

'Yes.'

'I don't think we heard you.'

'Yes! Yes, I turned the tape off. No, it wasn't off for long.'

'Temper, temper!' cooed Slonský. 'Would you like us to give you a moment to collect your thoughts?'

'There's no need. I'm perfectly collected, thank you.'

'Would you like a glass of water?'

'No, thank you.'

'Perhaps a biscuit?'

'No, thank you.'

'Do you have an anger management problem? I only ask because you're clenching your fists.'

'That's because I find you intensely annoying.'

'Just doing my job, sir. Trying to find the murderer of a young Czech girl whom you admit to having screwed just minutes before she was strangled.'

'We don't know it was only minutes before.'

'*You* don't know that,' agreed Slonský.

'That's it,' Banda announced. 'I'm not saying any more until my lawyer is here.'

'Fair enough,' said Slonský. 'Navrátil, call Sergeant Mucha and have the accused returned to his cell.'

Mucha and the young uniformed policeman escorted Banda to the cells. Slonský waited until they had gone, then turned to Navrátil with a broad smile on his face.

'That went very well, I think. Beer and a sausage, Navrátil?'

The bottle smashed against the brick wall, and the thrower sank back onto a bench in the square. A stout figure in a dark coat slipped onto the bench beside him.

'They killed my girl. Where were you when they killed my girl?'

'I know,' said Tomáš. 'Come on, I'll give you a lift home.'

'Aren't you going to arrest me like normal?'

'Not tonight, Václav. You're entitled to throw a bottle or two tonight.'

Chapter 10

The morning newspapers made interesting reading, thought Slonský. The sacking of the Minister and his arrest by the police were given due prominence on the front pages of all the papers, except one tabloid that chose to lead with a story about a television personality who had denied having cosmetic surgery. The press release announcing the arrest had come, by agreement, from the Prime Minister's office; the police had declined to give any details of the charge, nor to reveal where the ex-Minister was being held, though every resident of Prague knew where that would be. And the majority of them were wrong. If everyone arrested finished up at Pankrác, it would need a capacity bigger than the Sparta football stadium.

It was the best time of the day, thought Slonský, the half hour or so before everyone began arriving. Time when he could do his best thinking. Today his best thinking was devoted to one subject: why would an intelligent man like Banda, who had been the personification of caution all his adult life, do something as profoundly stupid as inserting nearly a quarter of a million crowns in his girlfriend's vagina? Was he two-faced enough to make love to her one minute, and despise her enough to humiliate her corpse like that a few minutes later? Well, he was a politician. Being two-faced probably came naturally to him. But even so …

Captain Lukas entered the room.

'Is it going to stick?' he asked.

'I'm not sure, sir,' Slonský replied. 'We'd best be cautious about what we say.'

'Thank you,' said Lukas. 'I'll make sure we are. What worries you?'

'I don't believe a man like Banda does silly things. And this was a profoundly silly thing to do. If Banda turned murderer he'd be better at it than this.'

Lukas pulled up a chair and sat down heavily.

'Josef, we've both known intelligent men do really stupid things.'

'Yes, I suppose we have. But this man does nothing by impulse. He's a cold, unemotional piece of flint. If he put the money inside her he did it for a reason. And I can't think what that reason could be. Until I can, I can't be sure he's our man.'

'The evidence tells its own story.'

They sat in silence for a few moments as Slonský revisited the evidence trail in his head.

'He seems guilty. I can't explain how he could be innocent in the face of the evidence.'

Lukas lifted himself out of the chair with a degree of effort.

'Well, we all know things aren't always what they seem.'

As the Captain headed for his office, Slonský repeated his words to himself.

'Things aren't always what they seem. No, they aren't. Why aren't they?'

When Navrátil arrived about a quarter of an hour later he found Slonský in a state not far off a trance. He was gazing fixedly at a blank wall and mumbling as if reciting his catechism.

'Are you all right, sir?'

'Never better. Lukas is a genius, you know that?'

'Captain Lukas? Our Captain Lukas?'

'Things are not always what they seem. That's what he said. And he's right.'

'Sir?'

'Navrátil, what do we know? We know that the Minister made love to Miss Gruberová, and that she was strangled very soon afterwards; so soon, in fact, that we can probably pin it on him. But we've been assuming he was alone.'

'He was, sir. He drove her back from the restaurant. And she'd hardly do … what she did … in front of an audience.'

'But suppose he'd arranged for an accomplice to be there. She was a fit young woman and he isn't exactly Samson, is he? How did a little runt like him pin down a girl like that? If he'd knocked her out I could understand it, but she was strangled. She fought — remember the leather under her nails? — so how did he subdue her? But if he had an accomplice, it's easy. He makes love to her, leaves the door open when he leaves; the accomplice comes in, strangles the girl, and there's no sign of forced entry. If the Minister is quick enough he can even get home to establish an alibi. Maybe his wife isn't lying; maybe he really was home when Irina was killed.'

'But if a third party did it, why insert the money? Wouldn't a hired criminal just pocket it? There's no hint that he was disturbed, and he disposed of the body as and when he wanted.'

Slonský mulled this argument over for a while to the accompaniment of mumbling and staring as before.

'Who wanted her dead, Navrátil? Who is most likely to want a mistress out of the way?'

'A wife, I suppose.'

'Exactly. A wife who gives her husband an alibi.'

'It's a pretty feeble, inexact alibi, sir.'

'Yes, but we can't prove it isn't true. We've been looking at the alibi as Banda's alibi provided by his wife. Actually, they're guaranteeing each other. And if they're in it together, it could be false as a ninety-crown note.'

'You've lost me, sir.'

'Mrs Bandová finds out about the girlfriend. She makes a scene. The girlfriend can't harm Banda's career — he'd shrug it off, like so many do — but if his wife divorces him and sells the story to the press, he's in trouble. He agrees to get rid of Irina, but Mrs Bandová knows of only one way to guarantee that he doesn't go on seeing his mistress behind her back. So they cook up a plan. He'll be the usual loving friend, take her to dinner, take her home, make sure he leaves DNA traces on her, make sure there is evidence tying him to the crime. Then he leaves and establishes an alibi while the murderer kills her. It might be Mrs Bandová herself or, more likely, someone she recruited. Now, here's the cunning bit. If we don't charge Banda, suspicion could fall on the real murderer, so Mrs Bandová's security depends on Banda being charged. The best guarantee of non-prosecution she can have is if we think he's guilty but got away with it. We'll devote all our efforts to nailing him and forget to look for anyone else.'

'But he might get convicted. How does that look so cunning?'

'Because he won't. We can't quite prove it was him. His lawyer will ask whether he is so stupid as to leave his sperm inside the victim, or to put money we can easily trace to him inside her vagina. He'll create just enough doubt to get his man off. Banda will threaten to sue the rear end off anyone who accuses him of having done it, and he's protected from a life in jail because he has already been acquitted and he can't be charged with the same crime again.'

Navrátil was unconvinced, but could not disprove the argument.

'So how do we test this theory, sir?'

'Cherchez la femme, Navrátil.'

'Sir?'

'The woman, lad. Let's go and talk to the Minister's wife. If she genuinely didn't know about the mistress, my theory falls to bits. But if she did know, we have to put the frighteners on them by hinting that we're after her rather than him. If she is in the dock, the sperm evidence and the money don't help her. Far from making her look too stupid to be guilty, they make her look like a jealous wife who gave a whore her earnings after she killed her.'

'I'll get the car, sir.'

'You do that, Navrátil. Meanwhile I'll go and get some essential detective equipment.'

'Sir?'

'A flask of coffee and some pastries, my boy. I can't think on an empty stomach.'

Chapter 11

Banda's wife opened the door herself. She was a tall, attractive woman, with chestnut brown hair that just brushed her shoulders, and some expensive-looking pearl stud earrings. Her eyes, though green in colour, flashed red with annoyance when she discovered who they were.

'Should I call my lawyer?'

'If you wish, but we don't intend this as a formal interview.'

'You say that now, but if I say something that helps your case against my poor husband, you'll use it, caution or no caution.'

'There are rules about that, madam. And I don't need to bolster the case against your husband. I want to hear your side of it all.'

'Mine? I have nothing to do with it.'

'Your loyalty to your husband does you credit, Mrs Bandová, particularly since he has admitted that he betrayed you with a younger woman.'

'Not to me, he hasn't.'

'Perhaps not. But you're an educated woman, and the Minister isn't the sort of man to spend his life with someone who isn't an intellectual match. You've got brains; you must have known something was going on.'

'Brains, yes, but not experience. I don't know what a man does when he has a mistress. He didn't buy her jewellery and leave it lying around, if that's what you're getting at.'

'What about your intuition? Didn't that tell you something? Aren't women supposed to know these things?'

She chewed her knuckle for a moment in deep thought, as if the action would help her keep something to herself. It failed.

'He had been a little distant.'

'Distant?'

'Undemonstrative.'

'You mean he slept in the spare room?'

'No! But it's certainly true that he showed less interest in me.'

'But you didn't know Miss Gruberová?'

'Certainly not. She wasn't the sort of woman I would meet socially, Lieutenant.'

'Your husband tells us she was helping him to plan your birthday party.'

'Does he? Far-sighted of him. It isn't for another eight months yet.'

Slonský smiled gently.

'Looks like he's slipped us both a pack of lies, then.'

'He's not a bad man, Lieutenant. He's been incredibly stupid, but he's not wicked.'

'I wouldn't argue with that assessment, madam, and coming from his wife it carries some weight. But was he stupid enough to kill?'

'Maybe. But he couldn't swat a fly. He hasn't the stomach to be a killer. If he was going to turn to crime it would be something like fraud, something where he could pit his wits against yours. Killing someone he didn't give a toss about isn't his style.'

'Didn't he love her?'

'Albert doesn't love anyone except himself, Lieutenant. He's fond of me and the children, but he's not a loving person.'

'So why have a mistress, if not for love?'

'I don't know. Because he can, because he likes the thrill of his little secret, because his friends have all got one. I don't know.'

'Forgive me, but I have to ask. Could it be just for sex?'

She gave a small, but mirthless laugh.

'His appetite did not exceed mine. If quantity was all he wanted, he could have topped up here. But he is a busy man and he was often "tired" at the end of the day.'

'So he'd rather have burger out than steak at home.'

'Indelicate but accurate. Steak was waiting for him.'

'Did you have Irina Gruberová killed, madam?'

'Irina? Is that her name? No, I didn't. I wouldn't have known where to find her.'

'You don't seem to bear her as much animosity as I'd have expected.'

'In what way?'

'You don't call her a whore or bitch.'

'If she'd been either of those things Albert wouldn't have touched her. He was fastidious, you know. Very fussy about things like clean white sheets.'

Slonský returned his hat to his head. His voice carried a definite tone of sadness as he told her what she already feared.

'Your husband could spend a long time in prison, Mrs Bandová. Maybe he didn't personally strangle Miss Gruberová, but it could well be that he ordered it to be done.'

'Both those thoughts had occurred to me, Lieutenant. Neither is pleasant.'

'What will you do?'

'I have no idea. He's my husband. I took a vow and I always intended to keep it. I can't give up at the first little difficulty.'

Slonský raised his hat, bade her a good evening, and walked back to the car with a heavy tread. After he took his seat, he remained for a few moments staring into the darkness in silence before motioning to Navrátil to start the engine.

'A remarkable woman, that. He doesn't deserve her.'

'You've given up on the idea that she might have organised it, then?'

'I never really thought it, but we had to take it into account. Did you see the family photographs on the side table?'

'No, sir. You were in the way.'

'Nice kids. Two of them. Unfortunately the boy looks like his father, but we all have our cross to bear. Put your foot down, lad, I could do with a beer or two.'

'Were you ever married, sir?'

Slonský turned in his seat to inspect Navrátil closely.

'Now what made you ask that?'

'Sorry, sir. Just curiosity. I've never heard anyone mention a wife but you talked to Mrs Bandová as if you knew a bit about marriage.'

'I talk to Novák about steeplechasing but I'm not a horse, Navrátil.'

'No, sir. Sorry, sir.'

'Yes, as it happens I was married, Navrátil. In my salad days, when I was green. Not long after I joined the police, I married a girl called Věra. Tall, blonde, bit of a catch if I do say so myself. We met at some Party function or other.'

'Love at first sight?'

'No, I don't really know what brought us together. Probably the local Party Secretary telling us both we should be thinking about getting married, so doing it with each other seemed the most labour-saving arrangement. He believed it was every Czech's duty to produce two little Czechs to keep the country populated.'

'Children?'

'No, puppies. Of course, children! We didn't get that far, though. A combination of shift work for me, a bit of grief about the Prague Spring and the fact that she found some leather-jacketed poet who persuaded her that getting shafted on a rug was an authentic piece of romance. She packed her bags and I was left on my own.'

'The Prague Spring, sir?'

'Surely you've heard of it, Navrátil. Or don't they teach you about our nation's history at school these days?'

'Yes, I've heard of it, sir. But I didn't understand why it interfered in your marriage.'

Slonský sighed.

'Pull in over there, lad, and let's have a sausage at that bar.'

Slonský took a large bite and chewed rhythmically.

'I wonder what domestic animal this is made from? Hand me the pickles, son.'

Navrátil sipped his beer, feeling a little shamefaced that he had asked the question in the first place. It was really none of his business, and he had no idea whether there was still an open wound in Slonský's heart, though it was very hard to think of Slonský as a man with tender feelings. It was rather like considering that a hippopotamus might enjoy ballet.

'How old were you when the Communists were turfed out, Navrátil?'

'Five or six, sir.'

'I thought so. It was grim, Navrátil. Grim, joyless, frightening, stifling, monochrome, all the things you'll have heard and more. I joined the police in 1967 as a young man. They didn't have the academy in those days, so I went in as a humble cadet. I must have been a bit younger than you are now. They gave me a uniform, proper boots for the first time in my life, a gun — and a fairly healthy wage by the standards of the day — in exchange for which I was expected to defend the motherland against capitalist aggressors, Yankee imperialism and old women crossing the road in the wrong place. Aren't you thirsty?'

'Just taking my time, sir. Don't let me stop you.'

'Don't worry, you won't.'

He waved to attract the waiter.

'Give the cat another diuretic and fill this up. So, Navrátil, our great nation was choking itself slowly, and then along came Dubček.'

'I remember him.'

'You remember him as an old man. He was impressive then, but as a party leader he was electrifying. For the first time we had someone who seemed to understand what a damn awful life lots of us led, and we believed he could change it. We had newspapers that told the truth. Some of them even contained some news other than tractor output figures and the various meetings of the bigwigs. We heard that not everything in our Socialist utopia was going exactly to plan. People managed to get on the television to say that the roads were full of potholes and they'd been waiting five years for a motorbike. It may not seem much to you, Navrátil, but it was a big deal to us. It was during the Prague Spring that I got married. It seemed like a time for new starts. Then we discovered the Russians were cheesed off about it all.'

'They invaded, didn't they?'

'No, lad, they were invited in to restore law and order and provide fraternal support to the Czech workers. Or some such claptrap. Yes, they invaded. Dubček was carted off and we got Husák. Two Slovaks, note, but one of them wasn't bad despite that. Husák didn't hold with all this freedom. Steadily he wound the clock back and repression was restored, and who do you think got the job of doing the repressing?'

'The Army?'

'Husák wasn't sure that they could be trusted, at least not alone. And he wasn't sure we could be either. But by getting the police and army to do it together and report on each other's performance, he kept us both in check. And that's when Věra started giving me a hard time. She said I was betraying the Spring movement and I ought to resign. I didn't think resignation was an option, unless you enjoy a stay in Pankrác. It seemed that everything that happened was a direct consequence of my inadequacies. When Jan Palach burned himself to death at the top of Wenceslas Square, I got the blame. She said it was people like me who drove him to it. As it happened, I was over the river and didn't even hear about it until she told me. I sometimes used to wonder if I had been there, would I have put the flames out to save his life, or let him burn so he could complete his sacrifice?'

'Would you?'

'I still don't know, and if I don't know now, I never will. It's been nearly forty years, and it seems like only weeks ago. When I finished work the next day I walked up to the top of the square. There were workmen scrubbing the ground to remove the charring. He hadn't died yet, but the doctors couldn't save him. I don't know how hard they tried. Alive, he was just a student, but dead, he spoke for all of us. I stood where he had burned and then — I don't know what came over me — I saluted.'

Slonský swilled his glass around and inspected the eddies in his drink.

'Policemen weren't too popular in Prague just then. You'd get barged in the trams and people would accidentally stamp on your feet. Someone spat on my back when I was on the beat. But when I brought my arm down to my side one of the workmen clapped his hand on my shoulder and muttered "You're all right, son". No praise I've ever had has meant as much to me as that.'

They sat for a while in silence. Navrátil felt that he should let the other man speak first.

'I think I've had enough, Navrátil. Let's go home.'

Chapter 12

Slonský was sitting at his desk in the morning, shuffling sheets of paper and drawing lines connecting phrases on them, when Navrátil approached him with an outstretched hand containing a paper towel.

'What's that?'

'I had a parcel when I got home. My mum's been baking. Try one.'

Slonský peered into the towel. There was a small strudel.

'I can't take your last pastry.'

'I've got a tinful.'

'Oh, well, in that case, thank you very much!'

Slonský took a bite and rolled it over his tongue.

'Your mum's not a bad pastrycook, Navrátil. You'll have a hard time finding a girl who can cook like that.'

'They're out there, sir. My generation's not that different to yours.'

'No, I don't suppose it is. We all think the younger generation is going to hell in a handcart. You will when you're my age. Listen to me, I sound like my dad.'

'Was he like you, then?'

'Depends what you mean by "like me". He had a heartbeat and testicles, but that's about it for resemblance, so far as I can remember. Now, to work, son! Last night I had a brainwave. Perhaps the Minister's car would have some traces of Irina's dead body in it, so I got forensics onto it first thing.'

'And?'

'I don't know yet. They don't seem to start till eight. The snag is, we know the live Irina was in the car, so I'm not sure if

114

they're clever enough to distinguish material from the dead Irina. It may just prove what we already know, but it's worth a try. Now, what are you going to do today?'

'Whatever you tell me to, sir.'

'No, lad, no clues! I want you to tell me what you think you should be doing.'

Navrátil had not expected an initiative test, and was momentarily nonplussed.

'Well, if the Minister did it, or caused it to be done, then he might have been spotted leaving.'

'Nobody owned up to that the other night. Waste of time doing more of the same.'

'Then we need to shake his alibi. See if we can get him rattled by making him repeat his story over and over to see if he forgets something.'

'Worth a try. But he's a politician, Navrátil. Telling the same lie repeatedly is something he can do with his eyes shut. We need to up the stress levels a bit. Why don't you ask Mucha for his mobile phone, then meet me in cell eight.'

'Eight? Who's in eight?'

'No-one yet. But there will be.'

'You can use my phone if you want, sir.'

'Thanks, Navrátil, but yours is a bit modern for me. Mucha has a particularly fine old phone.'

Navrátil was getting used to some unusual requests, but this one was a little more than normally abnormal.

Nevertheless, he did as he was asked and around half an hour later he bore a satchel into the corridor leading to the cells, and found cell eight at the far end on the left.

Slonský was washing some towels in a large bucket.

'Ah, there you are. Plonk it by the table there.'

Slonský spread a wet towel on the floor and stood an old metal-framed chair on it. Taking his handcuffs from his pocket, he attached one end to the chair and left the other dangling.

'Now, lad, be a little angel and tell Mucha we're ready.'

Ready for what, thought Navrátil as he walked back to the desk. The mind boggled.

'The Lieutenant says he's ready,' Navrátil announced. 'What for?'

Mucha shook his head and smiled.

'He's a naughty boy sometimes. You've got to hand it to him, life around Slonský is never dull.'

Navrátil returned to the cell and waited. Plainly nobody was going to tell him anything.

After a few minutes the door was pushed open and Banda walked in. He was naked apart from a large red towel.

As soon as he saw Slonský he turned on his heel and tried to leave, but Mucha blocked the doorway and pushed the ex-Minister into the room.

'Take a seat,' said Slonský. 'Cuff him to the chair, Sergeant — right hand only, he'll need his left hand. He's left-handed, you see.'

'What are you doing?' squealed Banda. 'What's going on? You said I was going to take a shower.'

Slonský reached into his trouser pocket and unfolded a piece of paper.

'Brno, last March. Remember?'

He began reading from the press cutting.

'"We must not forget the rights of victims. We cannot allow excessively liberal ideas of human rights to prevent our bringing criminals to justice. I will expect the police to be vigorous in pursuing, arresting and questioning suspects." I found that very inspiring. It sets a tone, doesn't it? One of your best speeches, if I may say so.'

'You didn't bring me here to ask for my autograph.'

'Only on a statement. Anyway, you and I are going to have a little chat.'

Slonský opened the satchel and extracted a brown bakelite box which he flipped open. He lifted out a telephone handset and put it on the table.

'We won't be needing that,' he said.

There was a roll of flex in the box, consisting of red and black wires twisted together. He unwound a few inches and attached the ends to the terminals on the hand-cranked generator of the field telephone.

'I'll do the business end, Navrátil. All I need you to do is to crank that handle a couple of times. It doesn't need much.'

Navrátil looked doubtful but did as he was asked. Slonský held the tips of the wires a couple of centimetres apart and appeared satisfied as a spark leaped between them.

'You just can't beat old-time Czech engineering, Navrátil. Can't have been used for twenty years and still starts on the button. Watch and learn, lad. It's very important to earth the wires before the next bit, or someone could get a nasty shock.'

He wrapped one wire round the metal handcuff and stood poised with the other.

'Now, where does this go?'

Banda tried to pull his arm out of the handcuffs.

'This is outrageous. I am not going to confess under duress. You know it won't be admitted in court.'

'I just want the truth,' said Slonský. 'Court can wait. Once we know what happened, we can find the evidence. Of course, back in the good old days, we'd just manufacture evidence if it helped us get a conviction. This takes you back, doesn't it,

117

Mucha? I didn't think we'd see our old friend again. Think of all the sterling service this little chap has done over the years.'

He smiled at Banda.

'If this terminal could talk he could reel off a list of celebrity genitals you wouldn't believe.'

Banda tried to get to his feet but the handcuffs hindered him and his bare feet slipped as the wet towel slithered beneath him. Mucha grasped him firmly round the shoulders and pushed him down onto the chair.

'No, don't!'

The ex-Minister was wild-eyed with fear. Navrátil stepped forward to intervene but as he moved he saw Slonský frowning at him.

'Did you arrange to have Irina Gruberová killed?'

'No! Why would I? We were having fun together.'

'So why pay her off? A parting gift?'

'I promised her a car. I kept my promise. I never intended her any harm.'

'So if you didn't kill her, who did?'

'How should I know? It wasn't me! You have to believe me.'

Slonský grasped Banda's chin and forced him to look into his eyes.

'You're wrong there. I don't have to believe you. I can believe what I want.'

Banda struggled but Mucha had him in a tight grip.

Despite squirming and throwing his upper body from side to side, Banda could not escape, and presently began to weep.

'Don't do this! I behaved badly, but I'm not a murderer. I ought to have cared more when she died, but I couldn't let you see how I felt. She was a sweet girl, and I would never have harmed her, I swear.'

Slonský nodded, and Mucha took a step back.

The prisoner continued to sob, and wiped his nose and eyes on a dry towel that Mucha gave him.

'Take him to the showers, Sergeant, and let him tidy himself up.'

Mucha steered Banda through the door, while Slonský picked up the wet towel and the field telephone and walked off down the corridor, Navrátil chasing him as he went.

'What were you doing there, sir? You can't do that to a suspect!'

'I just have. Worked, didn't it? Just like it always did in the past. If that wasn't the truth, I don't know what is.'

'He could report you.'

'What for? Helping him prove his innocence? I don't think so.'

'You threatened and humiliated him.'

'I don't know if he would have got that much of a shock, because I've never actually needed to do that. Just showing them the kit is enough. In medieval times the day before you tortured somebody you showed him the tools of the trade, then you left him to think. I wouldn't have given him a shock. But he had to believe I might do it. I was taking a chance because he might be stubborn enough to call my bluff, but you have to give it a try, don't you?'

'I don't believe what I've just seen,' Navrátil muttered. 'You terrorised him.'

'Don't come over all bleeding heart with me, lad,' snarled Slonský. 'I've got one aim, to find Irina Gruberová's killer, and that's what I'll do, whatever it takes. She deserves that. And, by the way, I wasn't the one who was turning the crank handle.'

He shoved the swing doors open and disappeared from view, leaving Navrátil standing in the corridor, confused and just a little bit frightened himself.

Slonský and Navrátil waited patiently as Lukas digested the information they had just imparted.

'You think he's innocent after all? I can't see the Prime Minister being too happy that he sacked a minister who turns out not to be guilty.'

'Everyone is guilty, sir,' offered Slonský. 'They may not be guilty of what they're charged with, but everyone has done something.'

'Cynical, and hardly reassuring,' Lukas observed.

'But true, sir.'

'You may be right, but I'm not sure that it will comfort the Prime Minister.'

'If we're asked, sir, the reason for the Minister's dismissal is surely that he failed to co-operate with our enquiries, thereby failing to meet the ethical requirements of his office.'

'That's very literate of you, Slonský. I'll just make a note for future reference.'

'On top of that, he's a lying little adulterer who didn't give a fig for his adoring girlfriend.'

'I won't make a note of that, Slonský.'

'Very good, sir.'

'So when are we going to release him?'

'Do we have to? He's stopped demanding his freedom. And he might not want to face the press. Besides which, the public may want us to arrest someone else if we let him go. All in all, it's probably better if we keep him banged up for a while.'

'There are limits, Slonský. If his lawyer kicks up it'll probably be only a day before he has to be set free.'

'I think we could probably still get a conviction with the evidence we have, sir. The fact that my private intuition tells me he probably didn't do it is irrelevant.'

Lukas cleared his throat noisily.

'Was that a meaningful harrumph, sir?'

'I think,' Lukas mused, 'that we might not yet discover the Minister's innocence and we could reasonably continue to think of him as the prime suspect.'

'Definitely, sir. He must be our prime suspect, because he's our only suspect.'

Slonský beamed benignly.

'There are times,' Lukas opined, 'when I think you may be the nearest thing we have to a Good Policeman Švejk, Slonský. Insubordinate, in an innocent, non-threatening sort of way.'

'Thank you, sir.'

'But where do we go now? If not Banda, then who?'

'I honestly don't know, sir.'

Navrátil was surprised to find that Slonský stopped only briefly at the office to collect his hat and coat before marching purposefully out into the street.

'Where are we going, sir?'

'To do some research, Navrátil. We need an environment suitable for deep thinking and reflection, free from distractions. And here it is.'

'A bar?'

'Beer, sausages, comfortable chairs — what more could we want? I need to think hard. Be a good lad and amuse yourself while I get my brain oiled.'

'There must be something more useful I can do.'

'No doubt. And when you think of it, do it. Just don't ask me for suggestions.'

With which, Slonský pushed the door open and was swallowed into the darkness, leaving Navrátil standing with his hands in his pockets and his mouth half open.

Navrátil had an idea. It was a peculiar idea, and he could not quite see where it would lead, but he had nothing else to offer, so he grabbed his file and marched upstairs to see if Klinger was free.

Klinger listened carefully to Navrátil's questions. They showed an uncommon degree of shrewdness, he thought. Someday Navrátil may have a future in the fraud department, provided Slonský did not ruin him with his addiction to beer, sausages and untidy mental habits.

As for Navrátil, he returned to the office with a sense that he had an expert's backing for the bizarre theory that he was beginning to form. He was no wiser about where it was leading, but in a landscape with no signposts, the smallest marker is a handy thing to have.

As it happened, Navrátil was crestfallen to discover that Slonský had independently arrived at the same odd notion.

'You think someone is out to frame Banda?'

'I can't see how else to explain it all,' Navrátil replied.

Slonský perched his feet on the desk.

'You're probably right, but it leaves us having to think of a perpetrator and a motive. I agree that he is being framed, but I can't think who would do it and why.'

'Someone who wants his job?'

'Another corrupt minister? Two, in the same government? Surely not! Navrátil, you'll get a reputation for cynicism. Still, it would be good fun to tell the Prime Minister he's got to sack another minister. Wouldn't do much for team spirit, banging one minister up for trying to frame another one.'

'But you understand the point I was making, sir?'

'Oh, yes, Navrátil. You did well. The Minister said what he said about the cash withdrawal, and it's a key bit of evidence. I just can't see who it points at.'

There was a critical story in the evening newspaper, claiming that Banda was unlikely to be charged and that the police were no nearer finding an alternative suspect.

'This is appalling!' Lukas protested. 'It undermines all we're trying to do.'

'Yes, sir,' agreed Slonský. 'It's true, too.'

'That is quite beside the point! This is speculation of the worst kind. We must answer it with action, Slonský. We must ram these words down the journalist's throat. I cannot imagine what he thought he was doing.'

Navrátil had not had the opportunity to read the article, but studied it as they walked back to their office.

'Doesn't this make your blood boil, sir?'

'You get used to it, Navrátil.'

'But where did they get this from? There's only you, me and maybe Mucha who could have known this.'

'As Captain Lukas said, it's speculation of the worst kind. Pure guesswork.'

'Who is this journalist anyway? Valentin?'

'Come along, lad. I've got to meet someone in the Old Town. You can come too.'

The meeting was, predictably, in a bar. The bar was, equally predictably, not particularly select in either its setting or its clientele. A scruffy middle-aged man sat in a corner trying to complete a puzzle in a scrunched-up newspaper, inexpertly folded. To Navrátil's surprise, Slonský bought three beers and placed one of them in front of the man.

'This, Navrátil, is Mr Valentin.'

Valentin nodded a greeting.

'Job suit you?' he asked.

'Very good. I especially liked the bit about muddled leadership of the investigation and whether the involvement of a minister had led to higher ranks becoming involved who no longer had day-to-day experience of murder inquiries.'

'That's word for word. You must actually have read it.'

'You mean in the paper, or when I helped you write it?'

'You disparage my talents, sir. I demand satisfaction! I have a reputation as a sozzled hack to maintain.'

'And you're doing it very well.'

Valentin pointed at Navrátil.

'Is he all there?'

'You mean that vacant expression? Yes, the brain works very well. He's a good lad, is Navrátil. One day I shall hang up my handcuffs and he'll slide effortlessly into my place, you mark my words. Navrátil, cultivate this old hack and you'll have a valuable ally. I take it that gormless look indicates that you're surprised by this turn of events?'

'You could say that, sir, yes.'

'Then let me admit you to my innermost thought processes while I can still remember what they are. How did we first link the murder to the Minister?'

'Someone sent us a photograph.'

'Exactly. Someone out there wanted us to know what was going on, and gave us the evidence to pin the crime on Dr Banda. Now, it seems to me to be a reasonable supposition that our penfriend wanted Banda fingered for the crime. It seemed plausible that if we let him or her know that Banda wasn't going to be fingered, he might send us a bit more evidence.'

'So this is a trick to get the original source to get back in touch with us?'

'A long shot, I admit, but maybe the best we have at present. And to give the story credibility, it couldn't come from us. If it came from someone unconnected with the police, it would carry more weight. Enter Mr Valentin here, who, for a modest amount of beer and first chance at the big story when we get it, was prepared to blacken our names in the gutter press.'

'To be honest,' said Valentin, 'for the chance to blacken your name I'd work for nothing.'

'Spoken like a true member of the fourth estate. Navrátil, Mr Valentin's glass is empty. Be a good lad and fill it for him, would you?'

'Can you manage another too?' asked Navrátil.

Slonský gave him a disapproving look and drained his glass.

Chapter 13

The following day, Slonský gave Navrátil the day off, once it became clear that there had been no response to the newspaper story. In the afternoon, Irina Gruberová was laid to rest in her home village, and the mourners might have noticed a slightly portly man in a crumpled overcoat standing in the churchyard, who appeared to be on speaking terms with Sergeant Tomáš.

'How's it going?' the sergeant enquired.

'Not well. The prime suspect is still the prime suspect; there's no good evidence to exonerate him, but I just can't picture him being so stupid. We're working on the principle that someone framed him.'

Tomáš nodded.

'Understandable. If I'd had something on him, I'd have framed the little sod myself.'

'But why would you do it? He loses his job, but how do you win?'

'It's just the pleasure of seeing another human being suffer, I suppose,' Tomáš shrugged. 'What is it the Germans call it? Schadenfreude? Joy at another's misfortunes.'

'Okay, I can understand that. But it takes some planning. And it costs an innocent girl her life. Why not accuse him of a tax fiddle, or corruption? Why harm someone else? Why not just kill the Minister?'

'Well, I guess whoever it was knew about the mistress and realised it could hurt Banda. He didn't have to create anything, because Banda did that himself.'

Slonský perked up at once.

'Tomáš, you're a genius! If I ever have a vacancy for a driver, I'll give you a call.'

'No thanks, I like it here. But what have I said?'

'You said "whoever it was knew about the mistress". That's right. And he knew he could go to that restaurant and have a good chance of getting a photo. How did he know that?'

Novák sipped his pear brandy.

'This is either brilliant or completely hare-brained, and I can't decide which.'

They were in the restaurant and Slonský had a tape measure in his hand.

'You understand this better than me. Where was this photograph taken from?'

Novák measured the height of a wineglass in the photograph, then a matching wineglass on the table. He scribbled some sums on a paper napkin, took the tape measure from Slonský, and started to walk backwards from the table where Banda and Gruberová had been sitting.

'That table there,' he announced, pointing at a table for two against the wall.

Slonský raised his eyebrows at the restaurant manager, who flicked through the reservations book.

'Table for one at 7.45, name of Lukas.'

'Did he pay by credit card?'

The restaurant manager clicked a few keys on a computer terminal.

'No, cash.'

'Remember him?'

'Afraid not. He can't have been here long, because we gave his table to a couple at nine o'clock.'

Novák drained his glass.

'Presumably, Banda didn't recognise him, or he wouldn't have let himself be photographed.'

'He'd have the cameraman slightly behind him. Probably didn't even notice he was there. In Banda's eyes, he was being very discreet. No hanky-panky at the table. Just a pair of business colleagues having a meal together.'

'They were lovers, Slonský! You can't disguise that.'

'Can't you? I remember a police captain who thought nobody knew he was shafting his driver. They kept a respectable distance in public and genuinely thought nobody had any reason for suspicion.'

'Nice girl?'

'Who said it was a girl? I can see Banda being just as arrogant. If he was trying to keep it secret, he'd believe he'd succeeded.'

'Okay, but humour me a minute. We're arguing that the man who took the photo knew enough to know Banda would be here with Irina. That argues for someone familiar with Banda and something Banda wanted to be discreet about. So surely if Banda saw someone he knew here, he'd know he'd been rumbled.'

'Then our source must have sent someone else to take the photograph. But how he used a camera in here without being noticed is a mystery to me.'

'But not to me,' Novák smirked, raising his mobile phone so that Slonský could see a photograph of himself waiting impatiently while the restaurant manager checked if "Lukas" had paid by credit card. 'You didn't know I'd taken that, did you?'

Slonský checked his own mobile phone.

'Can they all do that?'

'Your antique model is probably the only cellphone in Prague that can't.'

'Well, phones are for phoning. Who needs a camera in a phone anyway?'

'Our blackmailer does,' responded Novák. 'As you said, he couldn't do this without one.'

'It isn't blackmail,' Slonský muttered. 'The photo was sent to us a day or so after it was taken. That isn't time for them to call Banda and get him to pay them off. There's nothing he could do to stop this getting out. It wasn't a question of money. Someone wanted to bring him down.'

'Not necessarily. They may have been planning to blackmail him, then read that Irina had been murdered and realised they knew who the prime suspect was. Even if they aren't public-spirited citizens who want to help the police in every way, they'd know the chances that Banda would be able to pay up, even if he wanted to, wouldn't be good.'

'It's possible. The trouble is, too many things are possible.'

'Any significance in the name Lukas?'

'You mean he was expecting Lukas to get the case? Maybe.'

'Your Captain isn't that well known. Could the informant be a policeman?'

'That's possible too. But then why not claim the credit for nailing Banda himself? Why send it to me?'

'Maybe he's too far down the food chain.'

Slonský sat at the table opposite Novák and rubbed his eyes.

'I don't know. We're not getting anywhere.'

Novák held out his glass for another brandy. The restaurant manager obliged.

'He'll pay.'

Slonský sighed. It was not worth arguing about that either.

'Just a thought,' mused Novák. 'Have you shown the photograph to Banda?'

'Yes, to prove he must have known Gruberová.'

'And does he know when it was taken?'

'Yes, he volunteered that from his diary.'

'Then does he know who took the photo? You're assuming he didn't know someone was here, but that doesn't necessarily follow. He may have recognised someone here but not been worried about it, if it was a friendly face. But now he may know who set him up.'

Slonský's brain was racing.

'If he does, then no doubt he'll be in touch the first chance he gets. We could let him have a private phone call — all suitably tapped, of course.'

'Surely he's not so dim as to fall for that?'

'No, I suppose not. But then if the photographer knows that Banda recognised him and is about to be released, maybe he will give us something else to stave off Banda's revenge. I feel another little chat with Valentin coming on.'

The restaurant manager coughed politely.

'If you don't mind,' he said, 'I'd like to earn a living by letting some customers in. Paying ones,' he added pointedly.

'Novák, sort the man out,' Slonský snapped as he marched to the door.

An advantage of dealing with the gentlemen of the gutter press is that they are regular in their habits. They can usually be found in a particular chair in a particular bar at unvarying times of day, so finding Valentin would not have taxed even Captain Lukas on one of his bad days, Slonský reflected.

'I was just about to go home to bed,' claimed Valentin.

'At eight o'clock? I doubt that very much. Unless you're in a nursing home and they insist on it, of course.'

'My funds are exhausted. What is the point of staying?'

'Is this a hint that you'd like me to buy you a drink?'

'I wouldn't insult you by refusing your act of charity. In fact, I'm prepared to give you repeated opportunities to be charitable.'

Slonský ordered a couple of beers and explained what he wanted.

'If I do this, can I have a head start if your informant gets in touch again?'

'I won't lie to you, old friend. If I can do it, I will. But there's a chance I won't be able to release any information if it proves to be useful to the investigation.'

'I know that. And I trust you to tell me as much as you can, and perhaps a bit more if I'm a really good boy. Now, let's compose our little tale. Front page headline?'

'Let's be a bit more subtle. Late breaking stuff jammed in at the foot of the front page?'

Valentin sucked the end of his pencil in thought.

'That would imply we'd heard about it late at night, and I'm not clear how we could do that. Who's his lawyer?'

'Koller.'

'Old Koller or Young Koller?'

'Ye gods, there are two of them?'

'Son qualified last year.'

'It's the old man. The one who runs the tennis club.'

'Does he play in Armani, I wonder? Never mind, innocent musing that will enliven a tedious midnight hour sometime. So, that publicity-loving hound is unlikely to object if we run a story saying that he is vigorously defending his client and is confident he will soon be released due to lack of evidence.'

'Especially since he has actually done damn all for his client, so far as I can tell.'

'Ah, that's because he doesn't like being associated with clients who might actually go to jail. If it looks like going belly up it won't be very long before he discovers a conflict of interest that means he can't act on Banda's behalf — unless, of course, the fees are spectacular.'

'Banda can pay. I've seen his bank account.'

'No chance of a photocopy some time, I suppose?'

'That would be highly improper!' Slonský replied in an outraged tone. 'I'll see what I can do when this has died down a bit.'

'Fair enough. Refill those glasses with brain fuel and let's start writing.'

Chapter 14

Banda had not seen a newspaper for several days, but he was allowed to see Valentin's handiwork. He smirked at the thought that he might soon be released.

'I wouldn't read too much into that,' Slonský announced. 'I'm a notorious liar.'

'You don't have the evidence to hold me,' declared Banda. 'You can't have, because I'm innocent.'

'There's a non sequitur there, or do I mean a metaphor?' mused Slonský.

'I think it's a non sequitur,' replied Mucha, 'if I remember my Latin from school.'

'Something that doesn't follow? You mean, he may be innocent, but that doesn't mean we haven't got evidence that proves he isn't.'

'Nailed it in one, Lieutenant. It must be true, because our prisons are full but nobody who gets jailed is ever guilty, or so they say.'

Slonský shook his head.

'No, everyone is guilty of something. Not necessarily what we bang them up for, but everyone has some little secret they'd rather keep to themselves. Isn't that right, Dr Banda?'

'I've already admitted I could have behaved better, but that's a far cry from being a murderer.'

Slonský turned a chair round and straddled it while he rested his chin on the back.

'You may be right. But if you'll permit me to put a contrary opinion, here we have a young lady found murdered with your seminal fluid running down her leg, dumped from a car that is the same make and colour as yours, after having dinner and sex with you and after you failed to remember a flat you'd been to — unless the bedhead was outside when you were making love, which I find unlikely — and after you failed to report that you knew a young woman we were trying to identify and whose face was all over the newspapers. Not only that, but a quantity of money you withdrew from your bank, in full view of security cameras, was found in her vagina. A vagina to which, I remind you, you had recently had abundant access, and how many people can we say that about?'

'It only needed one other,' Banda remarked with a heavy sigh.

'So you're saying the murderer waited politely till you'd finished, then he ran in, strangled Miss Gruberová, found a large sum of money and, rather than pocket it, amused himself by shoving it up her before putting her clothes back on her and driving her five kilometres across town in a car just like yours to dump her by a busy railway station?'

Banda jutted his chin forward defiantly.

'Yes,' he growled.

'Fair enough,' said Slonský as he headed for the door. 'It's good to know what we're up against. If you happen to think of a name for this murderer, you might want to give me a shout.'

Navrátil heard Slonský's footsteps approaching and tried hard to look industrious, a task made appreciably more difficult by not having anything in particular to do.

'Ah, there you are, lad! Some of us have done a day's work by now.'

'Sorry, sir. I slept in.'

'Well, you've had a few hard days.'

'It won't happen again, sir.'

'Don't be daft. Of course it will. We all crash out from time to time. Occupational hazard of being a policeman. Just don't let me catch you making a habit of it.'

'Yes, sir. I mean no, sir.'

'We'll say no more about it, unless of course I want something off you. What did you get up to on your day off, then?'

'Saw my mum.'

'Jolly good.'

Slonský riffled through a few papers, had a good scratch while gazing at the large map on the wall, then sat in his chair with a loud sigh.

'Been baking again, has she?'

Mid-morning, Captain Lukas sauntered into the room.

'I've had a telephone call from Mr Koller,' he announced. 'He is concerned that his client has not yet been released.'

'What did you say, sir?' Slonský enquired.

'I said that I have a number of cases currently occupying me and I would make the necessary enquiries, which is what I'm doing now. We can't hold him much longer, Slonský.'

Slonský worried at his thumb with his front teeth.

'I know. I'm just hoping something will turn up.'

'If I remember this morning's newspaper, you were quoted as saying that you had no reason to hold Banda anyway. It's just as well Mr Koller hasn't seen that. Why do you so regularly put your foot in it?'

'I was hoping that the real murderer would give me something more to keep Banda under lock and key, sir. I know we can't wait long, but sometime today something may happen. If the real killer thinks Banda is getting off, he may help us a bit. In any event, he won't kill again if it means letting Banda off the hook because he is in custody.'

Lukas turned a sickly shade of white.

'You think this could be a serial killer?'

'I hope not, sir, but we can never be sure until he's locked up. Of course, Dr Banda is at risk himself with the killer still at large. Our cell is the safest place for him.'

Lukas recovered his composure.

'I may make that suggestion to Mr Koller. I'm sure he wouldn't want to insist on his client's release if there's a homicidal maniac out there waiting for him.'

'No sane person would, sir. But he is a lawyer.'

A little after two o'clock Sergeant Mucha called.

'Someone just delivered a package addressed to you.'

'It's not my birthday. Was it a tall, leggy blonde in a short skirt?'

'No, it was a motorcycle courier with greasy hair and a star tattooed on his neck.'

'So what did he leave?'

'It's addressed to you! How would I know?' Mucha sounded outraged.

'You didn't open it?'

'Certainly not. But I did ask who sent him. He says he was told by phone to go to a block of flats and look in a particular person's mail box. There would be an envelope there and if he opened it there would be something to deliver and a handsome fee for doing so.'

'And was there?'

'A padded envelope and a thousand crowns. Not bad for ten minutes' work.'

'We'll be right down. Or at least Navrátil will.'

Slonský put the phone down and smiled at his assistant.

'Better go by way of the canteen, lad, and bring some coffee and a sausage or two. I think somebody up there likes us.'

Banda's cell was looking rather more lived-in now. He had been allowed a table at which to write, and low piles of paper, meticulously sorted, covered half its surface. He was writing vigorously. Unfortunately he no longer had the gold fountain pen with the mother of pearl inserts in the barrel that he used at his desk at the ministry. It was now in a cardboard box that Mrs Bandová had been invited to collect so that his personal effects did not go missing before he was released. The Prime Minister's abominable secretary sniffily conveyed the message with an undertone that implied that the release could well be sometime around 2050. All Banda was allowed was a wooden pencil bearing someone else's teethmarks. Since he was not allowed an eraser, presumably in case he committed suicide by breaking it in half and ramming a piece up each nostril, he was obliged to consider his words carefully before committing them to paper, but Banda would have done that anyway. He finished the letter he was writing and called Sergeant Mucha.

'I'd be obliged if you would arrange for this to be posted,' he said. 'I assume I haven't been given an envelope so that you can read it before it is sent.'

'You assume correctly,' replied Mucha. 'There's nothing questionable in it that might offend my delicate sensibilities, I hope?'

'Of course not,' Banda growled. The man was insufferable. If he ever got his old ministry back there would be a few policemen put out to grass before you could say 'Welcome back, Minister.'

Mucha scanned the letter.

'I'm not posting that!' he announced. 'What kind of language is that to use about a Prime Minister?'

'Where?'

'There.'

'It says "Philistine".'

'Does it?' asked Mucha doubtfully. 'You want to work on your handwriting, mate.'

'It does. And don't call me mate. I'm not your mate.'

'Dead right,' said Mucha. 'I'm too fussy for that.'

Navrátil was pressed against the far wall as Slonský contemplated the envelope on his desk.

'Are you sure it's not a bomb, sir?'

'Why should it be a bomb?'

'It's in a padded envelope. And if he thinks you're getting close to him it's the kind of thing a murderer might do.'

'Navrátil, it takes a certain set of skills to make a letter bomb. Someone who strangles women is not a prime candidate for a cold-hearted bomb-maker. Besides, Mucha almost certainly steamed it open before he rang upstairs, and since there wasn't a hell of a bang from the front desk I feel fairly confident about opening it. But if you want to cower any further away, Lukas isn't in his office at the moment.'

Navrátil was barely reassured, but he did not wish to be thought craven, so he advanced three or four paces towards the desk as Slonský peeled the envelope open.

'I was wrong, lad,' he announced, causing Navrátil to flinch in anticipation of an explosion that failed to come. 'No, Navrátil, I was wrong about Mucha steaming it open. The seal was intact. Now, what have we here?' Reaching into the envelope, he slid out a large colour photograph and examined it closely. 'Weird. Why send this to me?'

Navrátil inched closer and accepted the photograph that Slonský proffered him. It took him a moment or two to understand what he was looking at.

'I know that man, don't I? The one in the pool.'

'Not in the biblical sense, I hope. It's the opposition's spokesman on finance, Daniel Soucha.'

'Who's the other man?'

'Don't know.'

'What's Soucha doing?'

'Well, I doubt he's checking if it's a whistle.'

Navrátil blushed.

'I mean, why is he letting people take pictures of him doing that sort of thing? There are still plenty of people who wouldn't vote for a gay man.'

Slonský stood up and arched his back to relieve the stiffness he felt more with each day that passed. The sun was setting behind the rooftops in a dramatic peach-coloured sky. There was a sharp chill in the air, but Slonský opened the window and leaned out. There was the profound quiet of a city muffled in snow, broken by chugging buses and the occasional whine of a spinning car wheel as it slipped on the icy road.

'It's not a new photo, Navrátil. Look at the garden through the windows — roses in full bloom, which is unusual in Prague come February. So why hang on to it that long? Why send it to a homicide detective? What they're doing is not a crime, assuming the dark-haired man is as old as he looks.'

Suddenly Slonský snapped his fingers.

'Right, lad, we'll get nowhere setting each other puzzles like that. Let's get some answers. Run it across to Spehar and let's see if it came from the same source as the first photo. Then we need to find out where it was taken. Judging by the angle I'd guess it's a still from a security camera in the roof over the pool. It's a pool in a private house, and I'll lay odds it's not Soucha's own or he'd have known the camera was there. So the first thing to do is to find out where it was taken.'

'I thought you said the first thing to do was to take it to Spehar, sir.'

'Yes. And this is the next first thing. Off you go, youngster. I'm going to find Valentin.'

Slonský returned within the hour.

'Didn't you find him, sir?'

'Of course I found him, Navrátil. I'd be a pretty poor detective if I couldn't find a toper who spends all his days in one of three or four bars within a few streets in town.'

'Could he help us?'

'I didn't ask. I just wanted him to find an expert for us. It's going to take a couple of hours so we've just got time to line our stomachs. I have a feeling it could be a heavy session tonight, so get some sustenance inside you.'

Valentin was sitting in a booth rather than his usual stool near the door.

'The chief problem with this seat is that you have a devil of a job catching the waiter's eye. My glass has been empty for nearly ten minutes,' he muttered.

'Let me fill it for you, old friend. No, I insist.'

'I wasn't arguing.'

'I know, but if people hear me say that they'll think it can't be you in this booth.'

Slonský smirked as he barged to the bar, returning with four large glasses of beer. He set one before each of them and put the fourth on a coaster in front of the seat opposite Valentin.

'You and I are having the outside seats, Navrátil. It's best if people don't get a good look at our guests.'

'Guests? Who's the other guest?'

A young bearded man in the next booth stood up and tapped Navrátil on the shoulder.

'I am. Shift over so I can get in.'

He extended a large hand and greeted each in turn. He plainly knew Valentin, who introduced him to Slonský and Navrátil.

'This is Martin,' announced Valentin. 'Be content with his first name.'

'Of course. Pleased to meet you, Martin.'

'I hear you have something I'd very much like.'

'I think so. But I can't give it to you. At least, not yet. It's evidence. But I'll see to it you get first option on it — assuming, that is, that whoever sent it to me doesn't publish it himself first.'

Slonský reached inside his coat and slid a folder across the table. Martin arched his eyebrows with curiosity before raising the flap and carefully examining the contents.

He let slip a low whistle.

'Do you know who this is?'

'I think it's Soucha.'

'So do I. That's dynamite.'

'You didn't know?'

Valentin waved a hand between them.

'Hello? I'm here. May I see, so I know what you're talking about?'

Slonský nodded, and Martin passed the folder across the table to Valentin.

'Well, I never knew that!' the old journalist exclaimed.

'Neither did I,' said Martin, 'and it's my job to know. If he's managed to keep this quiet for so long, and I haven't heard so much as a whisper, he must be very discreet.'

Navrátil could contain his curiosity no longer.

'What exactly is your job, Martin?'

'I trade scurrilous stories to the press. I used to edit an underground magazine, but when it didn't need to be underground anymore it switched to running exposés of corruption. Really big ones get sold on, like this one will when I can use it.'

'Is it a big story? There must be plenty of gay politicians.'

'Yes, but not in top jobs. This will finish Soucha's career. I can't believe he's been that stupid. And I can't believe I didn't know.'

Slonský drained his glass.

'I didn't know either. That's why I needed to check it with you. And if you didn't know, that suggests that only a very small number of people did. Since Spehar tells me the label on the envelope came from the same printer as the first envelope, it means we can narrow down our possible suspects. It's got to be someone who knew the Minister was having an affair and also knew that Soucha was gay. Not only that, he knew where he could collect photographic proof of both facts. He's an insider.'

'But there's one thing I don't understand …' Navrátil began.

'No, there are lots of things you don't understand. This is just the latest.'

'Point taken. But if these connections narrow down our possible killers, why draw our attention to himself by sending us the pictures? Does he want to be caught?'

Slonský stared at the ceiling in deep thought.

'That's a very good question, lad, and I shall ponder it carefully while you get us another round of drinks.'

'I'll help you carry them,' volunteered Valentin, and showed a surprising agility in sliding from his seat without disturbing Slonský.

Slonský rubbed his chin in thought while Martin examined the photograph again.

'Any idea where it was taken?'

'That's what I'm pondering. Nowhere I've been. It must be a big house to have a pool that size. But Soucha has a lot of powerful friends — bankers, industrialists and so on — so it wouldn't surprise me if he was a guest there.'

'But if he's discreet, as you seem to be telling me, then he can't risk someone just walking in on that. They must be alone in the house.'

'Or the other man owns it. But I have no idea who he is, and anyone who owns a house this size near Prague I would know.'

'Could it be taken abroad?'

Martin nodded slowly.

'Soucha travels quite a bit. There's only one way to find out. You'll have to ask him. If you need a shorthand writer, I'll make myself available any hour of the day or night just to see his face when you show him this.'

Slonský smiled.

'I think I'll have to manage with Navrátil, but thanks for the offer.'

Chapter 15

The next morning Slonský made an appointment to see Soucha, then told Navrátil they were going to make a detour.

'You won't need your coat. It's a detour inside this building.'

At the foot of the stairs they turned towards the cells.

'I just want to run something past Banda. Watch his reaction for me.'

Mucha opened the door and they entered. Banda glanced at them with an irritated expression.

'Have you come to molest me again?'

'No. I wondered if you felt like giving me some help.'

Banda put his pencil down carefully.

'Why should I want to help you?'

'So I can help you.'

'And how would that be, precisely?'

'Do you know Daniel Soucha?'

Banda pursed his lips.

'I know of him. He's by no means a friend.'

'I see.'

Slonský turned to leave.

'Why do you ask?'

'Oh, nothing really. It's just that he's having the same trouble with his relationships that you are.'

'Someone murdered his girlfriend? I can empathise. Are you going to lock him up too?'

'Not yet. We're going to have a coffee with him first.'

Mucha closed the door behind them.

'Well, Navrátil?'

'Nothing. But what was I supposed to be looking for?'

'He didn't doubt that Soucha would have a girlfriend. So he didn't know either. And if he didn't know, he couldn't have arranged to have the picture sent. And therefore, in my humble but conclusive opinion, he isn't the murderer. Quod erat demonstrandum.'

'Quod what?' asked Mucha.

'Erat demonstrandum. "Which was to be proved." It was a test, Mucha.'

'Oh. Did I pass?'

Soucha was a tall, slim man with a floppy shock of blond hair that repeatedly fell over his right eye when he moved his head. Cartoonists concentrated on that piece of hair which, in their representations, became bigger and more unmanageable as the years passed. In some versions now it jutted from his head like a cantilever, extending well beyond the tip of his nose and flopping across his right shoulder when it collapsed. He showed Slonský and Navrátil to seats around a low glass table and brushed his hair back as he unbuttoned his jacket and sat in a single fluid motion.

'I'll come straight to the point, sir. I'm afraid this isn't going to be pleasant.'

Soucha looked at each of them quizzically.

'Bad news? Someone in the family died?'

'No, sir. It's about you. Someone has sent me a document that I need to ask you about.'

If Soucha was concerned, he hid it very well indeed. He looked just like a man who had no idea what Slonský was talking about.

'Fire away, then.'

Slonský passed him the envelope. Soucha hesitated, as if unsure whether he was meant to look inside, then peeled back the flap and pulled out the photograph. As he realised its content his face passed from Mediterranean tan to Nordic white.

'Good God. I … Where…?'

'It was posted to me, sir. No covering letter. I take it that you recognise yourself as the gentleman on the right.'

Soucha swallowed hard.

'Yes. That is me.'

'And the other gentleman?'

'Look, we're not doing anything illegal. Why are you asking me about it?'

'We're investigating a serious crime, sir, and the circumstances in which this was received suggest to me that there is a connection. I just don't know what it is. I hoped you would.'

'Does this have to get out? I mean, you'll exercise discretion about who gets to see —'

'Oh, yes, sir. If my questions are answered satisfactorily no-one else need see it. Though, of course, the sender may have made other copies.'

If Soucha was pale before, he became rather grey now.

'Let's get it over with. What do you want to know?'

Slonský motioned to Navrátil to make notes.

'The other gentleman, sir?'

'I don't know him.'

'You seem to know him rather well in the photograph, if I may say so, sir.'

'I only met him a few days before at a party. He's called Mario.'

'Mario?'

'Presumably a nickname.'

'You don't say, sir? Mario. Write that down, Navrátil.'

146

'I think he's foreign. Austrian, maybe. He spoke Czech with an accent.'

'And you haven't seen him again?'

'Lunch a few days later. Then we lost touch.'

'Do you have a phone number for him?'

'He stopped answering.'

Soucha took out his cellphone and found the number, which he showed to Navrátil.

'Dial it, Navrátil.'

Soucha rubbed his hands together in a compulsive washing motion as they waited.

'Number unobtainable, sir,' Navrátil reported.

'Shame. Where did you meet?'

'It was a party at the National Theatre. I went to see a play and was invited to join the host for some wine and nibbles.'

'"Nibbles", sir?'

'You know, canapés. That sort of thing.'

'We're not big on canapés in the police, sir. They're rarely offered. But your host introduced you to Mario.'

'No, he was just there. I'm not sure who brought him. He didn't seem to be with anyone in particular.'

Slonský shifted uncomfortably in his seat.

'I don't mean to offend, sir, but I don't know anything about … that sort of lifestyle, and I need to understand how this happened. If nobody knew that you were that way inclined, how did you and Mario recognise that you were kindred spirits?'

'You just know, Inspector. When you're "that way inclined" you get a sense for who else feels the same way. Presumably Mario sensed it about me.'

'So he approached you?'

'Yes, I suppose he did. I was chatting to a few friends when I noticed him looking at me intently. It was a bit unnerving, to be honest. Then he smiled and when I detached myself he walked over to say hello.'

'And one thing led to another.'

'Not immediately. We agreed to meet at the weekend.'

'Where, sir?'

'Our original plan was to meet at a restaurant and see what progressed. But on the Friday I was talking to a friend who offered me the use of his summer house if I ever wanted it.'

'That's very generous, sir.'

'Yes. I said I'd like to do that one day, and he said he wasn't using it at the weekend, and perhaps I'd like to look it over. I would be doing him a favour because he hadn't had time to go out there for a few weeks and he'd like to know it was in good repair.'

'Was this recently, sir?'

'Last summer, I think.'

'So you agreed to go out there. Very helpful of you, I'm sure. Weren't there any staff in a place this size?'

'He said nobody lived in. There were a few people in the village who came up when he needed a cook or a gardener, for example, but it would be empty. He suggested I might like to take some company.'

'I imagine he didn't know about Mario, then.'

'No, he offered to fix me up with a girl if I wanted, but I said it would be good to get away to do a bit of writing.'

'Who was this kindly benefactor, sir?'

'Dr Sammler. Theodor Sammler.'

'And how do you know him?'

'He was quite a big donor to the party.'

'Was?'

'Could still be. But I met him first after he provided a lot of IT equipment for our central office. I gather he's some sort of wheeler-dealer.'

'Where would I find Dr Sammler?'

'I don't know. Central Office could probably tell you.'

Slonský mulled this information for a few moments, then picked up his hat and held out a hand.

'Goodbye, sir. Thanks for seeing us. Navrátil, pick up the photo, please. We'll see ourselves out, sir.'

As they strode to the car, Navrátil shook his head wonderingly.

'He just lent a stranger his house! Who goes around doing that?'

'Very kindly people, Navrátil. Trusting, gentle kindly souls. People like you, in fact. And, of course, the occasional complete villain. Let's see what we can find out about Dr Sammler.'

Chapter 16

Klinger's eyes narrowed and flicked from Slonský to Navrátil and back to Slonský again.

'Why do you want to know about Theodor Sammler?'

'Idle curiosity.'

'I believe the idle bit. I suppose you aren't going to tell me.'

'You know I'd like to,' Slonský said soothingly, 'but my lips must remain clamped together like a nun's knees.'

Klinger held his steepled fingers to his lips while he thought.

'At least answer me this. Do you have any evidence that Sammler has done anything that my department ought to know about?'

'No. But the fact that you ask suggests you have.'

Klinger got up and went to the filing cabinet, drawing out a slim folder with a number of coloured sticky notes protruding at the edge. Slonský noted with delight that a green sticker was out of alignment with the others, and watched silently as Klinger opened the file and carefully repositioned it, before closing the folder again and holding it up to check that the edges of the stickers formed a straight line.

'If I had, life would be easier. Sammler is a German businessman. He's lived here in Prague for about twenty years on and off. Daddy was a rich industrialist somewhere in West Germany, and we assume he bankrolled young Theodor, because the youngster first seems to have come here around 1986. He got a job with an Austrian bank and came back a couple of times over the next year or so. But he really comes to official notice after the Velvet Revolution when we privatised a lot of our businesses. Do you remember the coupons?'

Navrátil shook his head.

'Vaguely,' said Slonský.

Klinger smiled in anticipation of the opportunity to give these neophytes a lesson in financial matters.

'Briefly, any adult Czech could buy a book of vouchers for thirty-five crowns. They could then register it for another thousand crowns, in exchange for which they got points. The points were used to bid for shares in companies that the government was selling off. Most Czechs didn't understand the system and, frankly, couldn't be bothered, but a few banks hit on a way round this. They would manage your points for you, and even pay you a fee. You gave them your vouchers, and they did all the rest. Of course, quite often the return for the banks was huge, but all you'd got was whatever you sold the vouchers for. Sammler cooked up one of the first of those schemes, but it was actually rather clever. He borrowed money on the strength of the shares he had just bought, which enabled him to buy more shares, which pushed the price up, so he could then redeem his loan more cheaply. If he was slick it was money for nothing. Ownership of some large Czech assets passed to foreigners, and while we enjoyed the money coming in, there was an inevitable backlash.'

He paused to sip his coffee and invite questions, of which there were none. Navrátil had not understood and Slonský just wanted to get to the end of the story.

'Friend Sammler was clever enough to get out of voucher trading and offer his services to the government to get some of those assets back. He didn't have a lot of successes, but he didn't need many. A select few gave him a big return. He found foreign owners who needed cash, and he would buy a stake in something they owned. But the deal would include a clause allowing him first option on the rest of that asset if they ever sold it. Then, as sure as night follows day, there would be a collapse of the company's share price, and the asset would be quietly sold to Sammler's bank to get some cash in quickly and discreetly. It's estimated he may have paid only sixty per cent of the true value of what he bought. Sammler's bank became very rich, and he did quite well out of it too. What none of us knew then was that Sammler had owned the Austrian bank all along, or at least he controlled it.'

Navrátil wanted to ask a question, and was sorely tempted to raise a hand as if in class.

'Was any of this illegal?'

'Probably not. And I don't hear of anything now that is definitely illegal. I just wonder why he stays here instead of using his undoubted financial skills in Germany where he could make a real killing.'

'Maybe he likes Prague,' suggested Slonský.

'He doesn't seem to like much at all. He does the Prague Castle circuit, knows all the top people, but hates publicity, doesn't have expensive hobbies — not one for fast cars or flashy holidays.'

'He has a country house though.'

'Yes, he does. You heard that? Not exactly a cottage, is it? But there are bigger ones, and he doesn't spend a lot of time there, I understand. If I didn't know better I'd say he only keeps it so he can lend it out to people who might thereby feel they owe him a favour.'

'There you are!' exclaimed Slonský. 'I knew we'd agree on something if I came here often enough.'

Klinger leaned forward abruptly.

'You know something, don't you? You've heard a whisper. Come on, Slonský, out with it.'

Slonský sighed.

'Between us?'

'Between us,' Klinger confirmed.

'You know this murder we're investigating. It turns out that Sammler lent his house to one of the suspects. I just couldn't see why he would do that.'

'Is the suspect a politician?'

'Yes.'

'Well, there you are then. Why does Sammler do anything? Definitely not for charitable reasons. He's an arch-capitalist, Slonský. He believes everything has its price — and everyone.'

'Why did you lie to Klinger just then?' asked Navrátil as they trotted down the stairs.

'He brings out the worst in me. I can't resist telling him a little story.'

'But Soucha isn't a suspect for the Gruberová murder, sir.'

'No, but Banda is.'

'Has he visited the country house too, sir?'

'I don't know,' said Slonský. 'But it's worth asking, don't you think?'

Banda's scribbling was his sole amusement. Mucha had given up rationing his paper and had left him a ream of flimsy copy paper, which Banda had turned into some letters, a few complaints, and several chapters of autobiography. If he had hopes that the latter would prove a bestseller, they were sabotaged by his exclusion of any matters of general public interest, such as how he had murdered his girlfriend.

He glanced up briefly as Slonský entered the cell.

'Have you come to torment me again?'

'Only if absolutely necessary. Though I can't guarantee I won't hum a Sinatra tune or two.'

Banda laid his pencil down parallel to the top of his page and turned to Slonský to indicate that he was prepared to give him his full attention.

'How can I help?'

'I wondered if you knew a Dr Theodor Sammler.'

'Of course I do. Who doesn't?'

'I don't.'

Banda shrugged to convey that anyone who was anyone would know Sammler, but that Slonský might not fall into this group.

'Perhaps you would write me a letter of introduction.'

'If it helps me get out of this place, bring me a better pencil and I'll get onto it straight away.'

'I wouldn't be in too much of a hurry to get out if I were you. If you didn't kill Irina, whoever did might be upset if you aren't blamed for it, since he must have gone to such trouble to frame you.'

'I didn't kill her, and that's a chance I have to take. Though I hope that the police will ensure my safety by catching the real killer.'

It was Slonský's turn to shrug.

'We might, if we've got nothing better to do.'

Banda closed his hand tightly around his pencil and breathed deeply to dissipate his anger.

'I'm not sure I like you,' he hissed.

Slonský leaned forward until their noses were almost touching.

'I'm not sure I give a toss,' he replied.

The two men held their stares like boxers at a championship weigh-in, until Banda threw his pencil aside in annoyance.

'This is ridiculous. Ask me what you want, then leave me in peace.'

'Tell me about Dr Sammler.'

'I know very little about him personally. We met regularly, as you would expect given that he is a leading financier in the Czech Republic and has been very helpful to this and previous governments.'

'How regularly?'

'Perhaps once or twice a month. Rarely one to one, but we move in the same circles in the Castle district. However, if Sammler wanted to speak to me he had only to ring my office and I would make time for a man of his importance.'

'Have you ever been to his country house?'

'No. I don't even know where it is. I'm not sure he does either. He's not a country lover, Slonský. Dr Sammler is thoroughly urban.'

'Any family?'

'No, I don't believe so. Certainly I've never heard mention of any. I think he lives alone near his office, perhaps with a housekeeper.'

'Is he a socialite?'

Banda laughed.

'Sammler? A playboy? No, he's a German. He doesn't believe in fun. In a previous age he'd have been a Puritan.'

'So he didn't approve of your relationship with Miss Gruberová, then?'

'He neither approved nor disapproved, at least not to my face. He's a cultured man who is better bred than to comment on another man's private affairs.'

'Any idea how he feels about homosexuality?'

'No, nor do I know what football team he supports, his shoe size or his favourite wine. If you're asking me if he is one, the answer is no. If he needs a female escort, he has no trouble finding one. But he is a very self-contained man, Lieutenant. He seems not to crave human relationships very much, other than those devoted to business.'

'Money is his passion, then.'

'He's not a man to have passions. He likes an ordered life and hobbies and interests would just get in the way. Oh, he enjoys good food or a night at the opera, but he's just as happy with a plate of stew and reading a book. Now, will you tell me why you're asking me all this?'

Slonský opened the cell door.

'No,' he replied, and closed it behind him.

To Slonský's great surprise, Valentin was wearing a tie. It was greasy, stained and abominably knotted, but it was undoubtedly a tie.

'Are you meeting someone?' Slonský enquired.

'No,' replied Valentin, 'so if you're buying drinks I can accept without feeling I'm taking advantage.'

'Navrátil will see to it. He knows the drill by now. So, why have you got a dog's leash hanging round your neck?'

'You're the detective. Detect.'

Slonský rubbed his chin in a pantomime of deep thought.

'Well, it can't be a woman.'

'I'm hurt by the suggestion that it can't be a woman. It happens that it isn't, but I can still pull a woman if I choose to. I just don't choose to, that's all.'

Slonský looked more closely. Finding that this did not help, he stood, grabbed a hanging light and pointed it directly at Valentin.

'You've shaved. Recently. Certainly today, and probably early afternoon — or as you journalists call it, breakfast time.'

'Getting warmer.'

'You wouldn't shave because you wanted to, so it was expected by the person you were interviewing. And since nobody's opinion has the slightest effect on you except one man, I deduce that you were seeing your editor.'

'Bravo. And that's why a brandy wouldn't come amiss.'

'Not a happy man?'

'He wasn't, and I'm not. I need a big story, Slonský. Something for the front page. And I need it quickly. He's given me a week to find him something or he stops the salary and I have to go freelance. So, old chap, have you got a titbit for me?'

'I wish I had.'

'No chance this juicy murder of yours is going to be tidied up in a week?'

'Don't know. Not much sign of it.'

'And you're adamant I can't use the picture of Soucha and his little friend?'

'No! Definitely not. You know I'd give you something if I could. I will just as soon as I can, but at the moment I'm stuck. Maybe I'm losing my magic touch.'

'Yes,' agreed Valentin sourly.

They sat in silence until Navrátil joined them.

'Took me an age to find a waiter. He's on his way.'

'That's because you don't look like a drinker. They gravitate to the likes of me,' growled Valentin. 'Better pickings. With luck I may keel over and forget my wallet, then they'll help themselves to a big tip.'

The waiter arrived with the beers and was promptly sent to fetch a large brandy for Valentin.

'Tell you what,' said Slonský. 'I'm so sympathetic to your misfortune I'm even going to pay for this one myself.'

'If only I had a camera,' Valentin retorted. 'No-one will believe this without photographic proof. I might even have been able to get it on the front page.'

'Between bouts of sarcasm,' Slonský said, 'tell me what you know about Theodor Sammler.'

'German.'

'Knew that.'

'Banker.'

'Knew that too.'

'That's me done.'

'You? The greatest investigative journalist Prague has ever seen?'

'You're only saying that because it's true.'

'No, I'm laying the flattery on with a trowel to get you to try harder.'

'Not much point. Sammler is a grey man. He doesn't party much, he doesn't court publicity, he doesn't flash his cash around. He just knows a lot of people and makes a lot of money.'

'Legally?'

'A banker making money legally in Prague? Are you taking the —'

'No. I just meant is he the sort of person to get involved with shady stuff?'

'Not that I've heard. Crafty but legit, so far as I know.'

'So there's no scandal?'

'I don't think so.'

Slonský took a large slurp from his beer and fell silent for a few moments.

'If he's such a good money-maker, why stay here? He could be coining it in Frankfurt among his own kind.'

'His contacts are here, I suppose. It's taken him years to build up his address book. And I bet those Germans have got Frankfurt sewn up. He wouldn't get a look in.'

Navrátil was feeling as dispirited as the others.

'Looks like this line of enquiry is going nowhere then.'

'No,' agreed Slonský. 'The deadest of dead ends.'

Valentin leaned forward and dropped his voice.

'Look, I'll see if my paper's man in Vienna knows anything. That's where Sammler was between Germany and here. I'll need a few crowns for the phone call, though.'

Slonský handed him a note.

'That's my own money. Don't waste it.'

Mucha looked disgruntled.

'I was beginning to wonder if you were ever coming back,' he moaned.

'How nice of you to pine,' replied Slonský, 'like a faithful lap-dog.'

'You don't need a lap-dog,' Mucha mumbled. 'You need a guard dog.'

'If you'd said I needed a guide dog I wouldn't have argued right now,' Slonský sighed. 'We're getting nowhere fast.'

Mucha leant across the desk and whispered something to Slonský.

'Just what we needed. Okay, I'll deal with it. Give me a few minutes to think.'

'Well, don't take too long. I was off duty an hour and a half ago.'

'Off duty? You? I thought you slept here.'

'If I did I'd probably get more sex.'

'And on that happy observation I'll bid you good night,' Slonský said. 'I'll call you later.'

Navrátil was waiting in the corridor by the swing door.

'What was that about?'

'Never you mind. Just another complication visited on us from above. If you haven't already discovered it you'll soon learn that we solve crime despite the support of our superiors, not because of it.'

'Do you need me for anything more?'

'No, lad, off you go. I'll see you at seven tomorrow morning.'

He walked on a few steps, then turned and called along the corridor.

'Not here, though. I'll meet you at the Florenc metro station.'

Chapter 17

They sat in the car with their gaze fixed on an alleyway between two buildings.

'More coffee?' asked Slonský.

'I'd better not. I'll have to break cover and find a toilet if I do.'

'There's one in that café. And while you're there you can get me another coffee.'

'Why are we here, sir?'

'Because we had a tip-off, Navrátil. There's every chance someone will be selling some guns here. Can't ignore a hint like that.'

Navrátil squirmed in his seat, trying to allow some air to reach his back.

'Is the source reliable?'

'One of the best. Mucha's brother.'

Navrátil's alertness level rose sharply, propelling him forward in his seat.

'Mucha's brother? Is he mixed up in that sort of thing?'

'Of course not. But he's extraordinarily well-informed. He has some great contacts.'

'Such as?'

'You wouldn't expect me to reveal his sources, Navrátil.'

'I suppose not. But they're good?'

'Always have been in the past.'

'So has he been responsible for putting lots of criminals away, then?'

Slonský turned to face Navrátil. His deep frown disclosed some puzzlement at the question.

'None, so far as I know.'

'I don't understand. How can he be a great source if nobody gets nailed on his evidence?'

'The fact that we never catch anyone doesn't mean it's not Grade A intelligence, Navrátil. It must be — I've graded it that way. He has wonderful contacts and no doubt one day cultivating him will pay off. This could be the day.'

Navrátil scanned the alleyway while trying to assimilate the information he had just received.

'So are we spending a lot on him?'

'Not much. Today's snippet, for example, is costing us two tickets to the Sparta game on Sunday.'

Navrátil shrugged.

'Cheap enough, if it pays off.'

'It already has.'

'How do you mean?'

'I think it's time I initiated you into one or two secrets of the art, Navrátil. But first I must swear you to secrecy. Do you promise you won't reveal anything I'm about to tell you, even if Lukas threatens to pull out your toenails?'

'Of course not. The first sign of pliers and I'll squeal like a piglet.'

'Any sane man would. But the need for secrecy will be very clear, even to you. I have great respect for your trusting and honest nature, lad. It does you great credit. But it's a damn nuisance when it comes to fighting crime.'

Slonský took a sip from the cold coffee and winced as he realised that the last warmth it retained came from his hand grasping the cardboard cup.

'Mucha's brother told us that there is a good chance that guns, possibly including some used in unsolved crimes, would be traded here this morning.'

'Is that what Mucha whispered to you last night?'

'Not exactly. But if you inspect Mucha's log you'll see that his brother phoned to tip us off.'

Navrátil blinked furiously. This did not make sense.

'When? Mucha didn't mention it.'

'Indeed he didn't. But his log book does. And I'm entirely confident that you'll find an entry in there about a message from Little Sparrow.'

'Okay, so how did "Little Sparrow" know this was going on?'

'Because I told him. Close your mouth, lad, you look simple.'

'You made up an informer?'

'Of course not. Mucha's brother is real enough. He's a plumber in Vysočany, I think. Though whenever I want one I doubt whether plumbers really exist.'

'So how did you hear about the arms deal?'

'Ah, I made that bit up.'

'Why? We're wasting time when we've got a killer to chase.'

'Because what Mucha whispered to me was that a bunch of goons from the Director's Office were going to be paying us a visit this morning to go through the team's cases and audit their methods. That includes us. I don't want to sit there while some acne-ridden youth questions what we've been doing. I don't mind explaining myself to you — we're colleagues, and I'm meant to be teaching you — but I can do without that lot pulling all our files to bits. So the best way of avoiding that was to find something that got us out of the office and couldn't be put off. An arms deal fits the bill, wouldn't you say?'

'So you rang Mucha's brother...?'

'No, I rang Mucha and Mucha told his brother what he'd already written in the log book. Young Mucha doesn't mind — he gets two tickets for the Sparta game and if it doesn't work out he just says it's what he overheard in a bar and he never swore to its accuracy.'

'But hasn't anyone noticed that he has never provided a useful lead?'

'He did once, come to think of it. He reported a motorist for driving with defective headlights.'

'But nothing came of it, you said.'

'Of course not. Colonel Tripka is a very senior police officer. Nobody is going to arrest him for that. But it was a good laugh when the car ownership record was faxed through and pinned on the canteen noticeboard.'

Navrátil felt that his head was reeling yet again.

'But the bottom line is that we're sitting doing nothing useful when we could be chasing a murderer.'

'True. But the choice is that we either sit here doing nothing useful, or we sit in our office doing nothing useful and getting hassled by the Director's hit squad. So are you going to get that coffee or not?'

Slonský pushed the door open, walked through, then turned round and came straight back out again.

'They're still there. Let's go for a sausage somewhere.'

'How do you know?'

'Mucha's jacket is hanging behind the desk. That's the signal.'

Navrátil searched his memory.

'I've never seen Mucha's jacket hanging up.'

'That's what makes it such a good signal. Keep to this side of the road, lad, so they can't see us from the windows.'

There was a shrill ring as Slonský's mobile phone jumped into life.

'Don't recognise the number. It's probably the goon squad wanting to know when we'll be back.'

The phone stopped ringing, only to be replaced in seconds by the marimba that Navrátil used as his ring tone.

'Don't answer…' snapped Slonský, but Navrátil was too quick.

'Navrátil,' he said.

Mucha's voice snarled at him.

'Tell Slonský to answer his bloody phone.'

Navrátil looked at his phone in surprise as Mucha rang off abruptly.

'It's Mucha. He says I've got to tell you to answer your phone.'

Within moments, Slonský's phone rang again.

'National Theatre Box Office,' said Slonský.

'Good try,' said Mucha. 'Got a pencil? I've got a phone number for you.'

Slonský relayed the number to Navrátil who copied it into his notebook.

'Who is it?' asked Slonský.

'Someone called Peiperová.'

'Don't know her.'

'Yes, you do. You met her when you went out to Gruberová's parents' place.'

'Tall blonde with a ponytail?'

'How would I know?' Mucha spat. 'Just call her before the Spotty Ones realise I'm talking to you.'

'Good point,' allowed Slonský. 'Get off the line and stop holding me up.'

'Whose is the number?' enquired Navrátil.

'Officer Peiperová.'

'Oh, the tall blonde —'

'…with the ponytail, yes. Not that I noticed. But I bet you did. Watch yourself, Navrátil, hormones have been the ruin of many a promising young policeman. Now, read that number back to me so I can call her.'

Peiperová answered quickly, and explained that she had been trying to find out more about the murdered girl.

'I got the class list from school and managed to find about eight of the girls.'

'About eight? Either it was eight or it wasn't.'

'Sorry, sir. Eight.'

'Good work, Officer. Do you have a list?'

'Yes, sir.'

There was a hesitation in her voice.

'What are you not telling me, Peiperová?'

'I hope you don't mind, sir, but I spoke to them to see if they could help.'

'That depends on what you asked them. And whether any of them is the murderer, of course.'

If you can hear a blush, Slonský heard it in Peiperová's voice.

'Sorry, sir. I didn't think of that.'

'Never mind. It's done now. What did they have to say?'

'Four or five of them … four of them say they haven't spoken to her since they left school. One hadn't seen or spoken to her since she went to Prague. The sixth one used to go out with Gruberová's brother when she was about fifteen so she still drops by from time to time to visit the mother, and she says Irina was there when she last went about two months ago.'

'Did they talk?'

'Mostly family talk, but Irina let out that she had a boyfriend in Prague. Markéta pressed her to say who he was, but all she could get was that everyone would be surprised when it got out.'

'She said "When it got out"?'

'Yes, sir. Markéta was very clear about that. Irina was expecting it to come out at some time, not soon, but definitely at some point.'

'That's interesting. Very good —'

'There's more, sir. The other two knew a bit more. Maria said that Irina told her that her boyfriend was a married man in his late thirties. He had rented her flat for her. Irina wouldn't give her the address because she said she couldn't risk anyone turning up while her boyfriend was there, but she let slip that it was in Strahov. She didn't know how much the rent was because her boyfriend paid it directly to the owner every six months.'

'Good work —'

'So I rang a letting agent in Prague and pretended I wanted a flat in Strahov like she had, and he asked me how much I wanted to pay, so I asked what the going rate was and he reckoned I'd be lucky to get anything below eleven thousand a month.'

'You've been a busy young officer, Peiperová.'

'But the really interesting one was Julia, sir.'

'Julia?'

'Julia went to school with Irina, but she works in Prague, sir. She went with Irina when she got the job as a dancer, but Julia still does it. She didn't know who the boyfriend was, but she was worried that Irina might have hooked up with a gangster. She says you get some rough types in those clubs, sir.'

'You don't say, Officer.'

'So when she saw Irina out shopping, she tried to catch up with her for a chat. She was wearing heels so she couldn't run, and she saw Irina go into a small restaurant, and that was when she found out who her lover was, sir. Not a gangster at all — quite the opposite, in fact. It was —'

'I know who it was, Peiperová. Have you told anyone?'

'No, sir. Just you.'

'Good. Keep it that way. You've done well, Peiperová. Are you there for a while?'

'Shift finishes at six, sir.'

'Well, Officer Navrátil and I are going to come to see you and get all this on paper.'

'I've written it all out, sir.'

'Good. Then Navrátil won't have so much writing to do. But we'll come anyway. There's a limited amount we can do in Prague at the moment. We'll see you in an hour or so.'

Slonský snapped the phone shut.

'Now why haven't you done all that?' he barked at Navrátil.

Peiperová had gone to make coffee.

'Navrátil, could you try not to look quite so much like a puppy when she talks to you?'

'Sir?'

'She's a good-looking girl who also seems to have a brain, but you're not selling yourself too well sitting there with a mouth as wide as a waste bin and dribble running down your chin.'

'I'm not dribbling,' Navrátil protested, but ran his hand over his chin just in case. 'Anyway, we're here on business.'

'Good of you to remember that, Navrátil. This is no time for lovey-dovey stuff.'

Peiperová pushed the door open and backed into the room bearing a tray.

'If you weren't dribbling before…' muttered Slonský, earning himself a glower from a reddening Navrátil.

'Is Sergeant Tomáš around?' asked Slonský.

'In the other room, sir.'

'Then I'll just go and have a word. It's only polite. You two chat about something, but not the case. I don't want to miss anything important.'

Before Navrátil could think of anything to say, Slonský had left the room and was stomping along the corridor.

'Well, that went well,' Slonský announced as they drove back to Prague.

'Yes, sir. But couldn't Officer Peiperová have simply faxed her report to us as she suggested?'

'You astonish me, Navrátil. One minute you're complaining we're not working on the case, so I arrange a nice trip out for you, and you carp about it.'

'I just thought we might have been able to use the time more productively.'

'I could. But could you?'

'Sir?'

Slonský sighed deeply and pushed his hat to the back of his head in exasperation.

'Don't tell me you wasted that golden opportunity I set up for you.'

'Sir?'

'You don't think I actually wanted to talk to Tomáš?'

'Sir?'

'Will you stop saying Sir in that half-witted tone of voice? I was hoping you would use the opportunity to get to know Officer Peiperová better.'

'She is nice, sir.'

'I know, Navrátil. I know exactly how nice you thought she was, and if she'd been sitting on my side of the desk she'd have seen for herself how taken you were with her. You'll have to learn some more self-control, Navrátil.'

'Sir!'

'You're lucky you didn't tip the desk over. Never mind that, lad, did you get her phone number?'

'I already had it, sir. You gave it to me.'

'That's the station number, Navrátil. I asked about her phone number.'

'I may have done, sir. On a completely different matter, do you think you'll need me on Saturday? I thought I might take a bus out to Kladno and see the countryside a bit.'

'I hope you've arranged a local guide, young man.'

'Yes, sir.'

Spehar's report confirmed that the photograph of Soucha had been addressed using the same printer as that of Banda and Gruberová. The surprise in Spehar's folder was that he had shown some initiative. Realising that the picture had been grabbed from a security camera, he had asked Navrátil where the house was so that he could get copies of the videotapes. Navrátil had forgotten to mention this, largely because he thought Spehar was only asking so that he could complete his paperwork accurately.

The owner had been out, explained Spehar, but there had been a security firm's plate on the gate, so he had telephoned them and a guard met him at the house. He had been careful not to disclose the reason for asking, but said that one of the house guests wanted to prove he had been there on a particular day. The guard showed him where the recording equipment was, and Spehar had used one of his clever little gadgets to transfer the files to a portable hard disk. The videos were therefore still at the house, but Spehar had copies. He thought Slonský might find the enclosed DVD of great interest.

His curiosity piqued, Slonský went straight to the canteen, with two objects in mind. First, he needed something to eat. Once that was secured, he would look for someone who could work a DVD player.

Chapter 18

Navrátil slept as well as any man could whose dreams featured a police uniform being removed, fortunately not his own. If he felt that his life may be about to change dramatically, that was as nothing compared with the shock awaiting him when he arrived at work.

Slonský was wearing a suit. That is to say, he was wearing a suit that did not look as if he had been sleeping in it for several years. He also sported a new tie. Navrátil knew it was a new tie because Slonský had omitted to remove the price label that dangled behind it.

'Are you going somewhere, sir?'

'We both are, Navrátil. It's time we had a few words with Dr Sammler, I've got an appointment with him at ten o'clock. We're getting a full ten minutes, Navrátil. I hope you're impressed.'

'I wish I'd known, sir. I'd have worn something more respectable.'

'You're perfectly respectable, lad.'

Navrátil combed his hair carefully and decided that he had better mention the price label to Slonský.

'Damn. Got any scissors, Navrátil?'

'No, sir.'

'Then go and ask Klinger. Klinger will have scissors. Klinger has everything.'

Klinger had scissors. Not only did he have small curved nail scissors, office scissors, first aid scissors and large wallpaper scissors, he also had a small pair of scissors built into his Swiss army knife, and he was prepared to let Navrátil borrow one of his pairs, provided he received a full briefing first in case there was something about Dr Sammler the fraud department ought to know.

Navrátil decided that 'ought to know' could not possibly encompass the forthcoming interview, since the relevance of that could only be assessed after it had taken place. He also reminded himself that Klinger had assumed that Banda had been in Sammler's house, which was the connection that Slonský must be investigating, so he explained that Slonský believed that Sammler may have possessed information about Banda of which he could not have realised the importance. They were going to have a brief word with him this morning to clarify exactly what the relationship between Sammler and Banda was.

'There! That didn't hurt, did it? But if Sammler mentions the word "Switzerland" at any point during this morning's little chat, no doubt you'll tell me about it when you bring the scissors back later,' said Klinger, giving what he believed was a cheery smile. Navrátil found it acutely unnerving.

'What did you tell him?' asked Slonský.

'Sir?'

'I warned you about that yesterday, son. Try to sound intelligent if you can. What did you tell Klinger?'

'He wanted to know what was going on in the investigation, sir.'

'Of course he did. And you wanted his scissors, so he finally had a bargaining tool. So what did you tell him? Before you answer, bear in mind that I've got the scissors and I could ruin your fun with Peiperová with one little snip.'

'I told him we were going to talk to Dr Sammler this morning to find out what relationship he had with Dr Banda.'

'You make it sound like they were a pair of shirt-lifters, Navrátil, but that should keep Klinger happy.'

'You might choose your words more carefully, Slonský,' Captain Lukas announced from the open doorway. 'Has somebody died?'

'Sir?'

'The suit, man. For once you look as if you've made an effort.'

'We're going to see Dr Sammler, sir.'

'Ah. Good. First-class. Be careful, Slonský. Don't want to upset him.'

'Unless he's the killer, sir. Can I upset him then?'

Sammler strode from his desk, hand extended in welcome, and showed them to some fine antique chairs in front of his desk.

'No computer, sir?'

'Over there. I'll let you into a secret. I can't work at this desk. It's completely impractical. But it is handsome, isn't it?'

'Yes, sir.'

Sammler spoke Czech rapidly and without hesitation, though with a trace of a German accent. He was sloppy about the difference between voiced and unvoiced consonants, particularly "s" and "z", but he exuded confidence. To Slonský's surprise, he smiled readily and spoke quite softly.

He was a well-built man, conservatively dressed with a stiff white collar on his striped shirt and starched white cuffs that protruded from his jacket and revealed elegant oval gold cufflinks. If you had never met him before you would know he was a banker.

'I'm grateful to you for giving us some of your valuable time, Dr Sammler.'

'Not at all. If I can assist your enquiries it is plainly my duty to do so.'

'Thank you. I must ask you to regard this conversation as confidential. Do you know Daniel Soucha?'

'Yes, of course. Although he is currently an opposition politician, those of us in the financial world try to maintain courteous relations with all sides.'

'May I ask, sir, whether you have lent him your country house?'

'Yes, I did. I think it was last summer. He needed a break, poor man, and I offered him the house for the weekend. To be perfectly frank, it suited me too. I probably ought not to say this, but the staff get sloppy when I don't use it for a while. I thought it would sharpen them up before I had guests there.'

Slonský produced the photograph of the swimming pool.

'Someone has sent us this, sir. Is that your pool?'

Sammler studied the photograph carefully. His mouth twisted in a grimace.

'Yes, it is. And that is Daniel Soucha. Though I have no idea who the other gentleman may be.'

'He wasn't invited by you, sir?'

'No. Though I ought to say that I placed no restrictions on Mr Soucha inviting any guests he wished. I might have hoped he would have shown better manners than to use my home for this ... sordid connection.'

'Mr Soucha told us that you offered to send a girl to the house for him.'

'Yes, I did.'

'Would that be a prostitute, sir?'

'An escort, certainly. I had in mind someone who would offer a bit more than mere sex. But it wasn't my business where they finished up. I just wanted to give the man some relaxation.'

'Very friendly of you, sir. Have you ever done the same for Dr Banda?'

'I saw he'd landed himself in a spot of bother. No, I've never lent him my house. Of course, we know each other well, and in this business if someone influential asks you for a favour, you do what you can.'

'What kind of favours would those be, sir?'

Sammler hesitated.

'I hope I can rely on your discretion, Lieutenant. The lifestyle Dr Banda is obliged to lead is an expensive one. Before he joined the government he had a healthy income. Ministers of his level of experience and competence usually take a pay cut when they take office. They need an understanding bank manager.'

'So Dr Banda is a customer here, sir?'

Sammler smiled.

'I believe you already know that, Lieutenant. Didn't your Mr Klinger tell you?'

Slonský smiled back.

'There's a difference between gossip and fact, sir. Thank you for your help.'

'Not at all. It rather looks as if I've backed two poor horses, doesn't it?'

'Never mind, sir. There'll be other horses, no doubt.'

'No doubt,' agreed Sammler, as he held the door open for them.

'Well?' enquired Slonský.

'Well what, sir?'

'What did you make of him?'

'He seemed very German, sir. Not a bundle of fun.'

'He looked genuinely shocked by the photo. And he happily agreed that he offered the escort, so he obviously wasn't embarrassed by that.'

'So if he offered to arrange an escort, he plainly didn't know about Soucha's tastes.'

Slonský stopped walking and looked quizzically at Navrátil, who pulled up abruptly.

'What a quaint way of expressing it, Navrátil. His "tastes". I like that.'

'But if he wants to influence Soucha he'd want to give him something he values, and Soucha doesn't value a girl.'

'Yes, but Soucha doesn't want anyone to know about his "tastes", so he has to act as if he has been influenced, or he looks ungrateful. Even if he doesn't want the girl, he has to behave as if he does. So Sammler has no way of knowing that his bribe isn't the right thing to give, because Soucha will tell him it is.'

Navrátil punched the button at the pedestrian crossing.

'The girl would tell him, wouldn't she?'

'Would she? If you gave her five thousand crowns to have dinner with Soucha and spend the night there, and Soucha doesn't want you to do that, are you going to tell? Of course not, in case Sammler wants his money back. You'll join in the lie and tell anyone who asks that Soucha is a superstud who kept you up all night. You'll want people to think you really earned that cash.'

The traffic paused for a moment, and they crossed the road. Navrátil had to wait for a few moments for Slonský to catch up.

'We should have taken the car, son. I don't know why I let you talk me out of it.'

'I didn't say —'

'Now, the girl has a good reason to keep it to herself. But on the other hand, if she has discovered Soucha's secret, she can make a lot of money out of that knowledge.'

'Blackmail?'

'I think they call it "knowledge management" these days. But it's all academic, because there wasn't any such girl.'

'So that got us nowhere.'

'I wouldn't say that. We know that Banda banks with Sammler.'

'We already did. Klinger found out and we got a bank statement.'

'Yes, but how did Sammler know that Klinger had been asking about Banda's account? Klinger told us he'd called in a favour to get it, and he asked Banda's office. He didn't ask the bank.'

'I'd better check that with Klinger when we get back.'

'You do that, lad. I'll be across the street doing some quality control on their beer. Join me when you finish.'

'Klinger says he didn't contact the bank.'

'So who did he ask at Banda's office?'

'The Minister's private secretary. Presumably she told Banda about the so-called underpayment and he rang the bank.'

'Meaning he rang Sammler personally. And Sammler would wonder why Klinger wanted to know about Banda's account.'

'But when Banda was arrested, Sammler would know why we were looking at him.'

Slonský slurped up a mouthful of beer.

'That's yours.'

'Thanks.'

'Don't thank me. I told them you'd be paying.'

Chapter 19

There are some sights so startling that the human brain immediately refuses to believe them. Disregarding the evidence that it is receiving, it prefers to conclude that it is gripped by an hallucination. This explains why Slonský did not respond promptly when Klinger spoke to him.

'I said, I've been speaking to Technician Spehar,' Klinger repeated.

'What are you doing here?' Slonský responded. 'Has the garlic fallen off our doorpost?'

'Very risible. Now, is there somewhere in this filthy hole that I could sit down?'

Navrátil offered a chair, which Klinger swept with a few strokes of his handkerchief before sitting. There was then a brief pause while the fraud officer carefully refolded the handkerchief and returned it to his pocket.

'I have received an envelope through the post,' Klinger began.

'You too, eh? The Post Office is breaking all records for successful deliveries.'

'Please concentrate on the matter in hand.'

'Is this going to take long? Only I'll send Navrátil for some coffee if it is. I don't function too well first thing and the truth is, I've had a bit of a shock. I've never seen you on this floor before. I always assumed you came in through the front door and somehow rematerialised one floor above us.'

'It's a measure of the seriousness of the position that I have changed my habits, Slonský,' Klinger replied. 'Make the most of it — it may never happen again.'

'Do you want coffee or not?'

'If it's station coffee, then no, thank you. But don't let me stop you.'

'Navrátil — just two coffees then. And get one for yourself if you want. Pray continue, Brother Klinger.'

Navrátil was reluctant to leave, since it seemed likely that something earth-shattering was about to be revealed, and hovered just outside the door where he could hear Klinger's revelations.

'I have received a letter —'

'You said that.'

'A letter that contained some information of a most interesting nature, at least to me. Of course, I sent the envelope to the laboratories for examination, and Technician First Class Spehar has just telephoned to tell me that the envelope in question is identical to two that have been sent to you. He has suggested that we should meet to discuss this turn of events. That is what I am doing now.'

Slonský remained resolutely unexcited.

'It's true that I've had two envelopes. Didn't I mention that?'

'No, you did not.'

'Then I'll tell you the whole story. Navrátil, stop hanging around in the corridor and get yourself back in here. The coffee can wait.'

It was Klinger's turn to be surprised. For Slonský to defer refreshment of any kind was a rare occurrence.

Slonský produced a large folder and offered it to Klinger.

'You know that we are investigating the death of one Irina Gruberová, who was the mistress of Dr Albert Banda, of whom you may have heard.'

'And whose bank account details I furnished for you, at your request.'

'Yes, thank you. Or are you expecting hidden microphones to capture the fact that it wasn't your initiative?'

Klinger flapped his hand impatiently.

'The involvement of Dr Banda came to our notice because someone sent us a photograph of him having dinner with the victim on the evening of her death. That photograph came in an envelope that we passed to Technician First Class Spehar for examination.'

'Did the examination provide any useful information?'

'It was posted in the Ninth district, probably at a post office, and was addressed using a laser printer. Some time later, I received an identical envelope, this time containing a photograph of another prominent politician, Daniel Soucha.'

'Soucha! I know him.'

'Then you may not want to see the photograph. But it's in evidence envelope B2 if you do.'

Klinger riffled through the stack before him, extracted the envelope and examined the contents.

'I'm surprised. Financial circles gossip like any other, but I'd never heard any suggestion that Soucha went in for that kind of thing.'

'That seems to be the general reaction. Soucha was a bit surprised himself.'

'You showed him the photograph?'

'It seemed more tactful than putting it on the internet and inviting him to download it. The interesting thing about this photo is where it was taken.'

'The country house of Theodor Sammler.'

'You know it?'

'No, but I recall you asked me about it, and now I know why. And Sammler, as we know, knows Banda.'

'He's his bank manager, if that's the right word for someone who sits on the top floor making millions.'

Klinger drummed his fingers on the edge of the desk as he thought.

'There have been rumours for some time that Banda was under financial pressure. He was a very wealthy man before he joined the government, but his investments have not done well lately. With a reduced salary, and no change to his outgoings, it wouldn't surprise me if he had needed the help of someone like Sammler.'

'Yes, we know all that,' Slonský confirmed, causing Klinger to raise an eyebrow.

'You knew all this and you didn't tell me?'

'I thought someone with contacts like yours was sure to know it already.'

'Flattery will not divert my wrath, Slonský. I expressly asked young Navrátil to share anything relevant to my department.'

'Which he would have done, had we found any evidence of naughtiness. But being skint is not a crime yet, thank God. And of course poverty is relative. The Banda children are not exactly going round with their backsides hanging out of their trousers.'

'No,' conceded Klinger, 'but the holiday in the Mediterranean will probably have to be scaled down, which will hurt him just as much.'

'It will have to be scaled down,' agreed Slonský, 'because he's in cell five downstairs and we don't normally let remand prisoners hop off to the Med for a bit of R&R.'

Klinger indicated agreement with a sharp nod of his head.

'Do you think Banda killed her?'

'We haven't got a better candidate yet.'

'He doesn't strike me as the murdering kind.'

'Neither did Kvapil, who ran amok in the Roma camp a couple of years ago. One of the nicest chaps you could hope to meet, if you didn't have any gipsy blood in you. Which he, of course, corrected by letting it all drain out of you through your neck.'

'Kvapil and Banda are very different animals. Banda is a more cerebral type.'

'If you're going to follow the Lukas line that it's unthinkable that he is a murderer because he has a university doctorate, I beg to differ, and be warned that I'm prepared to use reasonable force to defend my position.'

Klinger held his hands up in a gesture of surrender.

'It's your case; not my business. My interest is in the little bundle I've had through the post.'

'Say more, gentle sage.'

'The envelope contains a set of documents showing large transfers of currency to a bank account in Liechtenstein. Ordinarily I would have no access to the details of that account, but our informant has helpfully provided a certificate of ownership.'

Slonský whistled.

'How did he get that?'

'I have no idea. Liechtenstein banking security is legendary. Only the bank where it's held would have that information and they wouldn't release it short of an Interpol warrant. Even then, they'd argue first.'

'And who is the lucky account holder?'

'One Leoš Holec.'

'Never heard of him.'

'You haven't. I have. Holec is a senior adviser to the Finance Ministry and the National Bank.'

'Does that mean that sneaking large sums of money out of the country is okay?'

'It means it definitely is not okay, especially if they're sums of money far in excess of anything that has been declared to the tax authorities. Holec has been banking more money in Liechtenstein than he has been earning in this country, yet he appears not to have any other income. Conclusion?'

'Some kind person has been sending him the occasional postal order.'

'For several million crowns at a time. And presumably Holec has been doing something to earn this largesse. And we further presume that whatever he has been doing, he won't want us to look into it. But we will.'

Navrátil interrupted to ask the obvious question. 'Could Sammler have known about these payments?'

'They weren't made by his bank — at least, not by the Czech part of it. And I can't imagine that bankers talk about this kind of arrangement openly. But if anyone could know, Sammler is the kind of person who might.'

Slonský rolled his pencil back and forth across his desk, an action that he expected would irritate Klinger intensely.

'Do you have to do that?'

'Sorry. It helps me think. So you'll call in Holec and try to find out who arranged this, but if it wasn't Sammler then tying Sammler to it is likely to be very difficult. We'd have to show that he definitely knew about it. It's the same problem we face with Soucha and Banda. Sammler doesn't seem to have known that Soucha was gay, and Banda says he showed no interest in his private affairs and therefore probably didn't know about Gruberová.'

'But if Sammler is the only link between them, he has to be involved,' offered Navrátil.

'Obvious, but false logic,' Klinger replied. 'He may be the only link we know about, but as soon as the defence find one other that's our case in ruins. And the connections between Sammler and any one of them are tenuous.'

'I hate to say it,' said Slonský, 'but Klinger is right. We'd never get a conviction based on our guess that Sammler knows three important people. And even if Sammler has this information, it only has value if he keeps it to himself. How can he profit by it getting out? If he knows about Gruberová or Mario —'

'Mario?' asked Klinger.

'The other man in the photo. To repeat, if he knows about Gruberová or Mario he has a hold over Banda and Soucha, but only so long as nobody else knows. Once the cat is out of the bag, his grip is broken, so he is the last person to want to let it out. There has to be someone else that we don't know about.'

'Agreed,' said Klinger. 'But who?'

'Difficult to say,' Slonský pronounced, 'since we don't know about them. But let's think about a strategy to plug some of the gaps in our knowledge. How quickly can you pull in Holec?'

'Given the sums involved, it could be sometime today.'

'Then you'll be able to ask him how these transfers were arranged. There can only be a small number of people who would know about this set-up. Then we take your list and cross-check it against Soucha and Banda to look for the links.'

'And if there are none?'

'Then Banda goes down for a very long time because there's probably enough to implicate him. Besides, I don't like the little greaseball.'

'Hardly adequate reason for imprisoning him, Slonský,' Klinger said.

'I don't know; it's pretty convincing from where I'm sitting.'

Navrátil felt moved to interject.

'But sir, if we've agreed he's being framed, and we put him away, doesn't that mean the real criminal has got away with it?'

'Don't be a nit-picker, Navrátil. We want a criminal, and we'll have found a criminal. There may not be a perfect match between what he has done and what he goes down for, but that's a small administrative detail. However, I take the point that in an ideal world we should only jail men for their own crimes and not other people's, so I promise I'll really try to find someone else.'

When Klinger had gone, Slonský decided that he had better brief Lukas on the latest developments. Navrátil was despatched to the canteen with instructions to wait ten minutes before he bought the coffee so it would still be hot when Slonský returned.

'I'm perturbed,' Lukas declared. 'This murder is becoming a complicated web of crime.'

'Exactly, sir.'

'It takes a lot to get Klinger to come down to this floor. He keeps muttering about dirty doorknobs.'

'I believe it's a recognised medical condition, sir.'

'Having dirty doorknobs?'

'No, being worried about them. But there's no doubt that Technician Spehar has done us a great service. If he hadn't been alert we might never have put these envelopes together.'

Lukas sucked the leg of his spectacles pensively.

'It's leaving things a bit to chance, don't you think?'

'Sir?'

'Well, I mean, if one chap is sending all these envelopes, and he wants us to realise that this is all part of one big plan, sending them to two policemen who might never speak to each other is a fairly inefficient way of getting that across.'

Slonský jerked upright in his chair.

'I didn't think of it as one plan, sir. I thought it was just information that came to hand being sent to whomever was best placed to pick it up and deal with it.'

'So murder stuff would come to you, and fraud stuff to Klinger, just because that's the natural way of things?'

'Yes. No point sending fraud papers to me — I don't know the first thing about financial crime, except that they keep putting the price of German beer up.'

'Hardly criminal, Slonský.'

'Matter of opinion, sir.'

'But — to return to my point — why send the picture of Soucha to you? If it's criminal, it should go to the vice squad.'

'I thought we agreed it wasn't criminal, sir.'

'Then why send it to us at all? If he wants a fuss, he should send it to the gutter press. He can't know that we're going to take a blind bit of notice of it.'

Slonský stood and thrust his hands deep into his pockets. He thought better when he walked, so he started pacing the length of Lukas' rug, back and forth, all the while thinking hard.

'So you're arguing that the key to this is the photo of Soucha, because it has no value on its own. Sent to us, we would ignore it. If it went anywhere else, it would provoke a reaction, but not the reaction the sender wants. The sender sent it to us because he wanted us to act upon it, but because it wasn't criminal there must be another reason why he thought we might follow it up. There's some link in his mind that we haven't worked out yet.'

'That's about the sum of it,' said Lukas, who was actually quite uncertain that Slonský's summary represented his own thoughts at all.

'Is he telling us Soucha killed Irina?'

'That's a bit far-fetched, Slonský. Why would Soucha do that?'

'But the sender forwarded both pictures to me. He sees a connection where I don't. Soucha and Banda have something in common.'

Lukas' eyes opened wide as a thought flitted through his head.

'Could it be that he has murdered Mario? Both men's lovers have been killed.'

'But then he would have sent the picture after one crime but probably before the other. We know he didn't send the first picture until Irina's discovery was in the newspapers, but there haven't been any gay Austrians killed in Prague for a while.'

'Get onto the report system, Slonský. See if there are any murder victims anywhere in the Czech Republic who could possibly be Mario. It's a slim chance, but it's all we have at the moment.'

'Get onto the report system, Navrátil. See if there are any murder victims anywhere in the Czech Republic who could possibly be Mario. It's a slim chance, but it's all we have at the moment.'

Navrátil scribbled a note to himself.

'Do you really think that's the link, sir?'

'I don't know, Navrátil. But neither do you, and we won't until you do the search, so shift yourself. I'll be down in the cells when you finish.'

Slonský flicked the door open with his foot and entered with a cheery 'Room service!'

'Very droll,' said Banda. 'Have you come to threaten me in some new way?'

'No,' said Slonský. 'I come bearing gifts.'

He handed Banda a 25cl bottle of red wine and a plastic beaker.

'I can't give you glass, I'm afraid, in case you smash it and slice your jugular with the shards.'

'I wouldn't give you the satisfaction,' Banda replied. 'But I should thank you for this s*mall* token.'

'Not at all. It's all part of our new justice system. Since the new Interior Minister arrived there have been some changes.'

'Don't rub it in. And, as one who knows the new minister personally, enjoy the honeymoon. It won't last.'

'Got any dirt on him we could save for a rainy day?'

Banda considered.

'It would be disloyal to share discreditable information about a coalition colleague. But if you have an idle moment you might want to consider how his son got a scholarship to a large American university.'

Slonský smiled broadly.

'I can see this heralds a whole new era of co-operation between the accused and forces of law and order. Mind if I sit?'

'It's your house. I'm a guest here.'

Slonský perched himself on the end of the bed. It was a tricky operation, since the cot was rather lower than Slonský had expected.

'I'd like to talk about your relationship with Daniel Soucha.'

'I don't have a relationship with Daniel Soucha.'

'I mean a professional relationship.'

'I don't have a professional relationship with him.'

'What's he like?'

Banda sipped his wine, not without an involuntary grimace.

'A populist of the worst kind. His grasp of economics is feeble, his approach to law and order is slack and his ethics are questionable.'

'In the interests of balance,' Slonský enquired, 'what are his bad points?'

'He is the darling of the chattering classes. Looks good on television. But there's no substance to him.'

'What could he have against you?'

Banda's beaker paused abruptly in its upward course.

'Against me? Why would he have anything against me?'

'You're a political rival.'

'Of course. I thought you were hinting at something personal.'

'I might have been.'

Banda sit in silence for a few moments, thinking deeply.

'You're suggesting that he might be behind the framing of me?'

'It doesn't sound likely, unless he then decided to do the same to himself in a sudden fit of even-handedness. But evidence has come to hand that suggests that there is a link between you. I can't begin to imagine what that could be, but the obvious answer was to ask you.'

'I wish I could help, but I can't think of any possible link between me and that serpent.'

'Apart from the fact that you're both in the manure in a big way.'

'If you say so. But I'm getting quite a lot of writing done here. If I could have some new curtains, perhaps a room with a view...'

'I'll have a word with the hotel manager.'

'That neanderthal on the front desk?'

'Sergeant Mucha? He's good at what he does. I've known him for years. Just remember that there are nasty people out there gunning for you, but so long as Mucha is between you and the outside world, you're safe in here.'

'Forgive me if I refuse to be comforted by that thought.'

'Do me a favour. Keep thinking about my question. The bottom line is that you don't get out until we bring someone else in.' Slonský rose from the bed. 'I have to take the bottle, I'm afraid. It's glass. Just promise me you won't do anything silly with the beaker and you can keep the wine.'

Banda raised his right hand.

'I do so swear.'

'Thank you. Now I must go and visit my other guests. We must do this again sometime.'

Holec looked unwell. He was perspiring, his colour was poor and his hands trembled as he mopped his brow with a large white handkerchief.

'I'm waiting, Mr Holec,' Klinger intoned, evenly but with a hint of menace.

'I don't know anything. I didn't open this account. I haven't made any payments into it.'

'Come now, Mr Holec. To open such an account, one needs a passport. Here is a copy of your passport attached to the application form. Do you seriously expect me to believe that you lent your passport to someone who looks enough like you to open an account in your name? And you didn't notice your passport had gone missing?'

'It's not my money,' Holec whined.

'It won't be now,' conceded Klinger. 'We'll repatriate it. And since you say it isn't yours I'm sure you'll willingly sign some paperwork allowing us to reclaim the cash and examine all the transactions connected with it.'

Holec bowed his head and began to wring his hands. Klinger sat patiently, something that he had perfected over a few years. Sit still, keep quiet, let them speak when they want to fill the silence.

'I didn't realise it was so much. I only did one thing for them.'

'Who are "they"?'

'It's an investment fund in Austria. They contacted me because I was organising the sale of a company here and their bid had been ruled out of time. They wanted to argue about the timetable and I said that it couldn't be changed but in any event there was a better deal about to come up, and told them about another sale. It wasn't illegal! I just gave them advance notice.'

'And?'

'They bought the company before it went on the market, and next thing I knew a bankers' draft for a hundred thousand euros was sitting on my desk. I obviously couldn't bank it here, so I asked around for ways of disposing of it.'

'You mean hiding it.'

'Yes, I suppose I do. If I'd known then what I know now, I obviously should have shredded it or sent it back. But it was a bit like a finder's fee. I didn't see anything wrong in it.'

'However, Mr Holec, that does not explain these other sixteen transactions, some for much larger sums.'

'I don't remember them all. The same firm used to ring and ask about investments in the old Eastern bloc.'

'I can't help noticing that one of these payments is for rather more than fifteen million euros. That must have been quite a profitable deal for them if they could afford to pay you that much commission.'

'That was a Romanian cement works. I didn't realise that their properties were sitting on top of an oilfield. They'd kept it quiet but the Austrians must have assumed I'd known.'

'And they were very grateful, it seems.'

'Yes. So it seems.'

'And it never crossed your mind to give this money back.'

'I didn't think I'd done anything illegal.'

'Well, you didn't pay tax on it. And there is an interesting debate to be had as to whether a government adviser should profit personally from the sale of assets. But in any event you know as well as I do that sending such large sums abroad without declaring them is an offence.'

'I'll willingly pay the tax,' Holec squealed.

'With what? The assets will be confiscated and, so far as I can see, your other accounts don't contain enough to pay this amount of tax. Oh, dear, Mr Holec, prepare yourself for a few years in jail.'

Holec began to sob.

'My wife!' he cried. 'The shame will kill her. She's not strong.'

Klinger pushed his chair back and gathered his papers together.

'You've got time to divorce her before the trial begins. Then she can tell her friends that she knew you were a devious little criminal and they'll congratulate her for finding you out before we did.'

Mucha entered bearing a cardboard box. Slonský glanced up from his paperwork and greeted him.

'Wife finally slung you out, eh? Well, you can't sleep here.'

'Ha-de-ha-ha. These are not my possessions. My life runs to more than a videotape and a couple of badly typed statements. Where's Navrátil?'

'Lying in a meadow somewhere plaiting wild flowers for his true love's hair. I couldn't stand the big sad eyes any longer so I sent him to Kladno to check something in one of the statements from Gruberová's friends. He's turned into a fearsome mythical beast, half man, half puppy.'

'Navrátil the were-puppy.'

'That's about the size of it. We'd better requisition some silver bullets in case he turns on us at the new moon.'

'I'll check the stores.'

'So what's in the box?'

'I thought it would be a nice simple case for him to cut his teeth on. Old dear at Smíchov burgled by three lads. One of them works for a television installation company. He had been there a day or two ago and rigged a window so it wouldn't close properly. He denies it, of course, but one of the boys is busy spilling all the beans he can.'

'How sweet. I love it when kids play nicely together.'

'The problem was that due to some illegal parking they couldn't get their truck down her street, so they parked it on an office forecourt and ran backwards and forwards loading it up. Unfortunately, they didn't spot the security cameras on the office building, so we have a nice clear videotape and a couple of confessions. One of them is holding out but I thought Navrátil would enjoy wrapping it up.'

'Will it keep till tomorrow?'

'I'll charge them all anyway.'

'Just leave the box on his desk and I'll get him on it as soon as he comes back. *If* he comes back, that is. Since he fell for

Officer Peiperová his brain has gone to mush. What is it with women, old pal? I'm no expert, but you've managed it. How many years have you been married?'

'Twenty-eight, and around half of them have been happy. I find it helps if I have as little as possible to do with her family. Her dad was a good type, but then he went and died on me.'

'Selfish so-and-so.'

'That's what I thought, leaving me alone with his wife and his other daughters. My wife's not a bad sort, but her sisters are harpies.'

'If it makes you feel happy I'll ticket their broomsticks if I see them parked around town.'

'You do that. Just watch for them turning you into a frog.'

When Mucha had left Slonský remembered another piece of security footage that he had watched several times without really understanding what he was watching. However, it spurred him to pick up the phone to Spehar.

'That clever gadget of yours — did it pick up any other days apart from the weekend that Soucha stayed at the house?'

'I copied the entire hard disk. However far it goes back, we've got it.'

Slonský flicked through his files and gave Spehar a date to check. He grabbed his coat and decided to take a walk, possibly taking in a sausage stall on the way.

Slonský ambled down the ramp to the underground garage, ducking under the black and yellow barrier that filled the whole of the opening. There was a small cabin at the back of the car park by the elevators from which a figure clad all in maroon emerged.

'This is a private car park, sir. If you're visiting anyone here I must ask you to go to the front door.'

'I don't do front doors,' replied Slonský, waving his badge at nobody in particular. 'Can we have a little chat in that palatial sentry-post of yours?'

The guard waved him ahead and offered Slonský a cup of instant coffee, which was accepted with alacrity.

'Quite a swish set-up you have here,' the detective said.

'State of the art, they tell me.'

'Do you open the barrier from here?'

'I can, but most of the time the number-plate recognition system does it automatically.'

'So it knows all the regulars?'

'Yes.'

'We're investigating a break-in earlier this year. It seems that the villains couldn't park outside so they must have hidden their vehicle off the street somewhere.'

'Won't be here, unless it was a skateboard. Nobody gets in or out without being checked.'

'Is there a log?'

'There will be. The boss is a stickler for that. The system itself logs all the entries by the cars it knows. We keep a separate sheet for visitors.'

He reached above him to produce a black folder which he offered to Slonský. Slonský fished in his pocket for a little slip of paper on which he had written a registration number that he carefully avoided letting the security guard see.

'How do I get to see the residents' log?'

'Surely none of them can be involved. They're all respectable people.'

'No doubt they are, but they may have disreputable friends who borrow their cars. I'd like to be able to exclude your tenants from my enquiries, but without the log…' He shrugged expressively.

The security man clicked a couple of buttons on his keyboard.

'What date?'

'Tuesday, 7th February.'

A few more clicks called up a list of entries and exits for the date in question. Slonský read it attentively.

'Can we go over to the next day?'

'There you go. Anything useful?'

'Oh yes,' said Slonský, then, seeing the guard's surprise he added, 'it's always helpful to be able to exclude someone from your enquiries. Could I make a copy of this just to prove the point?'

The guard printed off a couple of pages at Slonský's direction.

'Thanks. And thanks for the coffee. I'll see myself out.'

Slonský allowed himself a broad smile as he climbed the ramp to the outside world. This called for a celebration pastry. Shame Navrátil was not there to share in it, but Slonský could have one for him too.

Chapter 20

Slonský was no chess player, but he played a mean hand of *sedma* when his head was clear, and he knew the importance of not rushing the last few tricks just because you had made a breakthrough. It was simply too easy to mess up when it all seemed to be going well. Before making any further moves he decided to write out what he had discovered and run it past Navrátil, inviting him to look for holes in the argument. If it passed that test, the next step was to take it to Lukas, who would doubtless prove a less demanding hurdle.

The less demanding hurdle chose that moment to make an impromptu visit to Slonský's office.

'Ah, Slonský, a word if you please.'

Slonský tried to close the folder both hurriedly and nonchalantly at the same time, and was acutely aware that he must have looked every bit as guilty as he appeared to his grandmother at the age of eight when she was investigating a case of gingerbread theft and unexpectedly climbed up to his tree house.

'Of course, sir.'

'The Prosecutor's office has been in contact with me. The Prosecutor has been reading the newspapers, Slonský.'

'I've warned him about that, sir. They're a tissue of lies and ill-informed speculation. I believe you said so yourself.'

'Be that as it may, Slonský, he doesn't like what he is reading.'

'Has he tried changing his newspaper, sir?'

'It is what he isn't reading that disquiets him, Slonský. He isn't reading about an arrest, and he isn't reading about a charge.'

'It's his job to decide on a charge, sir, not mine.'

'Don't be obtuse, Slonský. His point is that the question is not even being asked of him, and he would like me to explain why.'

Slonský let out a deep exhalation of relief.

'That's all right then. For a moment I thought I was going to have to come up with something.'

'You do, Slonský, because I can't answer him unless you answer me.'

Slonský was not a small man, and when he decided to stand to attention in the centre of the office floor Lukas found the experience rather intimidating.

'Beg to report, sir, that I am keeping the Prosecutor uninformed as a mark of respect to his integrity, sir.'

Slonský could have sworn that Lukas mouthed the words silently as he mulled them over.

'A mark of respect to his integrity? What the devil does that mean?'

Slonský stood at ease.

'Who appointed the Prosecutor, sir? Dr Banda did. It could therefore be argued that the Prosecutor may be beholden to Dr Banda and any decision other than charging the ex-Minister would look to some eyes like a cover-up.'

'Ye-es…' began Lukas, rather uncertainly.

'But at the same time charging him may look like political opportunism of the worst kind — kicking a man when he is down.' Slonský bent close to Lukas so that he could drop his voice in revealing the full cunning of the plan he had just concocted on the hoof. 'By not giving the Prosecutor a decision to make until I have incontrovertible proof of either guilt or innocence, sir, I am protecting him from ill-informed public criticism and possible interference from higher circles.'

'Yes, yes, I can see that,' agreed Lukas. 'I'll put those points to the Prosecutor and see what he says.' In the doorway he paused. 'You, er, might just give me a written note of your argument — just so I don't forget to mention something important.'

'Certainly, sir. Within the hour.'

Slonský watched the door close and breathed another large sigh of relief.

'God,' he muttered, 'I hope he never gets promoted. I could never strike that lucky again.'

The unsuspecting prey was grazing contentedly, chewing slowly and silently, as the great predator sighted him and carefully weighed up the right moment to strike. With a coffee in one hand and the least disgusting of the available sandwiches in the other, Slonský dropped into the seat opposite Němec, who reacted instinctively by wrapping his hairy forearms around his bowl to protect his soup.

Slonský was generally given to formality, but Němec had always rated the familiar greeting.

'Ahoj, Josef.'

'You're looking a bit peaky. Everything all right?'

Němec was fairly sure that he looked in the best of health. Of course, he could do with losing a kilo or two — who couldn't? — but for his age he was doing pretty well, he thought.

'Yes, fine, thanks. Why the sudden concern for my health?'

'It would be such a shame if anything happened to spoil your retirement when you're so close to it.'

Němec tore off a mouthful of bread, sprinkled a little salt on it, and chewed it thoughtfully.

'Slonský, how long have we known each other?'

'Thirty-eight years, old pal.'

'That's right. We know each other better than any other pair in the whole police force, I reckon. So when I detect some kind of scheming going on, you'd better believe I know what I'm talking about. I know you dread retiring, so why should you think I'd be any different?'

'Because you have a family, and grandchildren to play with, and lots of things you've told me you want to do. You said you wanted to go skiing in the Alps, for example.'

'Slonský, I said that in 1976. We weren't going anywhere then. My skiing days are behind me.'

'Lots of breweries you haven't visited. That vegetable plot of yours — you work miracles on it in your time off, so think what you could do if you could work on it full time.'

'I don't like the heavy emphasis on "full time" in that last comment of yours. Why don't you just tell me what you're after? Then I can tell you to stick it up your backside and we can part the best of friends.'

Slonský took a mouthful of roll. To his horror, it proved to contain salad.

'Hell, that's like eating a hedge. Give me a napkin so I can spit it out.'

'You should have had the soup. I was enjoying that till you came.'

'The fact is, you have it in your power to do me a great favour at little or no cost to yourself. Have they given you a finishing date yet?'

'Last day of April. Why?'

'Advert out to replace you?'

'Internal selection.'

'Have you got your eye on anyone?'

'No. I haven't promised it. I don't see how I could, since it won't be my decision.'

'That's fine. Just wanted to know my plan wasn't a waste of time.'

'You have a plan?'

'Yes.'

Němec eyed Slonský with great suspicion.

'I'm just trying to remember any plan of yours that ever worked out well for anyone but you. No, I can't think of one.'

'There was the trip to go climbing in the Tatras with those young policewomen.'

'I broke my wrist, remember. Someone sitting not too far from me yanked on the rope when I hadn't fixed it to the pin and I slid down the rockface. Not your finest hour.'

'You persist in looking on the black side, Josef. Those girls were so impressed with the stoic way you bore the pain. If you'd played your cards right you could have got off with any of them.'

'I could, if I hadn't been in a hospital in Poprad getting my arm put back together without adequate painkillers while you lot were having a high old time in the mountains.'

'Point taken. But this plan will be for the good of the force, trust me.'

Němec slurped another spoonful of soup.

'No more broken bones?'

'Guaranteed.'

'I won't be retired in disgrace?'

'Not unless you've done something I haven't heard about. You haven't, have you?'

'You sound like a gossip columnist. No, I haven't. And I'm going to keep it that way, so if it involves bending the law, count me out.'

'Not in the least, old friend. What do you take me for?'

'Out of respect for our friendship, Slonský, I won't answer that.'

Navrátil had run off to play with the contents of Mucha's cardboard box, so Slonský was left to his own devices for a few hours. There were two things he had to do, so he tossed a coin to decide which to do first. It came down heads, so he tossed it twice more until it came down tails, then went off to see Captain Lukas.

Lukas read Slonský's memorandum carefully, then returned to the top and read it again.

'I see Captain Němec has put his name to this.'

'Yes, sir. It's typical of the selfless generosity of the man.'

'Indeed. A first class officer. We shall miss him. When does he retire?'

Slonský replied a little too quickly. 'Thirtieth of April, sir.' He added, as an afterthought, 'I think.'

'Well, I'm bound to say I'm rather surprised, Slonský. I had you marked down as a confirmed misogynist.'

'No, lapsed Catholic, sir.'

'It's certainly a novel idea. And it meets several of the Director's requirements for force development.'

That's not a coincidence, thought Slonský, who had spent his evening reading the damn things over and over until he could recite them in his sleep.

Lukas had suddenly grown suspicious.

'You don't have any plans to get rid of Navrátil, do you?'

'Certainly not, sir. The boy is a future star and I intend to mould him in my own image to further his prospects.'

Lukas clearly did not believe that modelling oneself on Slonský would further anyone's career, but he let the point go. The old detective obviously meant well, and there was no denying that Slonský and Navrátil were becoming a very effective team.

'I think,' said Lukas, 'that I shall add my name to this proposal and we shall see what our superiors make of it. If we're successful, have you anyone in mind for the job?'

'Oh, yes,' said Slonský, but then held his peace.

Navrátil was in the interview room, writing out some of the notes that he had scrawled.

'How did it go, son?' asked Slonský.

'Šmíd and Dort are singing a sweet tune, but I can't get anywhere with Jiskra,' Navrátil replied.

'Where's Jiskra now?'

'Next door, looking very smug. The other two won't implicate him directly.'

'Why not?'

'I think they're frightened of him.'

'Are you frightened of him?' Slonský's concern was obvious.

'No. He thinks he's hard but he hasn't met any of the real hard nuts.'

'Thought not. I'll be back in two minutes and then we'll sort this out together.'

Slonský paid a quick visit to the washroom and rejoined Navrátil. They pushed the door open and greeted Jiskra, who was slouching in a chair looking exaggeratedly cool.

'When do I get out?' he asked.

'Let's say around three years from now and counting,' said Slonský.

'You can't pin anything on me,' said Jiskra. 'I'm out of here.'

'No,' said Slonský, 'you're inside for three years heading towards four and if you give me grief I can make sure it's nudging five.'

'Yeah, well, I ain't getting convicted so it don't matter what the sentence might have been.'

Slonský growled.

'If I had my way we'd add eighteen months for grievous bodily harm to the Czech language. However, I don't get to decide on the length of your sentence.'

Jiskra grinned.

'But,' Slonský continued, 'I can recommend where you serve it. Present for you.'

He suddenly tossed a small bar of wet soap he had picked up in the restroom against Jiskra's knee. It dropped to the floor, and Jiskra leaned forward to pick it up.

'What's that?' he asked.

'That,' said Slonský, 'is the last time you'll dare to pick up a bar of soap you've dropped for the next four years.'

Jiskra's gaze flicked nervously between them.

'You're joking, right?'

'I'm joking, wrong,' said Slonský. 'Remember some of your cellmates won't have seen a woman since bubble perms were in fashion and everyone was going round in shell suits.'

'I'll ask for solitary.'

'You can't ask for solitary!' Slonský's scornful voice boomed across the chamber. 'They don't do single occupancy rates at Pankrác. You're damn lucky if you get a whole bed to yourself.'

'Don't matter. You can't get me put away without evidence.'

Slonský grabbed the arms of the chair and glowered into Jiskra's eyes.

'Even if you could enjoy the showers in Pankrác, what do you think it's going to do to Šmíd and Dort when I tell them about it in a few minutes? Do you think they'll be as fearless as you are? Or do you think they'll whimper like babes and sign anything that gets them a nice quiet prison in the country somewhere? Your call. You've got as long as it takes Navrátil and me to grab a quick coffee.'

Slonský steered Navrátil outside and they headed for the canteen.

'Do you really think he'll co-operate ten minutes from now?' asked Navrátil.

'I don't know. We never will, because you're not going back in ten minutes. We'll leave him alone for a good long time to work up a sweat. By the time you go back he'll have decided you've abandoned him to be the plaything of a bunch of hairy lifers and he'll be so pleased to see you he'll sign a blank confession. Now, where are we going for coffee?'

They left the building and were immediately accosted by Valentin, who looked anxious.

'I was trying to think how I could get you to meet me,' he admitted.

'We were just going out for morning coffee,' beamed Slonský. 'Care to join us?'

'Maybe something a bit stronger than coffee. There's a café on the corner.'

'I know,' said Slonský. 'Ghastly place, always full of policemen. Come on, this way.'

He strode across the road and soon had the three of them arranged around a small table with a coffee before each and a small brandy keeping Valentin's cup company.

'What's the big story?'

'I was hoping you'd have one for me. Remember my deadline? I don't want to go back to the days when I had to work for my living, Slonský. I need that retainer. And when I tell you what I've got for you, I think you'll agree I deserve a helping hand from the forces of law and order.'

Valentin savoured the first brandy of the day, oblivious to the tension he was generating in his audience.

'Well?' asked Slonský. 'We haven't come here to watch you drink.'

'You asked me what I knew about Sammler, and I admitted I knew very little, but I thought my colleague in Vienna would know more. So I rang him.'

'I know,' said Slonský. 'I paid for the call.'

'And you got your money's worth. The chap in Vienna had a strange, incomplete sort of story to tell, but it hinges on a photograph. Apologies for the quality — he faxed it to me — though truth to tell the original isn't much better.'

Valentin offered a black and white photograph. It showed four young people apparently sharing a picnic. To the right, a woman was resting her head on a man's shoulder. They were listening to a girl playing the guitar. In the foreground a young man had a notebook open and was writing something.

The woman cuddling the man had blonde hair reaching below her shoulders. He was the owner of a curly beard and a pair of rimless spectacles. Both of them wore a standard intellectual's outfit of roll neck sweater and jeans. The guitarist was wearing something lighter in colour. Her face could not be seen clearly because the picture showed only a profile. The writer had thick, dark hair and was wearing a corduroy or velvet jacket and jeans.

'Recognise him? That's Theodor Sammler, according to our man in Vienna.'

'Date of the picture?'

'I'll come to that, but probably around 1971 or 1972. Sammler had not long started as a student at Tübingen.'

Valentin took a further sip of his brandy, then noticed that it was empty. This discovery threw him into such confusion that he stopped talking until Slonský took command of the crisis and ordered another.

'The reason for dating it 1971-2 is the woman on the rug with the bearded guy. She is Gudrun Ensslin.'

The theatrical pause for a reaction produced absolutely nothing.

'We're obviously meant to know who Gudrun Ensslin is, but I don't. And Navrátil won't have any chance.'

'Gudrun Ensslin was one of the leaders of the German Rote Armee Fraktion. You know, the Baader-Meinhof mob.'

'Terrorists,' said Slonský. 'Sammler was hanging out with left-wing terrorists?'

'So it seems. It can't be before 1970 because he was still at home then, and in June 1972 Ensslin was arrested and never got out before she committed suicide in prison in 1977.'

'Date?' snapped Slonský.

'18th October. You'll remember that the Red Army Faction tried to engineer an exchange of prisoners by kidnapping an industrialist and then hijacking a Lufthansa airliner. When this failed to work, the leaders committed suicide in prison. Now, plainly the involvement of a leading establishment banker in terrorism would be big news, but there is absolutely nothing around to indicate that. He doesn't seem to have been at the kidnapping or the hijacking, and none of those who continued the Red Army struggle name him or even seem to know of him.'

'Interesting, but how does it help us?'

'First, because the story doesn't end there. It was whispered that Sammler was using daddy's money to bankroll some of the RAF's work. His father's reaction was to prevent young Theodor having access to any bank accounts except his own little allowance, but also to decide that he must be removed from Germany to break links with his former friends and get the West German police off the Sammlers' backs. Theodor had finished his doctorate by 1977 so he was sent off to Austria to work for a small bank there. He proved to be the cuckoo in the nest. Within five years he had more or less taken full control.'

'I can imagine that,' said Slonský. 'He wouldn't like being number two to anyone.'

'That brings me to the second interesting fact our man had for us. You were speculating the other day as to why Sammler doesn't go back to Germany to make his fortune on the bigger stage in Frankfurt. The simple answer is that he can't. The German police never formally closed their enquiry into his links with terrorism and he is worried he could still be arrested.'

'It's a long time ago,' said Slonský. 'Who would remember all that now?'

Valentin drew a long, satisfying slurp and smiled broadly.

'His father would.'

'Sammler's father is still alive?'

'Alive and in the pink. He lives in a retirement home in the Black Forest. He is ninety-three but still in full possession of his marbles, they say. And he hasn't spoken to Sammler since that day in 1977 when he put him on the train to Austria.'

Navrátil shook his head.

'I can't imagine your own dad not speaking to you for thirty years.'

Valentin ignored the comment.

'I got on to our man in Frankfurt, who gave me a few more details. By the way, you owe me for the phone call. I've got old Sammler's address in case you want a word. It seems that his prime concern was that his son was turning into a Communist fellow traveller, so the father's idea was to take him away from his circle of bad influences, and give him a healthy pile of cash to make his fortune. Old Sammler reasoned that when the money started coming in, Theodor would be hooked on capitalism, and so it proved.'

'So does this exonerate Sammler, or point the finger at him?' asked Slonský.

Valentin appeared shocked at the mere suggestion that he might know the answer to this.

'You're the cops,' he said. 'You work it out.'

'It's a tenuous link in the chain of evidence,' Slonský decided. 'A photograph showing someone who might be Sammler having a picnic with someone who might be a famous terrorist without anything to suggest that Sammler was ever a fellow traveller.'

'Except his dad's belief,' Navrátil added. 'Presumably his dad had his reasons.'

Slonský finished his beer with one long glug.

'Well, there's only one way to find out,' he told them. 'We'll have to ask him.'

'You want to go where?' gasped Lukas.

'The Black Forest, sir. It's in Germany,' Slonský added helpfully.

'I know where it is, Slonský. I also know how far away it is. It must be six hundred kilometres or more.'

'I've done some research, sir. That's the price of two flights, and that's the corresponding rail fare. But then we have to get to the nursing home, which is a fairly long taxi ride. Whereas if we take a police car, I reckon the fuel will come to that figure at the bottom. So all in all we'll be saving you around two thousand crowns by driving.'

'Very considerate of you.'

'So even with an overnight stay somewhere —'

'No! Six hours each way doesn't warrant a hotel.'

'But with an interview between the journeys, sir, and a lot of ground to cover —'

Lukas scrawled across the paper.

'Very well! One night, in a guest house, with a simple dinner and breakfast. And this had better be worthwhile, Slonský.'

'All approved,' Slonský announced. 'Now, key tasks before we go. Navrátil, you're in charge of the commissary.'

'I thought that was a big bird that couldn't fly.'

'That's a cassowary, Navrátil. A commissary is what you're in charge of — a big picnic hamper with ample bread and sausages to see us through our epic journey. We'll each take one small bag. I'll go down to the motor pool and see what kind of car they'll let us have. Anything I've forgotten?'

'Do you speak German, sir?'

'Only "Don't shoot, I'm a friend". You?'

'Not a word, sir. And I'd guess that our chances of finding a German policeman who speaks Czech must be slim, so shouldn't we take an interpreter with us?'

'Good idea, Navrátil. Organise it. We can't pay them, but there may be someone who'd like a free day trip to the Black

Forest. And I suppose I'd better tell the German police what we're up to, in case they discover we're there.'

Navrátil decided the best prospect of finding a German speaker was to ask Sergeant Mucha, who seemed to know everything that went on in the building.

'A fluent Kraut-speaker? I don't think so.' He scanned the duty roster in the hope that a possibility would leap out at him. 'Isn't Klinger a German name?' he wondered.

Navrátil tapped on the door, and waited for the crisp 'Come!' from within.

'Ah, Navrátil, isn't it? Have you come to seek a transfer? We're always on the lookout for likely lads in the fraud squad.'

'Not just at the moment, sir. I'm trying to find a fluent German speaker and someone suggested that you might be one.'

'Did "someone"? Well, you may tell Sergeant Mucha that I do indeed speak German tolerably well. What do you want one for?'

Navrátil summed up the discussion with Valentin.

'Well, isn't that fascinating? I can see why Slonský wants to speak to Sammler's father. Although what this has to do with the murder he's supposed to be investigating isn't at all clear to me, unless it's his contention that Sammler murdered someone in Germany before his father kicked him out.'

'I don't think so, sir.'

'When do you leave?'

'Tomorrow morning, sir. Seven o'clock sharp.'

Klinger sprang to his feet and marched briskly to the door, holding it open for Navrátil.

'I shall be ready at 06:50. And I hope that Slonský will have obtained a suitable vehicle instead of that battered insurance write-off he normally makes you drive.'

Chapter 21

Thursday dawned, and Navrátil and Klinger were waiting in the entry hall of the police headquarters when a slick white Volkswagen Passat glided to a halt on the yellow lines outside.

'Will this do?' asked Slonský through the open window.

'I'm impressed,' said Klinger. 'A 3.6-litre engine, I believe. How did you manage to get the use of this?'

'By swapping the keys for those of the eight-year-old Škoda Octavia they were going to give us.'

'You mean you haven't booked this out?' gasped Klinger.

'Of course I have,' said Slonský. 'Old Dlouhý asked me to read out the registration, so I read this one to him, and he wrote out the paperwork. Then we both signed it. When he discovers it he's hardly likely to tell everyone he's so short-sighted he can't actually do his job properly, is he?'

Klinger pursed his lips in a moue of disapproval.

'That seems to me perilously close to taking advantage of the lame and halt,' he said.

'Fair enough,' said Slonský. 'Shall I take it back and get the Octavia?'

'It's a matter for your conscience rather than mine. But the seats are rather nice, aren't they?'

'Right, in you get. Klinger, do you want to sit in the front with me, or have the whole back seat to yourself?'

'I'll be happy to spread myself out in the back, if that's agreeable to all,' Klinger responded, and climbed in before anyone had time to object. Navrátil put the bags in the boot and walked back to address Slonský through the driver's window.

'Have you forgotten your bag, sir?'

Slonský reached into the footwell beneath him and held up a small snap-top freezer bag.

'Pants, socks, toothbrush, razor. It's only one night, Navrátil, not an Arctic expedition. Now, get in before some overzealous traffic cop books us.'

Klinger had brought a book. He was the sort of person who always had a book on the go, usually of the kind that he would describe as "improving". In this particular case, he was reading an economics text by Hayek and not, as Slonský affected to believe, one by Hašek.

'Though I don't doubt for a minute that Hašek would have written an economics textbook if he had thought there was money to be made from it,' Klinger commented acidly.

'Ah, a true Czech,' said Slonský. 'Not one to let mere profound ignorance prevent him from expressing an opinion.'

'Or, indeed, teaching others,' Klinger added.

'Well, so long as you keep one step ahead — Jesus Maria! — Navrátil, take that car's number. Did you see that? Nearly had my wing mirror off. We'll ring it through to traffic when we get back.'

'Let it go, sir. I'm sure we'll see more bad driving as we go.'

Klinger muttered something about motes and beams, but since Slonský did not know what a mote was, and had not heard clearly anyway, he let it pass.

'I'll drive for the first two hours or so, then you can take over, Navrátil. Klinger, do you want a drive?'

'I'm enjoying being chauffeured around, thank you, but if you wish I'll take a turn. It will be interesting to experience a really powerful engine.'

'What do you normally drive, sir?' asked Navrátil.

'I don't. A car is such a millstone in Prague.'

'You don't drive,' said Slonský, 'but you're planning to take the two of us on a death spin along the highway?'

'I *don't* drive, but I *can* drive,' Klinger corrected him. 'The jury is still out on some others.'

The journey was relatively uneventful. Navrátil took over after a couple of hours, and was able to calculate that Slonský's average speed exceeded the speed limit at any given point in the journey so far. Rolling along at a more sedate pace, they reached the halfway point around ten o'clock, which prompted Slonský to suggest that a refreshment break was in order.

'We can spare ten minutes for a coffee,' he told them.

Half an hour, a coffee, a sandwich and a pastry later, they were back on the road. Klinger had purchased some tissues and was washing his hands with a gel from a small squeezy bottle he kept in his briefcase. Navrátil was wishing he had not been talked into having both a sandwich and a pastry. Slonský was regretting not having taken a few extra minutes to top up with a second coffee and perhaps a pancake.

'Did you see the state of those washrooms?' asked Klinger. 'Not a good advertisement for the country.'

'We've crossed the border,' said Slonský. 'They're German washrooms.'

'I know that,' Klinger replied. 'And they reflect badly upon German standards.'

'Tut, tut,' Slonský answered. 'The Sudetenland, the Holocaust and they've got a dirty toilet.'

'You may mock,' Klinger sniped, 'but standards are standards. It's in the attention to detail that we learn so much about the real priorities of a people.'

Slonský closed his eyes as if to take a nap, but suddenly turned to look fiercely at Klinger.

'What did you just say?'

Klinger carefully placed his bookmark between the pages, closed the book gracefully, and addressed Slonský slowly as if speaking to the local village idiot.

'I said that it is in their attention to detail that people give their priorities away.'

Slonský's face lit up.

'Nobody speak to me for a while. I have an idea, and I need to think deeply about it. To the untrained eye it will look as if I am asleep, but actually my brain will be running like a hamster in a wheel.'

As a result of Slonský's nap, and Klinger's total immersion in his book, Navrátil was still driving two hours later as they approached the turn to Stuttgart.

'Excuse me,' Navrátil said, 'but is anyone going to give me directions?'

'I don't have the address,' Klinger responded. 'You'll have to wake Slonský.'

'That's rather difficult when I'm driving,' Navrátil answered.

'Of course,' said Klinger. 'But you could pull up at the side of the road, wake him, then start driving again.'

'No need,' came a sonorous voice from the body beside him. Slonský's eyes were still shut, but he handed Navrátil a sheet of paper from his top pocket.

'That's the address. I got directions off the internet. They're on the back. Brilliant thing, the internet. I even got an aerial photograph of the nursing home.'

'That will be very useful,' said Klinger, 'if we fly over it. But since Navrátil is driving I expect us to continue at road level the rest of the way. Are they expecting us?'

'I didn't want anyone coaching him, so I haven't told them,' Slonský explained.

'You did what?' gasped Klinger.

'No, I didn't what,' Slonský said. 'And I accept that he may not be there when we arrive, though where else would he go?'

'Heaven,' snapped Klinger. 'Old people do that with the minimum of notice.'

'No consideration, some people,' agreed Slonský. 'But if he's popped it, we'll just turn back and enjoy the trip.'

'And how will you explain that to Captain Lukas, sir?' Navrátil enquired.

'I'll probably just leave a note on his desk saying it was a wasted journey because you forgot to ring ahead to check Old Sammler was still alive, Navrátil.'

'That's not fair, sir!'

'No, it isn't,' Slonský agreed. 'It's called life, Navrátil, and you're suffering from it. Though I suspect life isn't so bad when you consider the alternative.'

'I'll stick up for you, Navrátil,' Klinger interjected, though without looking up from his book. 'You need never fear this behemoth while I'm around to offer you a bolthole in the fraud squad.'

'Fraud squad?' spluttered Slonský. 'When did you become a squad? There's only two of you. How can two people be a squad?'

'There are only two of us *at present*,' Klinger conceded, 'but that is because we haven't replaced Kobr.'

'Ah, yes, Kobr,' said Slonský. 'When does he get out?'

'About two years, I think.'

'Bit long to hold his job open for him, then.'

Klinger looked at Slonský over the top of his spectacles.

'I fear Kobr's chances of reinstatement with the fraud department are not likely to be good. Other departments may be less picky. Criminal investigation, for example.'

'No, I think we'd go along with your judgement there, Klinger. After all, you know him best, having been colleagues and all that.'

'Colleague is, perhaps, a little strong,' said Klinger. 'We were not on terms of great fellowship.'

'Do you ever visit?'

'I think to do so might be … tactless,' Klinger answered. 'And difficult.'

'Yes, I can see that,' said Slonský. 'Must be an awkward conversation when one of you is a police officer and his former colleague is hanging from the wall in chains.'

'How very medieval of you, Slonský,' Klinger smoothly replied. 'Kobr is in an open prison where he runs the library, I believe.'

'Just so long as they don't let him run the prison amenities fund.'

Navrátil's curiosity was given full rein.

'What did this Kobr person do?' he asked.

'He overlooked a couple of bank accounts belonging to black marketeers, one of which had his name on it. Allegedly. And he delayed passing valuable information on to Klinger. Allegedly.'

'No, he definitely did that,' Klinger expostulated.

'And he allegedly did these things in exchange for allegedly having a wild night in a hotel with a couple of young dancers. Allegedly. Oh, hang on, that one was proved. Scrub the allegedlys.'

'In the interests of accuracy, it was four nights, Slonský, and seven dancers.'

'At the same time?'

'Working shifts, I believe.'

'Thank goodness for that. I was beginning to see Kobr in a whole new light. Navrátil, you see that big blue sign pointing towards Stuttgart? Well, that's the way to Stuttgart. You want to turn there.'

Two of the three had been expecting a Gothic pile, possibly a converted stately home, but the care home proved to be a very pleasant affair built on the side of a hill with a wonderful view across the forest.

'I wouldn't mind living here,' announced Slonský.

'I'll make enquiries about their waiting list,' Klinger offered, 'though I suspect the monthly rates may be beyond a police pension.'

The interior was a riot of carved wood. A few litres of petrol and a match and this could be the bonfire of a lifetime, thought Slonský. There were no nurses in uniform bobbing about, but a stoutly built lady in a grey business suit approached them wearing a name badge that suggested that she might be staff. Klinger dealt smoothly with the formalities, produced his badge, instructed the others to produce theirs, and they were all invited to sit on a large red leather sofa under the head of a confident-looking stag.

'I bet he didn't look that smug a few moments later,' whispered Slonský.

'That's the problem with being the alpha male,' declared Klinger. 'First go at all the women, but you're also the one the hunters want to take down.'

'Then I sympathise with you, Klinger, as the big alpha male of the fraud squad. Or was it department?'

'Tease me, and I shall deliberately mistranslate for you. I wonder how much help Mr Sammler will give you if he thinks you're from the Euthanasia Society.'

'Business before pleasure, Klinger. Then I'll use my police expenses to buy you a nice dinner. Or, given German prices, a tolerable starter and a glass of milk.'

The grey-suited matron was blocking out the light again.

'She says Mr Sammler will see us now,' Klinger said, and walked alongside the lady as she led them to Sammler's room.

'This isn't a room,' said Navrátil. 'It's a suite.'

'Very nice indeed,' agreed Slonský. 'The absence of a bed suggests this is just a sitting room.'

They introduced themselves to the old man who sat in a high-backed armchair, his legs swathed in a woollen rug. He was clearly very old, as shown by his sparse white hair, but his blue eyes, while slightly pale now, were keen and sharp, and his back was straight as he sat to attention in the chair. He did not appear to need anything that Klinger said repeated to him, and answered clearly and concisely.

'Please tell Herr Sammler that we are interested in the circumstances that led to his son's departure from Germany,' Slonský began.

The old man barked a few syllables back at Klinger.

'He wants to know why you want to know.'

Slonský handed Sammler the photograph of his son at the picnic. The old man held it tilted to the light, jutted his jaw out defiantly, and handed it back, before beginning to speak.

'That is my son Theodor. He is a man of not inconsiderable gifts. We were fortunate enough to be able to provide him with an excellent education, as a result of hard work and thrift.

There seemed to be a danger that Theodor did not value this grounding that we had secured for him. He became wayward, and began mixing in undesirable circles.'

'Yet he completed his doctorate,' Slonský remarked. As Klinger translated the old boy eyed Slonský shrewdly.

'I can see you're not a bumpkin like most Czechs I've met. Yes, Theodor stayed at the university when many others fell by the wayside. That is a tribute to my dear late wife.'

He pointed to a photograph on the sideboard. Slonský stood to view it more closely.

'A fine-looking woman,' he pronounced.

'Not only fine looking, but intelligent,' said Sammler. 'Not a bubble-headed gossip like so many women. Theodora was in some ways the brains of the family. I had technical gifts, if I may say so. But Theodora was well read, and her German was so cultured. She taught Theodor to write well. She would tell him again and again that it does not matter how fine a man's ideas are, if he is unable to express them clearly. It made a great impression on the boy, and from a young age he wrote and spoke well.'

'He speaks good Czech too,' Slonský conceded.

'His mother was born in Bohemia,' Sammler replied.

'She was a Czech?'

'No, she was a German, born in Bohemia.'

Klinger glossed the translation.

'I think he means she was a Sudeten German.'

Catching the word 'Sudeten' Sammler quickly agreed.

'Yes, German by birth and heritage, though at that time her birthplace was in Czechoslovakia. She spoke some Czech, and I don't doubt Theodor heard her. Her own nanny was a Czech woman, so most of the lullabies she knew were in Czech.'

'May we return to the photograph, sir? Your wife was obviously instrumental in keeping Theodor at his studies.'

'Yes, she persuaded him that whatever his views, a completed education would be an asset to him and that his campaigning would have even more force if he were a known scholar.' He chuckled drily. 'She used to give him an odd example. How did Stalin come to the top of the pile in Russia? She said it was because, unlike his fellows, Stalin had grown up in a seminary and had been taught to speak well. After all, Russian was not his first language, yet he was able to defeat the others in debate. It made an impression on Theodor. His life might have been very different if she had lived — although, of course, the fact that she did not live was largely the result of his betrayal.'

'Betrayal, sir?'

'They were very close. He was an only child. Do you have children, Lieutenant? I thought not. I was fond of him, naturally, but there is a special bond between a mother and her son. I had grown up knowing that work would take me away from my parents, that separation was a part of independence. Having been uprooted at the end of the war, a secure home was very important to Theodora. She felt Theodor's departure very keenly, whilst, of course, absolutely agreeing with me that it was necessary.'

'May I ask what precipitated it, sir?'

Sammler did not answer for a moment, but reached for a large golden cord beside him and yanked on it. A distant bell rang, and within a few moments a young woman appeared at the door.

'Some tea, perhaps, for my guests, fräulein. And no doubt there will be some cake.'

The young woman nodded and left.

'They don't give me cake,' the old man grumbled. 'They say it's bad for me. As if I should worry about what's bad for me at ninety-three. Now, to continue, gentlemen. You have seen this photograph. You have some idea of the company that Theodor was keeping. I may say that I was a man of some substance even then, and perhaps that protected my son to some degree. If he was not fully involved in their atrocities that may have been because he was not entirely trusted. They were not convinced that he really shared their ambitions, given the future mapped out for him. As a result, it was not until that lot were jailed that Theodor was able to progress in their filthy organisation. I do not know precisely what part he played. He has given me his word that he was not directly involved in any violence towards others. He has refused to give his word that he obeyed the law at all times. I should like to be able to accept his word as that of a gentleman.'

'You have doubts, sir?'

'I do not have doubts as such. Only worries. The consequences of his actions did not weigh with him. If he were capable of some of these barbarities one read about, he was hardly likely to baulk at lying to his father, was he? How many of us have done that without being in any sense a criminal? If these years have taught me anything, it is to regret that I did not make the effort to understand my own father better. We had some fearful arguments, gentlemen, when I was a young man. I was twenty-six when the war broke out, and I soon found myself in the army. My father had served in his time, in the Kaiser's army in France. To my mind, we were doing the same thing. We were both serving Germany. But my father, while initially a supporter of Hitler, turned against him when he was sent to serve in a prison camp in Bavaria towards the end of the war. The younger men were all needed for the front, of course, so father was brought out of retirement and served as a Major. He would not tell me what he saw there, but said that if it came out, it would be an eternal shame for the Fatherland. I replied that I had every confidence in the nation's leadership. He became angry with me, and our relationship changed.'

The old man gazed out of the window for a moment, before clearing his throat gently and resuming his rigid position.

'Naturally, one can see now that my father was right. I was wrong, and I did not know what I was talking about. I should have admitted it and respected my father's view. When Theodor and I quarrelled, I said as much to him, but he laughed at me. He said that I ought not to be so quick to assume that I was wrong, that maybe youth sees more than experience, or some such tripe.'

The tea arrived, and was dispensed by the smiling young woman. She offered cake to each, and was about to leave when Sammler reminded her that she had inadvertently missed him out. She smiled weakly and gave him a plate and a slice of cake.

'It's a charade, of course,' said Sammler.

'Of course,' replied Slonský. 'If she really intended to miss you out she would not have brought a plate for you.'

Sammler laughed out loud, dabbing his eyes with a large handkerchief he produced from beneath the rug.

'Excellent! I think if you are intent on snaring Theodor he may have to be on his mettle to escape you.'

'May I ask about your own war service, sir?'

'Modest enough. I did very little fighting. That, you must understand, was not the result of any desire on my part. It was determined at an early stage that I had some administrative skills, and consequently I was sent for specialised training in logistics. I served out the war keeping the army supplied as best I could. When the war ended, I knew where some stores had been kept. It did not seem that the Americans had great need of them, whereas our people were suffering dreadfully.'

Slonský asked his next question after some deliberation.

'Forgive me if I have misunderstood. Do you mean that you were able to profit by selling the supplies?'

'You want to know if I made my money as a black marketeer? No, sir, I did not. I didn't need to. I took no money from Germans, though I was willing to accept American dollars from soldiers who wanted souvenirs to take home. I bartered some, and I gave some away, and in this way I gathered a large group of people who felt in some way beholden to me. When conditions improved, and I set up in business, this goodwill stood me in good stead. People trusted me where they did not trust others. When they had a little money, it was my little bank that they gave it to. So much of banking is about trust, gentlemen! They trusted me with their pfennigs, and were not concerned about the return so long as it was safe. I carried the risk and reaped the reward. As time went on, their many little nest-eggs grew, so they found more money to deposit. I began buying stakes in companies, and in twenty years or so I had become a regional force. This work involved sacrifice, of course. I could not allow myself to marry until I could keep a wife well, so I was thirty-four before I married Theodora. She had been kicked out of Bohemia with nothing. She had been well-to-do there, but she had only a donkey cart and the small amount that it could carry. I told her that I could not marry her until I could provide properly for her, and you know what she told me? That she placed no value on anything beyond my company and my love, and believed that if she hitched herself to me I would do more for her than any other man could. She had lost all, and did not expect ever to have that life again, but if it were possible, I would be the one who

227

could make it happen. And I am proud to say that I did. I married her for better or for worse, and it was overwhelmingly for better, until Theodor spoiled it all.'

'You said that you quarrelled, sir, but that is not a reason to send your son into exile.'

'I believed that I was doing the right thing. I hoped that if he moved in other circles he would forget his infatuation with this left-wing tosh he had been imbibing. I thought that if he began to make his own money, his views would come more closely to approach mine. I told him straight that I would give him a fair share of my wealth so that he could follow his own path. If he chose to give it away to those hippies that was his affair, but he could set himself up well with it. However, I reminded him of the parable of the prodigal son, and told him that if he returned there would be no fatted calf.'

'You did not expect to see him again.'

'The police had begun to ask difficult questions. Naturally, one defends one's child, but I genuinely did not know if he had done any of these beastly things that were alleged of those people in the newspapers. But over the years I had made some good friends, one of whom was a very senior man in the police force. He telephoned one day and asked if we could meet in private. I kept a small flat in Frankfurt then, and we met there. My wife was at our main house. I explained to her that I would be late because I was meeting Max. That, perhaps, was a mistake. Would the young gentleman mind pouring me a little more tea, since he is nearest?'

Navrátil did so, feeling the need to bow slightly as he returned the cup to Sammler.

'A fine young man. They say the young are a waste of time, a disappointment to us, but they have always said that. My parents' generation said it of us, and look what we achieved in rebuilding Germany after the war! One day we have to get out of the way and let the young ones run things, and if they mess up then they will have their own youngsters to tell them so. Ach! It's unimportant. So much time wasted on stupid arguments. Now, back to business. As I told you, I met Max at my flat. He was serious, I would almost say pained. He told me that Theodor was under suspicion. He showed me the photograph that you have shown me today and that I hoped had been lost forever, along with some others. Theodor was too clever to do any of the dirty work himself. He followed his old man.'

Sammler gave a short, mirthless laugh and explained his last observation.

'He specialised in logistics. He obtained the things they needed. He could say that he did not know precisely what they were planning. That may or may not be true. But he made it possible. If they needed guns, he found them. Max produced a piece of paper that broke my world apart and killed my wife. He had an invoice for the delivery of some automatic weapons. Theodor had used my company's money to pay for these. To do this, he had not forged any signatures. He had signed the paperwork quite openly in his own name, but he had represented himself to the sellers as my agent. My name, my reputation, my entire business life was at stake. This could not be allowed to happen again. I assured Max that I had known nothing of this, and that eventually we would have discovered it, no doubt, during one of our audits and taken appropriate action. He said that any large ship houses a rat or two, and that he could probably ensure that this evidence was lost if I could guarantee that Germany would be rid of Theodor. He would, regrettably, have to keep it for a while to ensure that Theodor did not sneak back. He was apologetic, but I did not blame him. I would have done the same, and he was taking a considerable risk by speaking to me about this at all. And after it was done, he remained my friend, making no attempt to keep a distance from me. He knew how much it had cost me. A man needs friends like Max.'

Sammler paused for a moment. His eyes were damp with nascent tears which he dabbed away as he composed himself once more.

'When I arrived home Theodora asked me what Max had wanted. I told her exactly what I have told you. Of course, she was heartbroken, but she could see that there was no choice. Theodor must leave us. I told her that she could visit him, but he would not set foot in Germany again. To her credit, she sat beside me as I confronted Theodor a few days later. I told him to choose somewhere to go and offered to help. I thought he would throw it back in my face, but to my surprise he said he would be guided by me. I mentioned a small Austrian bank whose owner I knew quite well. Theodor thought that would be acceptable. I rang the man and told him that I wanted Theodor to get some experience outside the family firm so that he could prove that he had progressed on his own merits. I offered to pay his first year's salary if they would take him on. I said that they would be doing me a favour if they forgot that he was my son. Of course, they didn't understand what I meant, and thought I was just saying that I didn't want him given any special treatment.'

Sammler stopped speaking and licked his thin lips.

'I have regretted that conversation many times. I misled them. I had let a wolf into their sheep pen. Theodor took the bank off them. He proved to be incredibly ruthless in business. I hope that I had maintained proper standards in my own work. Certainly that was my aim. But Theodor had no such scruples. He has been successful, but at what a cost.'

'He has never married, sir.'

'So I understand. I am not surprised. Theodor does not seem to feel the need for relationships. He is not a clubbable man. He joins no societies, shares no interests. I once asked him why he did not have a girlfriend. His answer was deeply shocking to me. I will not repeat his exact words, but he said that every service that can be provided by a wife can be purchased from women more accomplished in those tasks, usually cheaper and without any continuing obligation. His language was extremely vulgar.'

'If I were to suggest that your son may have resumed his old ways, would it surprise you, sir?'

Klinger asked Slonský to repeat the question before he translated it.

'Are you sure you want to ask that?' he asked.

'Yes. I may be wrong, but I want to see his reaction.'

Klinger translated the question. The old man's eyes widened and he gripped the arms of his chair angrily.

'What my son does now, he answers for. I hoped he might have been cured, but is one ever cured of this infection? If it is as you say, it is all the more reason why he should not come back.'

Slonský leaned forward and spoke gently.

'I am sorry to have had to ask you that. It must have been distressing and I hope you will understand that I would have spared you that if I could.'

Klinger translated, while Sammler acknowledged the apology with a nod.

'A man must do his duty. I see that. This is yours. I see that too.'

'I hope that we will — that I will — prove to be mistaken. I have spoken to your son, and I shall have to interview him again. And now I think we should leave you to rest. I am grateful for your considerable assistance.'

Slonský stood, clicked his heels, and offered his hand. The old man shook it. Klinger followed suit, and then Navrátil shook hands too, speaking a few words of fractured German as he did so. Sammler smiled, patted the back of Navrátil's hand as he shook it, and his eyes filled with tears again.

Navrátil pushed past and left the room first, striding swiftly down the corridor.

'What did he say?' whispered Slonský.

Klinger looked puzzled.

'Something like "I'm pleased to have met your wife, sir".'

There was another rare event that evening. Slonský was not hungry.

They had left the nursing home in silence, and low in spirit. Slonský was not his usual ebullient self and climbed straight into the passenger seat without even asking who was going to drive. That'll be me then, thought Navrátil, whose emotions were confused and raw. He had genuinely liked the old man, who reminded him of the grandfather he would have liked to have had. His father's father had died when he was too young to remember, while his mother's father was a miserable old git. When the interview was over Navrátil could have cried, and hoped the others had not noticed. They had said nothing, of course, but that did not mean that his face had not betrayed him. He just wanted to go home now, but unfortunately he faced six hours in the car with Klinger and Slonský first, neither of whom was known for their delicacy when it came to other people's feelings. Being alone seemed so desirable, so Navrátil cut himself off and concentrated on his driving.

Klinger was angry. He believed that Slonský had had no business suggesting that Theodor Sammler had returned to left-wing terrorism without the slightest shred of evidence to back up such an assertion. If Old Sammler had asked Slonský for proof, what could he have said? And the allegation had come out of his mouth, albeit as an interpreter of Slonský's accusing words. He had given Slonský the opportunity to reconsider, but Slonský had blundered on regardless like the uncouth golem he sometimes seemed to be.

Slonský closed his eyes and rehearsed the interview. For some reason, while Slonský had difficulty with names, could not remember anyone's birthday other than his own and regularly forgot his PIN number when standing at a bank machine, he had a very good memory for conversations with witnesses. He could see now that his previous interpretations of the evidence were complete bunkum, and part of his brain was attempting to construct a verbal report for Lukas that would somehow explain that the new theory was actually just a subtle reworking of the old one, though differing in one or two minor details like having an alternative motive and killer. If he tried hard he could work through the events of that evening in early February and piece together a sequence that made sense. He could see where some of the evidence that filled the gaps would come from. But some of it would have to come from the murderer, and tricking them into letting it out was going to take a bit of nerve and a lot of low cunning. Fortunately, low cunning was Slonský's strong point. He could limbo his way past most villains' defences if he could engineer the right opportunity, and he turned his mind to setting up that encounter.

'Where do you want to stop, sir?' Navrátil suddenly asked.

'Let's grab a bite anywhere you see,' said Slonský. 'I don't fancy a night away if you don't mind, Klinger.'

'I'm always happiest in my own bed,' came the reply. 'Let's stop for a little freshening up, then press on. Even with an hour's break, we should be home around midnight.'

They covered about half the distance home before Navrátil saw an inn just off the road. Klinger declared that anywhere must be better than that insanitary hole at which they had stopped in the morning, and Slonský had no opinion at all. They ordered their food and sat in a quiet corner, Slonský holding a beer, Klinger contemplating a dry white wine, and Navrátil trying to look enthusiastic about a mineral water when he really fancied a very large vodka. The sort of vodka that guaranteed that you would forget the last day and a half and wake up when it had all gone away.

Klinger straightened the beermat and positioned his wine glass precisely at its centre.

'So?' he said.

'So what?' asked Slonský.

'Exactly,' said Klinger.

Slonský delayed his answer by taking a large mouthful of beer, swallowing it, and licking his lips.

'Herr Sammler cannot know anything of the events we are investigating, but he believes that his son could be implicated.'

'He said no such thing,' said Klinger. 'He only took your rash statement at face value. He belongs to a generation that respects the police, so of course he didn't argue. How could he? He hasn't seen his son for thirty years.'

Slonský's eyes were diamond hard.

'He didn't know why we wanted to know, but he didn't ask. Doesn't that strike you as strange? Not once did he ask what we were investigating or why we wanted to speak to him. I think he knew that it must be serious, and it didn't surprise him. He said he would like to take his son's word for the claim that he had not been directly involved in any violence, but he plainly couldn't. He worded it exactly that way. Not "my son told me this and I believe him" but "I would have liked to have taken his word". He couldn't take that word because he didn't believe it. He knows his son is capable of violence.'

'You're reading too much into that,' said Klinger. 'First, because he was describing events that happened a long time ago, and those distant events become distorted in our memories. Second, because he knows his son bought weapons and maybe he thinks, as any right-minded person would, that there isn't any real moral difference between killing someone and making it possible for someone else to kill someone. Third, because what you heard was what I told you he said, and perhaps my German isn't up to such subtle differences.'

'Then write down the German and we'll ask another translator what they think. Do it now while it's fresh in your mind. As to the weapons, someone who buys guns for others to use might be just the sort of person who would pay someone else to strangle a young woman. Doesn't do his own dirty work, but is quite happy to have the dirty work done for him.'

Klinger could see no point in continuing the argument. He merely snorted to show that he disagreed, then decided to realign his glass on the mat to return some order to a chaotic world.

'Why strangled, sir?' asked Navrátil.

'Because it's a built-up area with lots of people around and a gun would attract attention, even in the Prague of today,' Slonský replied.

'But surely strangling a woman takes time. A knife would be quicker. Putting a pillow over her face when she's asleep would be easier.'

'Knives cause blood and blood is messy, Navrátil. Novák would have got us a lot more useful stuff if there'd been a puddle of blood. The murderer would have been spattered and might have been seen leaving, in which event being covered in blood could be a disadvantage.'

'He might have been seen leaving anyway,' said Navrátil. 'He couldn't know that he wouldn't meet someone on the landing or on the stairs. If he killed her when Novák says, then there could well have been people about.'

'He couldn't leave it any later, Navrátil, or she wouldn't have answered the door to let him in.'

'If you're casting Sammler as the murderer,' Klinger interrupted, 'then show us some evidence that she had ever met him, because without that your case falls down. Why would she let a complete stranger in at that time of night?'

Slonský picked up his beermat and tapped it rhythmically on the table top, not so much because it helped him think as because he was fairly confident that it would annoy the hell out of Klinger. He was right about that, even if he was wrong about everything else.

'Not hungry, Slonský?' Klinger enquired. 'The schnitzel is really rather good.'

'I've lost my appetite. Help yourself to anything you like the look of.'

'Thank you, but no, thank you. I've never been keen on second-hand vegetables, however careful their previous owner.'

Slonský picked up his fork again and speared a carrot.

'I hate waste,' he said as he chewed. 'I hate waste even more than I hate carrots.'

Klinger drained his glass and Slonský immediately sprang to his feet.

'Coming?' he asked Navrátil, and strode out to the car.

Navrátil guzzled the last of his water and hurried to catch his boss, whilst Klinger decided that one of them really ought to pay the bill.

When Navrátil arrived at the car, Slonský was in the driver's seat and the engine was running. Klinger took his time, but finally appeared and had to scuttle to shut the door as Slonský took off with Klinger only partly inside.

'I paid the bill,' said Klinger.

'Good,' replied Slonský. 'I'd hate to think of you washing up all night while we drove home.'

'I'll give you the receipt later, when you repay me.'

'You can sign it off yourself.'

'Ah, but this is a homicide investigation, nothing to do with the Fraud Squad.'

'Only a small fraction of the homicide team is in this car, whereas we've got half of the Fraud Squad here, which just shows the importance you attach to it.'

'What it shows,' said Klinger, 'is that I am not divisible into any meaningful smaller units. And don't even think of experimenting with your penknife in a lay-by.'

Chapter 22

The morning sun shone low on the Prague rooftops, but appeared to have elevated Slonský's mood. After a night's sleep he was obviously uplifted by something or other, because he was charging around the offices like a young pony exploring a new field.

Lukas was more than usually nonplussed.

'I just hope you know what you're doing, Slonský.'

'Maybe I do, and maybe I don't, sir, but it's time to rock the boat and see who falls out.'

'That isn't a reassuring metaphor, Slonský. Let me remind you that I am the captain of this ship, and if anyone goes overboard it isn't you who is going to be called to account. Well, not you alone, anyway.'

'Banda isn't in the danger I thought he was, because if I read this right, the perpetrator has already got what he wanted from him. He doesn't want Banda to escape the criticism he'll get for having an affair and he achieved all he needed when Banda was sacked. He didn't follow up on his original photo because he had got what he wanted, to wit, Banda's backside on the steps of the government buildings.'

'And suppose Banda sues us?'

'For protecting him? I'll sweet talk him, sir. I'll get him to agree to a statement that he was never a serious suspect but we needed to keep him in protective custody for his own safety. He'll be more than happy to get public confirmation from us that he was never really in the frame for Irina's murder.'

'But he was, Slonský. You put him there. You were convinced he had done it. And I understand that there was some monkey business involving a threat to his person that I wasn't told about.'

Slonský waved the argument away.

'A simple misunderstanding on the way to the showers, sir. Let me have a few words with him, and all will be well. I'll turn on the charm.'

Lukas threw his pen angrily onto his blotter.

'Damn it, Slonský, you don't have any charm! You're a public relations disaster area for this police force in general and my department in particular. I've protected you for a long time, but if this goes wrong on us I'll be very happy to sign your retirement papers.'

Slonský was taken aback. Lukas had never said that to him before. That hurt. It was a definite low blow. Slonský was not afraid of much but retirement frightened the hell out of him.

He rose slowly from his seat and picked up his folder.

'It won't go wrong on us, sir. I'll take full responsibility.'

'That goes without saying,' Lukas replied.

Banda was as surprised as Lukas had been.

'I can go? Just like that?'

'If you want. I don't think you're in any physical danger. The perpetrator wanted you humiliated, not dead.'

'Well, he certainly got that.'

'I'll be happy to issue a press release that your innocence was quickly established and that you remained here solely to give you protection.'

'And my wife?'

'She was never a suspect.'

'I mean, what will you say to her?'

'The same.'

'She's not a fool, Lieutenant. She knows you suspected me for some time. In fact, so far as I know she still thinks you do. Unless, of course, you've told her otherwise.'

'No,' admitted Slonský. 'But she never believed you'd done it anyway, so she doesn't need my word for it.'

Banda pursed his lips and thought deeply for a few moments.

'Very well. Give me a few minutes to get my papers together, bring me my own clothes, take me home and issue your statement and I'm happy to forget the whole thing.'

Slonský relaxed, until Banda continued.

'Provided, of course, that you tell the Prime Minister I'm innocent and I need a job.'

Lukas was apoplectic.

'Why should I go to tell the Prime Minister you've let Banda go?'

'Well, you arrested him, sir, not me.'

'On your recommendation!'

'But you insisted on reviewing the evidence yourself, sir. You said the evidence was sound. At the time, that is.'

'And I suppose you want me to make the Director go with me like last time?'

'I don't think he will, sir. But we could ask.'

'You let him go, you can tell the Prime Minister.'

'That would undermine your authority, sir.'

'Undermine ... how?'

'Because if you arrest him and then I let him go, it looks like I'm criticising your decision, sir.'

Lukas stood so he could look Slonský squarely in the eye.

'If I go, then when I come back, I will take out your personnel file and drop a little note to those concerned to point out that you're ready to retire.'

Slonský could not avoid a small, but visible, shudder.

'Do you mean that, sir?'

'I certainly do.'

'Then I suppose I'd better go to see the Prime Minister, sir.'

Slonský managed to get a five-minute appointment within the hour, and was only two minutes late for it. He remained standing as he explained that Banda had been framed, and he hoped that the real culprit would soon be charged.

'So Banda didn't do it?'

'No, sir.'

'He'll want his job back, damn it.'

'But he did fail to co-operate with a police inquiry into a serious crime, sir. You were right to sack him for that.'

The Prime Minister doodled for a moment or two.

'You sound like Komárek,' he finally said. 'That's the sort of twaddle he talks when the opinion polls come out. You're absolutely sure Banda was framed?'

Slonský handed the Prime Minister the photograph of Soucha and Mario.

'The same person who sent us the photograph of Dr Banda with Miss Gruberová sent us this picture too, sir.'

'Good Lord! That's Thingummy, isn't it?'

'Daniel Soucha, sir.'

'God in Heaven! And I thought kissing babies for votes was bad.'

'I don't think he's electioneering, sir. The other gentleman doesn't have a vote here.'

'Soucha resigning?'

'I don't know, sir. He was very keen that this photograph should not get out.'

'I bet he was.'

The Prime Minister thought for a moment or two.

'Is Banda going to sue you for wrongful arrest?'

'He said he wouldn't if I told you he was innocent, sir.'

'What will he do now, I wonder?'

'I don't know, sir. It isn't going to be easy for him to carry on as if nothing had happened.'

'Leave him to me. There's a nice little job in Brussels I could offer him. The Deputy Director of the National Bank thinks he's going to get it, but I like him even less than I like Banda.'

'Thank you, sir.'

'Was there something else, Lieutenant?'

'May I ask a favour, sir?'

'Why should I do you a favour, Slonský?'

'Because you're a decent man, sir.'

'And in return?'

'I'll give you a weather forecast.'

'What is it you want?'

'I have a journalist friend who needs a scoop. If you were willing to give him the news of Banda's forthcoming appointment before anyone else gets it, he would be very grateful indeed.'

'A journalist?'

'Yes, sir.'

'Name?'

'Here's his card, sir. Telephone number on the back. Will it be this week, sir?'

'Yes, no point in dithering.'

'Thank you, sir. I'm very grateful.'

The Prime Minister cocked his head and raised an eyebrow.

'The weather forecast?'

'Very stormy, sir.'

'And why is that?'

Slonský told him what was to come. They parted cordially.

Navrátil was waiting for Slonský in the office.

'Sir, how would I go about getting a transfer to Kladno?'

'You come and ask me, and I tell you not to be so stupid and to get your brain back in gear.'

Navrátil held out an envelope.

'I just thought I'm not sure life in Prague —'

'Cobblers! You didn't think, your groin twitches every time Kladno is mentioned. Don't think I don't know what's behind this sudden interest in the Central Bohemian Police, Navrátil. It's tall and blonde and it has a backside like two coconuts in a sack.'

'Sir!'

Slonský took the envelope and threw it in the waste bin.

'Navrátil, you're a detective. Stick with me and you could become a really good one. But in this case your brain has gone soft, lad. Kladno doesn't have a detective department worth the name. It has a good dog-handling school, I grant you. If your idea of fun is running around in a padded jacket waiting for a German shepherd to sink its teeth into your arm, Kladno is the place for you. But if a crime is committed in Kladno, where is the regional police headquarters?'

'Zbraslav, sir.'

'And what is Zbraslav's address, Navrátil?'

'Prague 5, sir.'

'Prague 5, sir, yes, sir. It's just across town. So if you want to be a detective in Kladno, what the hell is the point of moving? This is the Kladno detective department.'

'Maybe I'm not cut out to be a detective, sir. Maybe I should try something else, you know, get a bit of wider experience.'

Slonský sighed and flopped heavily into his seat.

'I'd hoped I wasn't going to have to do this, Navrátil, but you leave me no choice. Sit down, lad.'

Navrátil obeyed, and Slonský picked up the telephone. He dialled a number that he had written in the back of his notebook and waited for it to be answered. When it was, he wasted no time on the customary civilities.

'I'll give you one thing,' he told the person on the other end, 'you can keep a secret. I've got Navrátil here. If I don't let him in on our little scheme he's going to blow the plan by moving to Kladno. Explain it to him.'

He handed the phone to Navrátil, who listened with increasingly wide eyes and an open mouth. At the end of the call Navrátil acknowledged that he had understood all that had been said. He had taken it all in, he claimed, and as he hung up he sat back in the chair and goggled.

'Well, don't sit there gawping, lad. Get us some coffee and get back to work. I take it you no longer want a transfer, now that Officer Peiperová has accepted a job here?'

The sausage tasted unusually good today, thought Slonský, and Navrátil's appetite appeared to have returned.

'But how did you work it, sir?' the younger man asked, his cheeks bulging with bread roll.

'Captain Němec is retiring. That left a vacancy, but in the current financial climate they couldn't afford another captain. They planned to do a bit of reorganising, bump someone up and do without a lieutenant. I argued that we needed another woman officer more than we needed a lieutenant, and I'm pleased to say the good captain agreed and persuaded Lukas.

With two captains supporting the proposal and a bit of money saved to boot, it went through very quickly. And when I told Lukas of the good work Peiperová had done on her own initiative in interviewing those girls, he agreed that this was just the sort of young woman we needed. Brings the average age down, helps with the gender balance, all that sort of equality stuff. If she'd been a black lesbian it might have helped but you can't have everything.'

'Thank you, sir. We won't let you down.'

'Navrátil, during working hours there will be no "we". There will be you, and there will be her, but there will be no "we". Any of that sort of stuff and you'll both be out on your ears.'

'Understood, sir.'

'And try to cure yourself of the puppy look when she comes near you.'

'Yes, sir.'

'Ever heard of bromide, Navrátil?'

'No, sir.'

'They put it in soldiers' coffee, Navrátil, so they wouldn't have carnal thoughts. If you can't control them, get some.'

'Sir.'

'Navrátil, I'll say this just once. I'm not getting any younger, and Lukas is threatening to put me out to grass. If I don't bring this one in, it could be very soon, but I hope we'll get over this and I'll go on until they can't keep me any longer. When that happens, there'll be a vacancy for a lieutenant. Set your eyes on that, lad, and get yourself ready to make a real play for it when the time comes.'

'Yes, sir. Thank you, sir.'

'And if Klinger comes sniffing around offering you all the kingdoms of the world, tell him to get lost. You'd be wasted in the Fraud Squad.'

Navrátil nodded his agreement.

'Sir, did you say you'd let Banda go?'

'Yes, lad. He wasn't the killer.'

'When did you decide that, sir?'

'When I got Novák's post-mortem report.'

'That was ages ago, sir! It's at least three weeks.'

'I know, Navrátil.'

'So how did that clear Dr Banda?'

'Because Novák told us that the strangler was right-handed. Whereas we know that Banda is very much a left-hander.'

'So that's why you didn't want to be around when Internal Affairs came to read the files? You knew they'd ask why we were holding Banda if there was clear evidence to exonerate him. So why didn't they?'

'Firstly, because Novák kindly gave me a replacement report which I put into the file. And secondly…' Slonský produced a folded sheet from his inside breast pocket.

'What's that, sir?'

'Insurance, lad.'

'You didn't even show me this version. All that time you were putting the frighteners on Banda, you knew that he hadn't done it. Why, sir?'

'Oh, come on, Navrátil! How often do you get to arrest your own boss? I couldn't let a chance like that pass me by. Don't look so po-faced. I've never been as popular at the station as when we gave Banda a hard time. And don't forget it worked. He confessed to the affair, and before that he'd been a hard little nugget. And on top of that, it's true that Banda hadn't strangled her with his own hands, but he could have hired someone else.'

'So why have we let him go, sir, if he could have hired a killer?'

'That's your fault, Navrátil.'

'My fault, sir?'

'Yes. Or at least you and Klinger. But mainly you. You're too sharp for your own good, my boy. You gave me the security footage from the bank. Now, Dr Sammler is a technophile. He likes having all the best kit, and his bank has some of the finest security money can buy, including some high-definition video cameras. You and I watched that footage, and you concentrated on the time and date. But I watched his hands, Navrátil.'

'His hands, sir?'

'Navrátil, you'll have to curb this irritating habit of repeating what I've just said as a question. Yes, his hands. The picture doesn't let us see the notes, but we can see that the teller is counting them out. What's the biggest note in circulation, lad?'

'Five thousand crowns, sir.'

'That's right. So to make up two hundred and forty-nine thousand, two hundred and fifty crowns, what's the minimum number of notes you could use?'

'Well, I … five times ten is fifty … then you'd need … er.'

'I'll save you the trouble, son. You need forty-nine notes to make two hundred and forty-five thousand, then a pair of two thousand crown notes, a two hundred note, and a fifty. However you look at it, you can't do it in less than fifty-three notes. That's why it was such a fat bundle in the little plastic bag Novák showed us. But if you watch the cashier counting it out, there are nothing like fifty-three moves. I've counted them several times, and the best guess I have is that she gives him nineteen notes. That would be consistent with eight lots of five thousand, nine one thousand crown notes, a two hundred and a fifty. That's forty nine thousand, two hundred and fifty, exactly what Banda says he drew out. Why would he pick that particular number if he was lying? So far as I can tell, he really was giving her the money for the car, and no doubt she was grateful and that's why they finished up in bed. It makes no sense at all for him to kill her half an hour later. And if I teach you anything at all while you're with me, Navrátil, I'll settle for this. Criminals don't usually do things that make no sense. It may make no sense to you or me, granted, but they have their reasons for what they do, just like you and me. The big problem is that most of us have a crowd of people who have a reason to kill us. Looking for a person with a motive doesn't help in that sense. But if a suspect doesn't have a motive, they probably didn't do it.' Slonský chomped contentedly on his last mouthful. 'Unless they're a psychopath, of course,' he added. 'Then my theory is stuffed.'

Much to Slonský's surprise, there was a note waiting for him when they returned.

'I only wrote it down,' said Mucha. 'I'm not responsible if it makes no sense.'

'Oh, it makes perfect sense,' said Slonský. 'Who'd have thought Adamec would have had it in him? Mind you, it's taken him weeks to get round to it.'

Navrátil stretched his neck trying to read the note, but Slonský stuffed it in his pocket and charged up the stairs.

'Navrátil, go and see your friend Klinger and ask him if he knows who Gold Lion Property Investments are. If he doesn't, ask him to find out. If I'm not in the office, ring me when you get the answer. I'm going to make an appointment.'

Navrátil did as he was asked. Klinger called up an online database and clicked a few times.

'Why does Slonský want to know?' he asked.

'I don't know, sir. He had a message from the Strahov police station and immediately sent me to see you.'

'Strahov? Isn't that where the young woman lived?'

'Yes, sir.'

'Then I know why he wants to know. And so should you, Navrátil.'

Klinger wrote some names on a sheet of paper and passed them to Navrátil.

'Those are the directors of Gold Lion Property Investments. But I believe that only one of them will interest Slonský. And the other is just a stooge to keep the thing legal, I think.'

Slonský was invited to enter and led through to Sammler's inner office, a curious little cubicle behind his main office. There were no windows and the walls were painted black. Sammler sat in his shirtsleeves at a functional desk and invited Slonský to take the other chair. The personal assistant closed the door as he left.

'It's a bit claustrophobic, isn't it, sir?'

'I don't find it so, Lieutenant. I can do a lot of work here, generally free from interruptions. I'm sorry, that sounded ungracious. I know you have a job to do and you were good enough to make an appointment. What can I do for you?'

'I need to tidy up a few puzzling snippets of information, sir.'

'That sounds ominous,' Sammler smiled. 'Do I need my lawyer here?'

'Only if you have something to hide, sir.'

'Then fire away, Lieutenant.'

'I should begin by saying that everything I have with me is a copy, sir. I'm not allowed to bring the originals out of the evidence store.'

'Of course.'

'You see, sir, when we received a photograph of Dr Banda with Miss Gruberová, our scientific team told us that the envelope had been printed by someone who had not attempted to put the haček in our address. That led us to wonder if the sender was not a Czech.'

'There must be a lot of non-Czechs in Prague, Lieutenant. One sees them everywhere.'

'Indeed you do, sir. Not so many tourists in February, of course. Then we were able to narrow down the time of Miss Gruberová's death. Dr Banda told us that he had left her some time before that. He had an alibi provided by his wife.'

'Surely times of death are only approximate, Lieutenant. And don't wives often give their husbands alibis, wittingly or unwittingly?'

'No doubt, sir. But we were a little confused as to why Miss Gruberová let her murderer into her flat. If Dr Banda killed her, then he made love to her, waited an hour or so, then killed her, dumped her body and went home. His cellphone gives him a better alibi, because he used it at 22:48 that evening, and it was within fifty metres of his house when he did so. We can track that by some technical jiggery-pokery I don't begin to understand, sir.'

'I do, Lieutenant. You can tell which particular mast he was nearest to when he made the call. By triangulation you can work it very precisely. So that lets Dr Banda out. But what has that to do with me?'

'Well, no matter how friendly a young woman is, I doubt she'd answer her door at midnight. I was surprised that there were so few signs of a struggle. Just a few bits of leather under her nails where she had clawed at a pair of black gloves. It seems logical to suppose those were the murderer's gloves, don't you think, sir?'

'I suppose so. She'd wash her hands before bed, no doubt, so the leather must have got under her nails after that.'

'No doubt, sir. I'm glad you agree. To return to the question of why she let her murderer in, the answer, of course, is that she didn't. He didn't need her to, because he already had a key. Most landlords keep a spare key, don't they, sir?'

'Do they?'

'Miss Gruberová didn't pay any rent, so far as we could see. Dr Banda's bank accounts don't show any sign of any rent being paid. It looks as if the kindly landlord was letting the young lady live there rent-free. So I wondered who these paragons were, and we discovered that the flat is registered in the name of Gold Lion Property Investments.'

'And you will have discovered, I'm sure, that I am one of the directors of Gold Lion Property Investments.'

'Just so, sir. It's very good of you to help a young lady like this.'

'The young lady was incidental, Lieutenant. I was helping Dr Banda. He was very grateful. It does no harm to have a sympathetic hearing from a politician or two. And I may have a key, but I rather doubt it. I own quite a lot of property, and the keys are kept by a management agency who do all the spadework for me. Perhaps they could tell you who had it. I'm sure they keep records; I'd be very upset if they didn't. I'll give you their name.'

'Thank you, sir. Then Miss Gruberová's body was taken to the rear of the train station at Holešovice and dumped there. A beige German car was seen in the area at around the time the body was left.'

'Seen "around the time", Lieutenant? That's a bit vague, isn't it? And no doubt a German car led you to think there must be a German driver, so here you are. I'm sure there are quite a few German cars in Prague. And mine is registered here.'

'We didn't have a registration number with the sighting, sir. We don't know where the car was registered. Just that it was a German make. Let's move on a little. The body was left in the early hours of Wednesday, 8th February. This is a DVD taken from your country house's security system, sir. It shows you arriving there at 03:48 on that morning. Here's a still of you leaving your car. I note you're wearing black gloves, sir.'

'So I am. I own a lot of pairs of gloves, Lieutenant, but you're welcome to search the house for them.'

'I doubt we'll find them, sir. I'm sure whoever the murderer was, he'll have burned the gloves long ago.'

'And I wonder how you obtained this DVD, Lieutenant. Would it be admissible in court, do you think?'

'Your security company volunteered it, sir. May I compliment you on the clarity of the pictures, sir? It's a very good system.'

'German, of course. I own the company. If you ever want one, I could get you a special price.'

'Very kind, sir. I doubt the police would allow me to accept, unfortunately. And I don't have anything worth stealing.'

'Personal safety is important, Lieutenant. Allow me to point out that if Miss Gruberová had owned a security system you'd have had video of whoever it was entering her flat.'

'Yes, but allow me to point out that the murderer doesn't seem to have worried about that — as if he knew there wasn't one there, wouldn't you say?'

'Your words, not mine. Maybe he just wasn't of a suspicious nature.'

'Maybe. Oh, I almost forgot. Your city flat has a very good security system too, doesn't it? It recorded your car leaving the car park that night at 22.16. That's a little late to be going out, isn't it, sir?'

'Is it? I don't sleep very well. And it was a night like any other. I can't remember why I went out on that particular night at that particular time, before you ask.'

'Then we have the curious matter of Dr Banda's withdrawal from your bank. I'm obliged to my assistant for this part. You see, Navrátil doesn't know much about banks, so he asked our fraud expert to describe what happens once someone fills in a withdrawal slip. That slip, by the way, can't be found.'

'It happens. There are thousands of them. We lose the odd one here and there.'

'You see, Dr Banda's bank statement shows that he withdrew two hundred and forty-nine thousand, two hundred and fifty crowns. Exactly the same amount was found in Miss Gruberová's vagina. Leaving aside the question of why the murderer didn't steal it, unless he had plenty of money of his own, the coincidence is striking, isn't it? It clearly pointed at Dr Banda. Except that Dr Banda is adamant that he only withdrew forty-nine thousand, two hundred and fifty crowns, precisely the amount he had promised Miss Gruberová to buy her a car. Now, our expert says that if this was a mistake by the teller, it would have been discovered at the end-of-day reconciliation, whatever that is.'

'It's when we add up all the money that went in or out and check that it tallies with the amounts in hand at the end of the shift.'

'Thank you. I'm learning a lot today. So Klinger deduces that the alteration took place after the withdrawal slip went through to the back office. And to alter that someone would need some pretty serious authorisation rights on your computer system. I'm not clear why the alteration was made, unless it was to make it absolutely certain that we would link the withdrawal with the vaginal deposit. After all, Banda might have used a bit of it to get himself a bar of chocolate.'

'Naturally, the bank will be very keen to get to the bottom of this unauthorised withdrawal. I can guarantee our full co-operation with any inquiry.'

'I'll pass that on to Mr Klinger, sir. And Dr Banda will be keen to see his money returned.'

'If he can show that he only withdrew the smaller sum, that will follow as a matter of course.'

'I've spoken to the teller involved, sir. She supports his claim.'

'That's very helpful.'

'Then we come to the second photograph we received, which you may recall. It was taken at your country home.'

'How could I forget that?'

'It can't be easy, sir. A very limited number of people could have access to your security system to produce that photograph, wouldn't you say, sir?'

'Apparently not. You got one easily enough from the company. How do we know who else was able to do so?'

'Then there's the question of who knew there would be a picture there worth collecting. Mr Soucha told me he met Mario at a party. What he didn't tell me, but I have subsequently discovered, was that you were there too.'

'Was I? I don't particularly like parties, Lieutenant, but I have to go to a lot. It wouldn't surprise me if most of Prague had been at a party with me at some time.'

'But the thing that really puzzles me, sir, is why this photograph was sent to me? Homosexuality isn't illegal. And if the aim was to discredit Mr Soucha, surely the press would be more interested than the police. Then I thought it was a particularly crafty idea, because if I showed the picture to Soucha, as I was certain to do, he would know that this would hang over him all his days, so it would give a blackmailer real power. But the problem with that argument is that it works much better if he just sends the photograph to Soucha directly, because he avoids even the slight chance that I might put it in the bin. Not to mention that it's an unusual blackmailer who doesn't give the victim any way of getting in touch with him. Without a line of communication, how can there be blackmail?'

'It's a fascinating conundrum, Lieutenant. When you find the answer, perhaps you'll put me out of this suspense.'

'I think I've got the answer, sir. But bear with me a moment. I just want to have a little chat about the third envelope. This one contained some documents showing that Leoš Holec had been creaming off large sums into a foreign bank account. I'm sure you know Mr Holec, sir.'

'Certainly I do, and I must say I'm very surprised. He's a respected adviser to the government.'

'Yes, it does seem strange. What seems even stranger is that he keeps very detailed notes of his transactions, not being a practised criminal. It never occurred to him to hide the evidence. Thus he was able to tell us that these sums were payments from an Austrian investment trust called Salzburger Prudent Investment Trust. The curious thing is that the Austrian authorities say that this trust was closed some years ago. Its official address was at the head office of your bank, sir. Somehow it has continued to make payments when it no longer has any known bank accounts. How can that happen?'

'It's hard to see. Every transaction must have a counter-balancing transaction.'

'Yes. Of course, our Mr Klinger wondered if there is an alias account somewhere containing these balancing transactions that will never be claimed because actually nobody really owns it. It might be discovered one day on an audit, but that's a remote chance really. The samples are so small compared with the number of accounts you have. You could take samples for a generation and never hit on this one. And if you did, what would it prove? An oddity, certainly, but not definite illegality. I suppose it would have to be a fairly senior official in the bank who was able to keep issuing payments against an account that didn't really exist.'

'Someone like me, you mean.'

'I couldn't possibly say, sir. I'm completely untutored in the ways of banks.'

Sammler rocked back in his chair and gave a slight, tolerant smile.

'All right, let us suppose that I am some sort of criminal mastermind who kills a young woman and frames a friend for it. I admit none of this, it goes without saying, but let's play at pretending.'

Slonský smiled encouragingly.

'Yes, sir, that would be good.'

'The question you haven't answered is — why?'

'You're absolutely right, sir. I haven't explained why. I was hoping you might do that, sir.'

'And how could I know why someone would do this?'

'I thought we were playing at pretending, sir. Make something up. You see, I can only see one plausible reason for it. But it sounded so bizarre that I needed someone to confirm that it could be correct. That's why I interviewed your father yesterday, sir.'

The effect of this statement on Sammler was very gratifying, thought Slonský. He looked shocked and concerned, however fleetingly, before recovering his composure.

'You will have heard that my father and I are estranged, Lieutenant. I'm not sure that he is an unbiased source where my shortcomings are under discussion.'

'No, sir. But he didn't argue about the underlying basis of what I think happened. You see, I think the key to understanding this chain of events is the picture of Soucha. Why would anyone send me that? The Vice Squad, possibly. The press, certainly. What can I do that the press can't do more efficiently to humiliate Soucha just as Banda was humiliated? The only possible answer is that I can put someone in court. If someone's plan was to get these three men into court, then there must be some illegality that I'm not spotting about Soucha and Mario. And the only idea that came to me is that Mario is younger than he looks. If our correspondent knew that Mario was under age, and could produce Mario after the story hit the press, that would really cause Soucha some problems, wouldn't it? First he is exposed as a gay man, then it turns out that Mario is under age, so the police's hand would be pretty well forced, wouldn't it? We'd have to prosecute or the tabloids would never give us a moment's rest. Then there's just too much evidence against Banda for us not to charge him too. It doesn't really matter whether we can make it stick or not, because the stench will follow even if a charge doesn't. And there's poor Holec. Maybe what he did wasn't illegal, or not intentionally so, but it certainly looks bad, and our fraud colleagues can't ignore the sums involved. That's the link between them.'

'How inventive!' said Sammler. 'I'm finding this very entertaining. Do go on with this nonsense.'

'A government minister, a senior opposition politician, a civil servant, all in the dock. They're all as bad as each other. The whole system is rotten to the core. It all has to happen in a short time or the public might not jump to that conclusion. But if all three were on trial at the same time, that would really damage the system, wouldn't it? And that brings us to the little difficulty I had earlier. I knew who did it, but I couldn't work out why. And the why is now clear to me. Our murderer did it all to discredit the whole Czech political system. It took years of planning, slowly building up trust so that it could be betrayed, accumulating the cash for a very expensive series of pay-offs, giving free apartments to curry favour, but it would all be worthwhile if he could finally be proved right. If he could show that his former colleagues had been justified, if he could complete their work to deliver what he wanted, the millions of crowns would have been well spent. If people lost faith in their democratic institutions, then the ideological war that appeared lost for so long could be fired up again. The only question left is: who would do such a thing? An hour with your father, and I knew the answer to that. Am I right, sir?'

'I'm not a litigious man, Lieutenant, but you will realise that if you repeated this outside this room I would be entirely justified in suing you for defamation.'

'Yes, sir. Although, of course, it is a defence that I can show my claims to be substantially true and in the public interest.'

'Can you? Can you really, Lieutenant?'

Sammler's voice was louder, more forceful, slightly higher pitched as stress began to pull at his vocal cords.

'You've heard the evidence, sir.'

'Ah, yes, so I have. It boils down to a piece of video showing I went out late, but you don't know where. Another piece of video proving I went to my other house, and it was the early hours before I got there, but you don't know where I was between these times. You have no forensic results. You have a bank statement proving that a customer took money out of his account in my bank — so what? That's what it's there for. The withdrawal slip is missing, which could be suspicious, but since you don't have it, that's going to be fairly hard to establish, don't you think? You know that I rented the flat to Dr Banda's mistress and you don't know how she paid for it. It was a favour, Lieutenant. It makes me a good guy. I lent my home to another man who betrayed that trust by using my house for some tawdry coupling with an unknown person. And even if I pointed the finger at Holec, aren't I the sheriff in the white hat hunting down evil in its many forms?'

'I'm sure we'd all be very grateful for your public-spirited action, sir, if that was your motive. But I think your motive was very different. It's an elaborate plot requiring resources that hardly anyone else in Prague could bring to bear. To pull it off you'd have to be rich, well-connected and totally committed to the cause. And you're all those things.'

'I had a youthful flirtation with some excitable fringe groups. A lot of people did, but they didn't all become ideologically committed communists.'

Slonský nodded his agreement.

'That's what makes you special, sir. You did. You started as one, and unlike so many after the Wall came down, you remained one.'

'And your evidence for this is…?'

'Twenty years of working with people just like that. You get to know the type. Of course, a lot of our homegrown communists have either seen the light or gone to jail. There are still a few around, but they're losing hope, don't you think?'

Sammler's answer came back just a little too quickly.

'There are more about than you would think, Lieutenant. There's nothing to be ashamed of in wanting to bring about a more equitable distribution of wealth. If that's a crime, I'll gladly plead guilty.'

'Of course not, sir. I'd sign up for that myself, especially since a lot of people have more than me. But the Czech Republic has tried communism and decided it doesn't like it.'

'No, Slonský, it tried a watered-down imitation of communism. It tolerated a cadre of opportunists and incompetents. But when communism returns, this is exactly where it will start.'

Sammler spoke rapidly, occasionally mispronouncing the Czech words as he lectured his audience of one.

'The Czech Republic has a long tradition of social democracy and left-wing politics. Between the wars there was solid support for proletarian social justice. Remember that this was the only country where communism was voted in at a free election after the war. Look at the 1946 election. Over forty per cent of Czechs voted communist, and over thirty per cent of Slovaks. We didn't even have to cheat. The President nominated a communist Prime Minister. Around one in every four adult Czechs was a party member. Nobody made them do that! They believed in the cause. It's in their blood, Slonský. Give them leadership, and they'll be the first to return to the fold. One more push, a firm line from the top, serious socialist reform, and this will once again be the socialist nation it used to be. And once socialism has a beachhead in Europe, it can recapture the hearts and minds of the many who have become disillusioned with Western-style democracy. All those millions who struggle every day and watch the few amassing great fortunes and blowing them in a tasteless display of conspicuous consumption. And they will be grateful to the Czech people for leading them back to the road to socialist equality. The Czechs embraced communism, Lieutenant.'

'With respect, sir, that was before they'd tried something else. A generation has only known capitalism, and they seem to like it.'

'Like it? How can they like what their country has become?'

Sammler had jumped out of his chair and was animatedly addressing Slonský as if he were a large, sceptical crowd.

'Look at Prague! The big glitzy shops, the clubs, the bars. And, in front of them, the beggars kneeling for a crust. All those new cars, some built here, but Czech only in name, because everything that matters is in foreign hands. All those tourists coming here — is it for the culture, to admire the Czech contribution to civilisation? Of course not. They come for cheap beer and sex clubs. Is that what your bourgeois Czech Republic wants to be, Slonský? Are you proud that your young women are the easiest in Europe, that so many of them earn a living in this way? Have you seen that vile place in Smíchov, "Big Sister"? A brothel where everything is free because people pay to watch what you do live on the internet. A city with the history and culture that Prague has, and it's known to the world because you can watch tarts being screwed there from anywhere you like. Is that "success", Slonský? Is it "reform"? Is it what Havel and those other idiots fought for? In all those underground years were they itching to turn their country into a place where English yobs come to drink cheap beer and paw Czech women? Can you picture them plotting in their squalid little rooms to fill Prague with unemployment and all-night casinos? I didn't make those men behave badly. I didn't trick them. They did what they were going to do anyway. All I did was bring it into the light.'

'I'd have no quarrel with that if Irina Gruberová was still alive.'

'That stupid bitch! If she had co-operated and sold her story to the press she would still be alive now. She was willing to take Banda's money for the car, and let Banda pay for the flat. And when I pointed out that I paid for her flat and if I took it away Banda couldn't do a thing about it — and he wouldn't try anyway — she threatened to go to the police. With what, I asked? A complaint that I'd offered to make her rich by telling the truth? She said that Banda was a good man and she loved him, and he was going to leave his wife and marry her. As if! Then she said she would accuse me of breaking in and assaulting her. She began tearing her clothes and was going to scream. As if I'd be interested in molesting a dirty little cow like her. The only thing she loved was my money, so I helped her make love to my money.'

Sammler fell silent, and the awkwardness of the quiet in the room caused him to subside into the chair.

'Would you like to put that in a statement, sir?' asked Slonský.

'Of course not,' Sammler replied. 'I won't say any of that outside this room.'

'How do you know I didn't record it, sir?'

'You wouldn't have got into this room with a wire on your body. It's a special shielded chamber, and the small corridor behind my main office door contains all sorts of scanning equipment. As you enter, I know you're clean. You didn't record, and if you repeat it I'll just tell everyone you've made it up. As I proved to you before, you don't have a shred of evidence. You'll never prove it, and I'll never go to court. One day, this country will return to the true path, and I may be able to do you some good. Remember that, Slonský.'

Slonský picked up his hat and stood up.

'I'll be long since retired, sir. And I don't think I want someone like you to do me any good. I'll see myself out, sir.'

Slonský had not talked to himself since his childhood, but he drew some curious looks from passers-by as he stormed along the road towards the metro. People who swear and mumble often do. He was annoyed with himself for letting Sammler know that he had only circumstantial evidence against him, and although Sammler had lost his temper and said more than he might have planned, he could use none of it in court. Without Navrátil there, he had no witnesses either, but then if Navrátil had been there Sammler would have clammed up.

Maybe he didn't lose his temper, thought Slonský? He heated up and cooled down very quickly, yet he is supposed to be very self-contained and controlled. Maybe it was for show. Maybe he wanted me to understand the link between the cases because he was worried that no-one was getting it.

But if he couldn't nail Sammler, what then? That was the really uncomfortable part, because Slonský knew there was a bit of truth in Sammler's claim that the Czechs were egalitarian by nature. It was quite likely that if communism was going to make a comeback in Europe, Prague would have to be the starting point, because if you couldn't foment socialist revolution there, you would never do it anywhere else. And Sammler had started a snowball that might become an avalanche. If those three men appeared in court, the people might very well decide that the whole system was not worth preserving. Slonský closed his eyes to visualise where the future was taking him. How would Navrátil fare if he had to go through the years Slonský had himself faced? What would happen to all that Slonský had learned and worked for? Somehow he had to derail Sammler's plan. He had to stop the three stories hitting the press at the same time. As the escalator carried him up to street level, an idea came to him.

Slonský took out his cellphone and notebook. He had never liked keeping numbers on the phone in case it got lost, not to mention that he did not know how to enter them anyway, so he needed to riffle through the black book to find the number he wanted. To his relief, it was answered quickly. Time was of the essence, and there was not enough of it to allow him to think through his next steps. He had to work by instinct. But his instinct had rarely let him down before.

Chapter 23

The morning newspaper was a sensation. The photograph was reproduced in gorgeous colour right in the middle of the front page, though decency required that so much was blacked out that it could have shown almost anything.

Valentin was looking more than a little self-satisfied as he held court in his favourite chair, acknowledging the fellow journalists who came up to ask if there were any more revelations to come, particularly any more photographs of Soucha, and how he had ferreted this information out.

'Happy?' asked Slonský, as he slipped into a chair by Valentin's side.

'Contract should be in the bag, thanks. I knew I could count on you.'

'That's not what you said the other day.'

'I was under stress. I wasn't feeling myself. I had every confidence that my old mate wouldn't let me down. And that was a lulu. I wasn't expecting the go-ahead to print that.'

'Just remember you never spoke to me about it. Our copy is under lock and key at the office and no doubt the concerned citizen who sent it in sent you an entirely separate copy. I almost drew a moustache on him so people would know it wasn't our photo you'd got hold of.'

'Glad you didn't. It was fun trying to stick the black rectangles on so you couldn't see what he was doing but you knew who he was.'

'Have you heard from Soucha?'

'No. Surprising how quickly you can get a flight if you need to. We gave him an hour's start, unofficially. I think he may have gone to Turkey, but it doesn't matter. The key thing is that I got my scoop, and the editor is happy as a pig in poo.'

Slonský made to get up, but Valentin grabbed his arm.

'In view of the extreme joy of this occasion, I am prepared to buy you a large beer of your choice, with my own money. How about that, then?'

'Old friend, I would love to accept your kind offer, which I realise may never come my way again. I've waited thirty years for it, and I probably won't live another thirty. But your story should have started a tidal wave, and I need to be in the office to watch the ripples hit the beach.'

'There aren't any beaches in Prague. We're landlocked.'

'Then I'll have to look all the harder. But there will be ripples, Valentin. I don't know what will happen, but something will.'

Slonský sat patiently as Lukas read the morning paper.

'I'm appalled. Of course, the man will have to resign. As you say, this changes things.'

'If I'm right, sir, Dr Sammler must be very angry now. His plot needs all three stories in the news at once, and he held this one back from the press to maximise the impact. Now one story will be a nine days' wonder, over and done with before the other two get anywhere. He knows now that Banda won't be charged, and although Holec will be, a fraud trial takes months to set up.'

'Especially when Klinger is writing it up,' agreed Lukas. 'He'll want to cross-reference and index every item of evidence he has.'

'So the fact that this has unaccountably got into the press takes the timetable out of Sammler's hands, and I can't see how he can get control again.'

Lukas sucked the leg of his spectacles in deep thought.

'I'm not quite so sure that I would use the word "unaccountably", Slonský. I trust this department is not connected to that development?'

'Only Navrátil and I have access to the original, sir, and it's safely locked in my filing cabinet. Of course, copies may have been made in the lab. Who can tell where it came from? We'll probably never know.'

'So what does Sammler do now?'

'It's a little hard to say, sir. I've never been a fanatic or a murderer. But he can't influence the Gruberová or Holec cases, unless he decides to confess to killing Irina, which I think is unlikely. I think he has two alternatives. As I've told you, he knows I'm on his trail, so he may try to discredit me in some way to take his revenge, or he may realise that the game is up and that his plan failed.'

'Be careful, Josef. If you're right and he has already killed once, who knows how he will get his revenge on you? I think you should carry your gun, just in case.'

'I've got it on me, sir.'

'And have you remembered to put a magazine in it?'

'Brand new, never been used, sir.'

'Good man. Don't take this the wrong way, but you might want to think about checking it actually works. I doubt you'll have cleaned it for a while.'

Slonský took it from its holster and placed it on the desk for inspection. Lukas deftly checked it over.

'I'm very cautious about my own safety, sir,' explained Slonský.

'Good. Tell Navrátil to do the same. I wouldn't put it past Sammler to punish you by taking it out on Navrátil.'

Slonský's heart gave a little skip. That thought had not occurred to him. He could live with being dead, but having to carry the guilt of Navrátil's early demise would be a real burden.

'I will, sir. In fact, I'll do it now, sir.'

'You do that. I'm going to see the Director. If Sammler decides to try to frame you, it would be as well to launch a pre-emptive move by making sure the Director knows why that might be happening.'

'Thank you, sir. Sammler will be desperate. Who knows what he might do?'

'Who indeed? Anything is possible with a man like that.'

Navrátil was sucking the top of his pencil in rapt contemplation of a set of particulars supplied by letting agents.

'Didn't your mother tell you not to suck pencils, or the lead will go your nose and enter your brain?' asked Slonský.

'She may have done,' agreed Navrátil. 'She warned me against all kinds of unlikely accidents. If I'm ever shot on duty I've got to get someone to check my underwear is clean before they take me to hospital.'

'Funny you should mention that,' commented Slonský. 'What's your shooting like?'

'I doubt I could match the Cat-Murdering Priest of Žižkov, sir, but if I'm ever attacked by a cardboard cut-out of a man, I'll be okay.'

'Good. Get your gun cleaned, oiled, loaded and on you. We don't know what Sammler will do next and whatever it is, I don't want him doing it to you.'

'Actually, sir, I think we do know. Valentin rang. He'd like you to call him back.'

'Call? Not meet? Where do I call him? He doesn't have a mobile.'

'He's at the newspaper, sir. The number is on your desk by the telephone.'

'Valentin? At the newspaper office? During daylight?'

Slonský dialled and asked to speak to the reporter, who sounded sober. In fact, he sounded scared and sober.

'Thank God you rang. Something very odd is happening here. I've had a phone call inviting me to follow up my story this morning. A young man called claiming to be Mario. He says he'll meet me at Kobylisy metro station if I come alone.'

'Did he have an accent?'

'Not really.'

'"Not really"? What kind of answer is that? Either he did or he didn't. Soucha said Mario was Austrian. Where did he get that from unless Mario had an accent?'

'I don't know. Look, all I want to know is whether it's safe to go.'

'I can't tell you that. We know Sammler must be rattled. I thought that if I couldn't stop his plan, I could mess it up by speeding one part along. Feeding you Mario now is probably a way of trying to regain the initiative. I'm just wary that it may be a stand-in, because we don't know where Mario has been. But you've got a photo of him, so you can check if he looks like the right young man.'

'Oh, great!' scoffed Valentin. 'I can hardly unfold that in the middle of the street to see if he looks right, can I?'

'Then scan it in, blow it up or do whatever you need to do to get a good image.'

'I can't improve a picture that actually doesn't show Mario's face clearly anyway. The attention is on Soucha — his face is plain as day. Mario's head is thrown back and to the side so you barely see it.'

'Then use your wits. Try asking a question or two, like proper journalists would. I can't see Sammler trying anything in a public place like a metro station. After all, if this is the real Mario he wants that story told. Just refuse to get into any cars. Stay in public. I'll get a few undercover police there. They won't be able to bring rifles, but they'll have handguns. We'll send them by metro rather than by car. When are you meeting?'

'Fifty minutes from now.'

Slonský growled down the line. 'Fifty minutes? Give us some notice, Valentin. It doesn't give me long to put this in place.'

'Hardly my fault. I rang half an hour ago but apparently you were kissing someone's backside.'

'Reporting to my chief and kissing his backside are two entirely separate things. Well, different, anyway. Just get there and we'll sort something out. Keep in touch.'

Slonský barked some orders at Navrátil and swept out of the room, flinging his coat over his shoulders as he went. Navrátil was a little put out, because he had no idea where he was going to find six guys with plain clothes and revolvers. However, the name Mucha came to mind.

Whatever happened at Kobylisy, Slonský had no intention of being there. If there is a trap, he thought, the one person they will be looking out for is me. The one person they might risk shooting in public is me. Not only that, the sausages are much better in town. If Slonský faced imminent death, he had no plans to die on an empty stomach. He was gnawing on a pork rib when his phone rang.

'Navrátil? You okay?'

'I'm fine. Nothing happened.'

'You mean he didn't turn up.'

'No, he showed as planned. And if it isn't Mario it's a very good lookalike.'

'So what's the story?'

Navrátil paused. His mouth sounded dry as if he did not want to tell the tale.

'Mario is a Roma boy.'

'You say "boy"? How old?'

'Nineteen.'

Slonský relaxed a little.

'But he's a ward of court. It seems he has personality problems so his parents couldn't cope with him and being on the move all the time meant he wasn't getting his treatment. He was in a home until he was seventeen, then he ran away. They caught him and put him under legal protection.'

'So how did Sammler find him?'

'Mario doesn't recognise the name Sammler. He says that his home found him a job but he doesn't like being indoors all day. Then someone said he would give him a job looking after horses. All he had to do was to say that his uncle was coming for him. One day he was called into the director's office and a man he had never seen before was waiting to take him to the horses.'

'And the home didn't check?'

'Doesn't sound like it. I've spoken to the woman in charge. She says she wasn't involved —'

'Funny how they never are.'

'— but the man seemed respectable, had some papers that seemed to show that he knew Mario, and Mario didn't say he didn't know him.'

'Because Mario was thinking about life with horses again. So does he know where he was taken?'

'Not a clue. He's actually not slow-witted. He just hasn't had much schooling and he gets angry because he can't express himself, says Valentin.'

'How did Mario get to the metro?'

'He says his uncle dropped him by car nearby and told him to wait there until he was collected at lunchtime.'

'And did we follow him when he left?'

'He got into a taxi that was already occupied. Olbracht tailed him on his bike but lost them. When he found the taxi again, it had a different fare. The driver told him he set them down at Florenc.'

'So they could have gone almost anywhere in Prague. Damn! What about Valentin?'

'He says he'll meet you in the cellar, and you would know where he meant.'

'Yes, I do. I only hope I get there in time.'

'You think he's in danger?'

'Yes, but I also think he's planning on getting very drunk.'

In fact, Valentin was relatively sober when Slonský arrived, having been collected by Navrátil on the way.

'Don't ever give me a scoop again,' he whined. 'My nerves won't stand it.'

'You wanted it,' said Slonský.

'That was before I knew I was going to get threatened over it.'

'Threatened? Who threatened you?'

'Mario said his uncle wanted me to tell his story, and I had to do that even if you tried to stop me, otherwise his uncle would be very angry with me.'

Slonský had a coffee, having once more refused a beer. Valentin wondered if he was sickening for something. Slonský stirred it slowly with his spoon, having dumped a ridiculous amount of sugar in it.

'You going to drink that or ice a cake with it?' Valentin asked.

'Hush, I'm thinking. Tell me what Mario said about himself.'

'He said he was nineteen, under the Court of Protection, has to see someone regularly, doesn't know where he lives. What else do you want to know?'

'When did he meet uncle?'

'End of last year. He says it was before the snow came.'

'That could be August in some places. He can't do better than that?'

'No. But he says it wasn't too far from here. Originally he came from somewhere to the east, because he remembers being taken to Frýdek-Místek as a boy. He thought it was a funny name.'

'Did you show him the photo?'

'I showed him the censored version from the newspaper. He thought it was funny.'

'Funny? Why funny?'

'Well, because they hadn't got any clothes on.'

'Did you ask him what happened in that swimming pool?'

'No, because it seemed unkind when someone had taken advantage of a young man to put him in that position.'

'You idiot! You empty-headed, balding drunken idiot!' snapped Slonský.

Valentin was more than a little hurt.

'I'm not balding,' he complained. 'Thinning a bit on top, maybe. But not balding.'

'That's not Mario! Damn! I should have seen this.'

'Seen what?' asked Navrátil.

'He'd probably told the real Mario to make himself scarce, so the chances are he couldn't find him again in a hurry. Even if he knows where he is, he's probably back in Austria waiting to be summoned when the occasion arose. There wasn't enough time between my seeing Sammler and your story appearing for him to get Mario back. But Sammler had a spare Mario up his sleeve. He probably spotted there's enough resemblance to pass a quick inspection, given that we don't have really detailed photographs of Mario. But he invited you, with no photographer. That's what he meant by alone. He wasn't warning off the police particularly — he wanted you to come without a photographer. No photos, no video, just your word for it that you'd met Mario.'

'Well, how was I to know? I never met the original Mario.'

'Exactly. But Sammler knew that if Mario 2 just told the truth about himself, that would be your story. And he frightened you into publishing it, because that generates the crime that hadn't been committed before.'

'Come again?'

'I told Sammler that the Soucha picture didn't show a crime. Sammler didn't know that the age of consent for these things is fifteen here. But if Mario is under the Court of Protection, Sammler doesn't need a crime. He just broadcasts what a scandal it is that the Czech Republic can't protect its mentally-deficient people from this kind of abuse. It becomes a story about Soucha taking advantage of a simpleton and the State not being sharp enough to prevent it. Damn!'

Navrátil was confused. 'How do you know it's not the same person, sir?'

'I know some youngsters with mental problems are uninhibited, but they know what they've done. Mario didn't react as if he knew what was happening in the photo. But more to the point, the photo was taken in the summer — remember the flowers? — whereas Mario says he met uncle before the snow came. If he's a Roma boy, he'll know the seasons. "Before the snow" is late autumn, not summer. Mario 2 was a late addition to the plan. More likely, he's Plan B, to be fished out if Plan A went tits up.'

'So what happens if I write that he was an impostor?' asked Valentin.

'Sammler gets angry. We need to keep you safe somewhere.'

'So what if I write that he wasn't an impostor?'

Slonský considered this option for a moment.

'You'd be an even worse journalist than I took you for. But I suppose Sammler would be happy, and it can't harm Soucha more than he's already hurt.'

'But it gives the initiative back to Sammler, sir,' protested Navrátil. 'How does that help us?'

'It gets him off Valentin's back. And Sammler might relax if he thinks the plan is back on track.'

'He can't relax, sir. He has to press it home while it's in people's minds.'

Slonský muttered a few words that he must have picked up in the street when he was younger.

'Okay, this is what we'll do. Valentin, get your editor to trail the story. Run something in tomorrow's edition saying you're going to have a really big story the day after. You can even say it's an astonishing development in the Soucha case. That should keep you safe, because Sammler won't polish you off when you've declared your intention of running the story he wants.'

'One extra day. Big deal. Pardon me if I don't turn cartwheels.'

'It's one extra day for you, but it's enough for us. Come on, we'll drop you by your office. Sleep there tonight.'

'Sleep in the office? How can you get any sleep in a newspaper office?'

'I'll buy you a nightcap.'

Slonský headed for the car while Navrátil and Valentin trotted along behind.

'Am I balding?' whispered Valentin. 'Would you call me balding?'

Chapter 24

Slonský rarely slept well, and his brain clicked over relentlessly as he rolled back and forth across his pillow. He recalled the first sight of Irina Gruberová's purple face, the grey snow beneath her, the policemen who refused to leave their warm car. Gruberová's eyes fixed on his, begging him to help her by catching her killer. He saw the body on the slab, the photograph of the intimate dinner, the look on Banda's face as he dropped his coffee cup into the evidence bag. Every moment of the enquiry was compressed into a single, short, restless night. Towards the end the visions started to cycle, always ending with a laughing Sammler walking free as Slonský found himself behind bars, looking out at a failure. He knew Sammler was guilty, but he could not prove it. And yet the evidence must be there somewhere. Whenever a crime was committed, evidence was left behind. All he had to do was find it. The proof is out there.

He turned his pillow over to find a cool side. Sammler is running this now. Sammler calls the tune, and we react to him; we have to wrest the initiative out of his hands and grab it for ourselves, Slonský told himself. But the Slonský in his dreams had no idea how that might be done. Putting the story in the newspaper bought them time, but it meant Sammler was still making the pace. Things were happening because he wanted them to. Slonský had to find something unexpected that threw Sammler's plan out of kilter. He pictured a smoothly running piece of black, antique machinery; pistons moved, cogs turned, steam hissed, and the machine pressed implacably on; Slonský had a large spanner and planned to push it into the gearing. He had no idea whether it would work or not, whether the engine might explode or even suck him in, but it was the only way of stopping the engine that he had. It had to be tried, because not to try was unimaginable. Slonský waved the spanner above his head like a banner, thrust it fearlessly into the slowest-moving gearwheels, and let go. That was when he woke up, and hence failed to discover what would happen if he did that.

Valentin's story ran as a lurid red splash across the corner of the front page. He had interviewed Mario, it said, and the exclusive interview would appear tomorrow, when they could devote enough space to do it justice. There would also be an exposé of the incompetent management of a certain young people's hostel, which one of Valentin's colleagues was working on.

Slonský was cleaning his gun once again. Parts littered the desk.

'Can you put that back together again?' Navrátil enquired.

'In my sleep,' said Slonský. 'It's pretty well all I did during my national service. Take them apart, put them together; take them apart, clean them, put them together.'

'Sir, I know it's not my place to question —'

'Then don't. Do I know what I'm doing? No. I'm flying by the seat of my pants. Last time he confessed, but there were no witnesses. This time there will be. He won't confess if he knows you're there, so I'll have to ensure that you aren't there. But you won't be far away. I'll be miked up and you'll be listening in.'

'Why don't we just bring him in, sir?'

'Because he'll shut up until his lawyer gets here, then they'll walk out of the door. Simple as that. If we want to nail him, he has to think it's an even game. He has to think he can taunt me with what he's done and get away with it.'

'Shouldn't you have a recorder, sir?'

'Too bulky. I couldn't use the recording anyway without a caution and all that jazz.'

'But you can't use my statement either.'

'I can if he doesn't object. And once he realises you've heard it, he'll know that the game is up. He can argue all he likes about circumstantial evidence, but if two policemen heard him confess, it's hard to claim he didn't.'

Navrátil nodded and got out of his seat.

'Can you give me ten minutes, sir?'

'Half an hour until we move off. Where are you going?'

Navrátil jerked his thumb.

'Church up the street, sir. Thought I might pop in and … collect my thoughts.'

Navrátil gently closed the door behind him.

'Say one for me while you're there,' mumbled Slonský.

Slonský telephoned Sammler's secretary to make an appointment. It was all terribly difficult, he was told. Unfortunately Dr Sammler had a string of very urgent appointments today. Slonský expressed the opinion that this might be a stalling tactic. How about 11:30? No, Sammler would be in a meeting with the Deputy Secretary at the Ministry of Finance. It started at 11:00 and was expect to last an hour. Then, after lunch, he had a meeting planned with some German businessmen who were funding a shopping mall. That couldn't possibly be postponed, because they were on their way there from Berlin. It would certainly take all afternoon until 16:30. Sadly, he would not be free then either, because he had to prepare for a speech he was giving at a dinner that evening for an Austro-Czech Society of some kind. Lunch? No, Prague Businessmen's Circle, meeting at 12:30 across the river. It would take time to get there and back given the traffic.

Slonský said that he understood, and that tomorrow would do. Half an hour should be more than sufficient. He had some new evidence that he needed to put to Dr Sammler that seemed to contradict the statement he gave the other day. A few moments later, Slonský had an appointment for 11:45 next morning. He allowed himself a small smile as he returned the handset to its cradle. The pressure on Sammler was building.

Navrátil was waiting by the car when Slonský emerged.

'Where to, sir?'

'City police office, District 1. It's on Letenská.'

'Why there, sir?'

'It's got a car park.'

Slonský climbed in, which seemed to leave little option for Navrátil but to do the same.

'Put your foot down, Navrátil. It would be good to be there by half past eleven.'

'Why, sir?'

'Navrátil, this investigation is henceforth being conducted on a need-to-know basis. And you don't need to know. At least, not yet. Patience, lad, patience.'

Navrátil pulled up by the police office and waited as he had been instructed. Slonský emerged after a few minutes with a uniformed city policeman and approached the car, motioning to Navrátil to wind the window down as he came closer.

'Right, Navrátil, listen carefully. I'll turn the mike on now. Can you hear it through your earpiece?'

'Yes, sir.'

'Good. I'm going to stand just past the bend there. This officer has his instructions. Your job is to follow me when I tell you. Is that clear?'

'You'll be in a car, then, sir?'

'That's the plan. Either that or I'll be running bloody fast to keep up with one.'

Slonský and the police officer marched up the street past the Ministry of Finance and disappeared from sight around a right-hand bend. Navrátil had very little idea what might be planned, and the small amount he understood did not appeal to him in the slightest.

The policeman busied himself ignoring the traffic chaos developing around him and keeping an eye peeled for the beige Mercedes. Slonský's instructions were unusual, but since they amounted to doing his job particularly well, he was happy to follow them. His boss seemed to know Slonský and had vouched for him, so that had to be all right.

The Mercedes had pulled out of the Ministry of Finance and was coming along the road towards them. The registration number was right, so the policeman stepped off the traffic island waving his arms to flag the Mercedes down. It came to a halt and the driver wound down the window.

'Is there a problem?' he asked.

'Yes. You pulled straight across that lane without signalling. Just because you're driving someone important doesn't mean you can ignore the rules of the road, you know.'

'I did not!' protested the driver.

'Right, out you get. Hands on the roof of the car.'

Sammler leaned across to speak through the window.

'Officer, I have an important meeting. Please send the fine to my office and we'll pay it.'

'It doesn't work like that, sir. Endangering other road-users can mean you lose your driver's licence.'

'I didn't endanger anyone,' the driver argued.

'I'm not arguing here,' the policeman replied. 'We can continue this at the station. It's just down the road there.'

'And how am I going to get to my meeting?' Sammler expostulated.

'I don't know, sir. But he isn't driving you. I suppose you'll have to drive yourself.'

Sammler snorted in annoyance, then opened the nearside rear door and walked round to the driver's side. He had to watch those other idiots who might have taken his door off, so it was a surprise to him when he sat down to find Slonský sitting beside him, who promptly clicked the central locking button.

'Good morning, sir,' said Slonský. 'Move off in your own time.'

'And why should I do that?' asked Sammler.

'Because I'm pointing this at you,' replied Slonský in his most guileless tone, holding his gun in his gloved hand.

'You wouldn't use it,' Sammler replied scornfully. 'It would be plain murder.'

'Not if you were armed too, sir. There's a gap in the traffic now.'

Sammler pulled out and began to follow the flow of cars.

'But I'm not armed, am I, Lieutenant?'

Slonský dug deep into his coat pocket.

'Fortunately I have a spare, sir. If I'm forced to shoot you, I'll casually drop this by your body as I perform the kiss of life very ineffectively.'

'That's not standard issue, is it?'

'No, it's a Makarov pistol. The East Germans had them. I got this one off an East German army officer I helped during an exercise.'

'Helped? How?'

'I stood him upright and took the weight of the heavy gun off his chest.'

'You stole it?'

'Technically, I took it off him because he was too drunk to use it safely. Call me old-fashioned if you like, but I have a thing about letting drunks get into fights when they have semi-automatic weapons on them. I just never got round to giving it back. It's their own fault. The Germans told us to make ourselves scarce before the military police got there. I thought being a patriotic gentleman you'd appreciate the attention to detail, sir, giving you a German gun.'

'I don't want a gun of any kind, Slonský, German or otherwise.'

Slonský could see that this was going to be difficult.

'You have to have a gun, or I can't shoot you. But you don't have to have it until after you're dead, otherwise you might use it.'

'This is preposterous,' Sammler growled. 'What's to stop me just running the car into a wall, or stopping to ask a policeman to arrest you?'

'The fact that you're an intelligent man, sir, so you'll see that anything other than falling in with my plans results in your lying dead somewhere. I may be under arrest, but that won't give you a lot of satisfaction. Dead men don't crow over their enemies.'

'Where are we going?'

'I thought somewhere quiet where we can talk. Somewhere in the countryside. Head westwards, please.'

'This is the end of your career, you know.'

'Yes, it could be,' agreed Slonský. 'Alternatively, it could be its finest moment, depending on whether I can get you to confess.'

'You know a confession obtained under duress isn't admissible in court.'

'Duress? What duress? You said yourself you didn't believe I'd shoot. So either you lied, and you think I really would shoot, or you aren't under duress. Can't have it both ways.'

Slonský glanced in the mirror. Navrátil was two cars back, keeping pace nicely.

'Right turn here, please. We'll go out on the highway. You can put your foot down if you like. But don't think of drawing attention to yourself by speeding. My fingers twitch when I'm driven too fast.'

Sammler's hands were glistening with sweat.

'I'm a personal friend of the Minister of Justice, you know.'

'No relevance to me, sir. Justice looks after courts; it's the Minister of the Interior that would impress me, if I hadn't already locked one up for a murder you committed. Incidentally, I think Dr Banda has a bone to pick with you. Don't expect a Christmas card this year.'

'It's a matter of indifference to me. He's one of yesterday's men now.'

'It takes one to know one, sir. You might want to start moving over to the right-hand lane, sir. We'll take Route 7 to Dejvice.'

'I'll have been missed by now, you realise. I have an appointment for lunch.'

'I shouldn't imagine you're too hungry just at the moment. I'll ring in a little while and ask them to keep it warm if you like. Turn right towards Jenerálka. Navrátil, go back to Prague and await further instructions.'

'Are you sure that's wise, sir?' Navrátil asked, before he remembered that it was futile because he did not have a microphone. He pulled off the road and feverishly considered his options. Should he obey his head, or his orders? He could not believe that Slonský seriously proposed to maltreat a suspect to get a confession, but on the other hand his boss had been perfectly happy to fake a beating and you could hardly overlook his treatment of Banda. Perhaps if Navrátil had not been so new and so junior, he might have decided differently, but he saw no alternative to doing what he was told, however much he felt that he ought to intervene. Then again, Slonský was hardly in a position to argue that an officer should always do what he was told. Several of their colleagues had described incidents when Slonský had ignored an order or "creatively interpreted" an instruction.

Navrátil sat at the side of the road and evaluated the alternatives as quickly as he could as he watched Sammler's car pull away from him.

Slonský glanced in the mirror again to confirm that Navrátil had pulled up.

'Ignore the village, sir. Follow the sign to Horoměřice.'

The road began to snake around between thick woods. Apart from the occasional house, there were trees on each side.

'This would be a good place to pull in, sir. Let's go for a walk in the trees.'

Sammler stopped the car, and Slonský immediately grabbed the keys.

'Just in case you were thinking of running back to the car and driving off, sir. Shall we go?'

'This is a nonsense,' protested Sammler. 'You plainly intend to shoot me in cold blood. Why should I co-operate?'

'Because if you co-operate I won't have to shoot you. I'd have thought that was clear. I'd much rather have you behind bars than in an urn on my mantelpiece. I want to have a little chat on neutral territory. We can debate the issues and perhaps come to an agreement. When you get out, twenty years or so from now, I'll probably be dead, but if I'm not you can come and hold me at gunpoint in return. Can't say fairer than that, can I? After you.'

Sammler trudged through the mud. The warmer weather had caused a thaw that turned the snow to water, and the frozen ground to black mud. Slonský indicated a drier patch alongside a rivulet. Sammler noticed that Slonský had stopped for a moment, and turned to see the old detective putting protective disposable overshoes on his feet.

'A little trick I learned off you, sir. You leave fewer footprints this way. That's what you did in the snow, wasn't it? Novák was stumped for a while till he did some experiments with rubber overshoes. Size 47 overshoes over size 44 shoes, he thought, reducing the definition at the edges. Was he right, sir?'

'Fantasy, pure fantasy.'

'I don't really need your confirmation, sir. Novák experimented until he could reproduce what he saw in the snow.'

'Then why waste your breath and try my patience?'

Slonský ignored the enquiry. He had never had much time for stupid questions.

'Then I puzzled over how you'd left no real tyre tracks in the snow, till I saw on the closed circuit cameras at your flat that you put a broom in the back of your car. A quick sweep would blur them quite nicely, wouldn't it? But why would you have a broom in your car? I notice you don't have one today.'

'There's no snow today, Lieutenant, or haven't you noticed? It's all circumstantial, and none of it convinces. How much further?'

'Tell you what, sir. Is the microphone putting you off? I wouldn't want you to feel inhibited about expressing yourself. I'll leave it here, shall I?'

Slonský placed the microphone on a tree stump, much to Navrátil's annoyance. Now he could not hear any of the dialogue between them. He hoped that Slonský was just trying to frighten Sammler into a confession, but he decided that he had better act quickly, just in case. He did not want Slonský's career to end like this.

'This is far enough. Let's talk.'

'Talk? About what?'

'About life, the universe, the price of fish, I don't know. Oh, and why a pretty young Czech girl is lying in a grave near Kladno fifty years too early. You know more about that than any man alive. Don't you feel any guilt?'

'No. Why should I?'

'Because you killed her. She was going to scream and you killed her, you said. But then I thought, no, that makes no sense. You couldn't let her live once you'd invited her to help with the plot, so whether she screamed or not, you were going to strangle her. You killed her and wrapped her in her own sheets to look like a laundry bundle. When you arrived at the back of the metro station you rolled her out like Cleopatra inside the carpet, and threw the sheets in the car, leaving her in the dressing gown and the first pair of shoes you could find for her. She must have put them out for the next morning, rather than having just taken them off, because they wouldn't have matched the outfit she was wearing in the photo. You knew there weren't traces of you on her clothes, but you couldn't be sure about the sheet because you'd knelt on it while you squeezed all the young life out of her.'

'A very colourful picture you paint. But you can't prove any of that.'

'Would you really sacrifice your life for communism?'

'Of course. A man needs something to believe in. What do you believe in, Lieutenant? The rule of law? Oh, I forgot, you interpret that as allowing you to shoot suspects. What happened to your oath, you hypocrite?'

'My oath, sir? My oath was to uphold justice, not the law. I spent twenty years of my life enforcing laws I didn't believe in. All those years of knocking on people's doors at three in the morning. They thought we did it to cause terror. Rubbish. We did it because people were less likely to be out then. We'd kick the door in then stand aside to let the security police do their dirty work. That was called upholding the law. I never believed there was any "justice" about it. My generation did that in every walk of our lives. We took bribes, but we were just as guilty if we gave them. There were just so many examples of the law turning a blind eye, not being applied fairly. Think of those show trials — Slánsky, Clementis, Margolius, Horaková. They didn't deserve to hang. The state has said so. Admittedly a bit late, but they've been formally exonerated, and much good did the pardon do them. They ended on the gallows, and the law of the day put them there. I upheld that law, but it wasn't justice. When the Wall came down and we made a new start, that was the most important thing for me. "No more upholding the law, Josef," I said to myself. "Your job is giving people justice." And I've tried to live by that. I've got a lot to make up for. No more than many and a lot less than some, but it's never going to be put right. All I can do is my best. And that's why you're here now. I want justice for Irina Gruberová, and you can give it to her by confessing.'

'Go to hell,' snarled Sammler. 'If the bitch is dead, so what? You can't make an omelette without breaking eggs. There are always collateral victims. Your precious capitalist west has littered Iraq with dead civilians who just happened to be next door to the wrong building. Was that justice? You make me sick. Such hypocrisy! We offer a new way, Slonský. No private property means no theft. International solidarity between workers means no war. There is another way, Slonský, and you and your kind are an obstacle to it. Mark my words, one day the red flag will fly again over Prague Castle. I hope you live to see it. It'll give you something to do while you twist in the wind dangling from a lamp-post.'

'If I thought that would stop you in your tracks, I'd settle for that. Here I am at nearly sixty, and I've finally found something worth dying for. I'd have willingly taken Irina's place to save her from the death you bestowed on her. I'd do anything to see you locked up.'

Sammler jabbed his finger violently at Slonský.

'That's it, isn't it? That's what you can't stand. It's not really about poor little Irina getting killed. It's the fact that I'll never face trial for it. It's the fact that you don't have any useful evidence — no forensics, no witnesses, no accusatory letters, not a thing. I could stand here and shout that I killed her, and you'd have to let me walk away. Free! And if you kill me, what does that make you? A common murderer. Is that what Czech law does for you? Is killing unarmed civilians okay with you? Is that what you want to be, Slonský? My murderer?'

Slonský stared into the spiteful eyes before him.

'I can live with that,' he said, taking a stride forward and firing left-handed into Sammler's right temple. Sammler looked uncomprehending for a moment before slumping back against the tree trunk and sliding down it. Moving quickly, Slonský peeled off his thin evidence glove, turned it inside out, placed it on Sammler's right hand and rubbed it vigorously to transfer any powder residue. Removing the glove again, he wrapped Sammler's fingers around the butt of the Makarov, pushed the car keys into Sammler's pocket, kicked some rotting leaves over any traces he may have left, and walked back to the main road, picking up the microphone as he went.

'You can come for me now, Navrátil,' he said, and began to walk along the road towards Jenerálka. A bus went past, but he ignored it. The only person he wanted to see was his young assistant, but Navrátil was not to be seen.

Slonský had been walking for about forty minutes when the car came towards him, and Navrátil stepped out. They stood facing each other in silence for a minute or so, then Navrátil held out a piece of paper.

'Receipt for the two coffees and pastries we had in Prague this afternoon,' he explained.

Slonský took it unsmilingly, and slipped it into his wallet before getting into the car.

Epilogue

In the wake of Sammler's death, Slonský had made a strange promise to himself. He would not lie about what had happened. If anyone realised that he had shot Sammler, he would admit it. It was not something that he was ashamed of. All he had done was rectify a failing in the law. Of course, he would go to jail for it, but the only person who knew, Navrátil, had kept his mouth tight shut. In fact, Navrátil had rationalised it away by telling himself that if he knew for certain that Slonský had killed Sammler he would have to report it, but by avoiding asking about it he could keep himself in ignorance and thus have nothing that he needed to report. It therefore suited both men not to mention the subject and they never had. From the moment that Navrátil picked Slonský up by the side of the road after the death they had said not a single word about that day.

Dr Novák's report had been unequivocal. The gun was in Sammler's hand, and had only Sammler's prints on it. There was some powder residue on Sammler's thumb and index finger. The bullet had undoubtedly come from the gun found at the scene. It was an open and shut case.

The body had been found after a bus driver reported that a car had been by the side of the road for several days. When Slonský had turned up at Sammler's office on the following morning for their pre-arranged interview, Sammler's secretary had been forced to confess that they did not know where he was. Slonský had duly reported as much to Captain Lukas, so Lukas had asked all police to look out for the car and its owner. Once the car was traced, a few policemen walked up into the nearby woods and found the body against a tree. Lukas was convinced that Sammler had realised that the game was up and had taken the easy way out rather than go to jail for a long time. The only slightly untidy part was that Sammler's secretary had deposed that Slonský had asked for the appointment, claiming to have important new evidence, but the old detective had admitted to Lukas that this had been a bluff. It had obviously frightened Sammler, and Lukas contented himself with the thought that this just proved the man's guilt, since he plainly believed that there could be important new evidence, whereas if he had been innocent he would have demanded to know what it was before agreeing to the interview.

The atmosphere in the office had been difficult for a while, but Navrátil was brightening considerably as the day approached when Officer Peiperová would be free to take up her new post in the detective division. Of course, she would not work directly for Slonský, but at least they were in the same building. Navrátil had not yet broached the question of sharing a flat with her, but the girl had to live somewhere and his own small flat was highly unsuitable. His mother would be shocked if Peiperová moved in, largely because she had never heard of her. He really must get around to mentioning it someday. Just not quite yet, he thought.

A NOTE TO THE READER

Dear Reader,

Thank you! You have generously given your time to read about Josef Slonský and his colleagues. How much time depends, of course, upon your reading speed, but whatever it was I hope you feel it was time well spent.

This story is set in 2006 because it was then that my wife and I first went to Prague. I had an idea in my head, but it was only when we went to an ice-hockey game that we walked the route that Bear walks on the first page, and the action became set in Prague. I sat down to write one Saturday morning, and on the cinema screen in my brain where I see the scenes a battered old car pulled up and Slonský climbed out. All I had to do was describe him.

Slonský lived the first half of his life under Communism and he recalls what he was told to do then. He knows his hands are dirty, and he assumes that is true for all people of his age. That explains the difficulty he has in showing respect. He is coming towards the end of his career and dreads retirement, so his boss has a small hold over him. If he wants to stay on – and he does – he has to accept a trainee. Navrátil, young, intelligent, moral, earnest and devout, equally sprang fully-formed onto the page.

Other characters then began showing up and doing whatever they thought fit, and I had to try to keep up with them. They have their quirks, whether it's Klinger's obsession with order or Mucha's avoidance of his sister-in-law's visits by judicious arrangement of the duty roster that he has never admitted to his wife he prepares. Plainly these are fictional people and they do not represent or reflect on the police in Prague. Maybe that's a shame, because if I were murdered in Prague I'd be comforted to know Slonský was on the case.

He is slovenly, cynical, humorous and cunning. He likes beer, sausages and pastries. He is good company. He can tell a story. Above all, he is Czech, and proud of it, and I hope my portraits of him demonstrate my affection for Slonský and his people.

If you have enjoyed this novel I'd be really grateful if you would leave a review on **Amazon** and **Goodreads**. I love to hear from readers, so please keep in touch through **Facebook** or **Twitter**, or leave a message on my **website**.

Všechno nejlepší!

Graham Brack

Sapere Books is an exciting new publisher of brilliant fiction and popular history.

To find out more about our latest releases and our monthly bargain books visit our website: **saperebooks.com**

Printed in Poland
by Amazon Fulfillment
Poland Sp. z o.o., Wrocław

55020381R00174